11.95

Helen Windrath has been an edit
1992. Prior to this she worked
west community publisher, base
London.

Also edited by Helen Windrath from The Women's Press:

The Women's Press Book of New Myth and Magic (1993)

READER, I MURDERED HIM, TOO

HELEN WINDRATH, EDITOR

First published by The Women's Press Ltd, 1995
A member of the Namara Group
34 Great Sutton Street, London EC1V 0DX

British Library Cataloguing-in-Publication Data
A catalogue record for this book is available from the
British Library

ISBN 0 7043 4363 0

Phototypeset in 10/12pt Times by Intype, London
Printed and bound in Great Britain by
BPC Paperbacks Ltd
A Member of
The British Printing Company Ltd

Contents

PENNY SUMNER

Dead-Head

'We're accomplices then? You'll help me keep him dead and buried?'

The walled garden smells of rotting apples and ripe compost; a bumble-bee hovers dreamily nearby. 'Yes,' I answer.

'And the other business too? You'll help with that?'

The other business is the relatively minor matter of blackmail. 'That too.'

A heavy red rose is cradled in a wide, stained palm. 'You know, it sometimes strikes me that this is how Isabella must have felt.'

'Isabella?' Things are complicated enough already. 'Who is . . .'

'Isabella and her pot of basil,' the voice is teasing. 'As in Keats.'

Looking at the thick-petalled rose I'm aware of feeling the faintest bit queasy. 'Of course,' I hear myself say, 'Keats.'

That's how the story finishes, in a garden at the end, or maybe the beginning, of the world. It starts three days earlier in my first floor office, halfway between the Barbican and Charterhouse Square. The electric fan is humming on the green filing cabinet, a mug of abandoned coffee weighs down a pile of papers in front of me, and the only flower in sight is the Georgia O'Keeffe calendar hanging on the wall opposite. It's eleven o'clock on a Monday morning and I'm interviewing a new client.

'Let's face it,' he's saying, 'the reason I need to employ a private detective is because the police simply aren't interested unless you can produce a body.' Running a manicured hand through an expensive haircut he looks straight into my eyes, and smiles. 'Can you help me, Miss Cross? Please say you can.'

A woman's gotta do what a woman's gotta do: holding the eye contact I smile right back. Okay, so from where you're sitting you can tell already that the guy's a complete sleazeball. But from my side of the desk there are two factors to take into account. Factor one: even sleazeballs have a right to get concerned when their big brother disappears. Factor two: business has been quiet and the agency could do with a paying customer.

'Mr Williamson . . .'

'Please,' he leans slightly forward, 'call me Gerry, short for Gerard.'

'Gerry, I quite understand that you're worried and if I can assist you I will. What we need to do now is make sure I've got the story right. Now you say you haven't seen your brother for a long time. Exactly how long?'

'Miss Cross . . .'

'Tor,' I cut in.

He looks blank.

'Short for Victoria.'

'Oh,' his laugh is what you'd describe as boyish, should you be so inclined. 'Tor, I haven't seen Rupert for – well, it must be over a year.'

And only now is he asking why? I haven't seen my brother, Tim, for almost four years, but that's because he lives in Australia. Gerry Williamson, however, has already told me that his residence is in Hampstead while his brother's is in Kentish Town. Which means there must be all of a mile and a half between them.

I glance again at the photo I'm holding: Rupert Williamson's smile is wide, the grey eyes laughing. He's a handsome man in his mid-thirties, about the same age as me. 'How frequently did you see him before that, Gerry?'

'Oh, we met at family gatherings. To be honest we've never really been close – largely, I suspect, because we were sent to boarding school. Rupert was six years older than me and was already at prep when I began registering anything.' His shoulders rise and fall in a well-practised shrug, 'Since school we've moved in different worlds: Rupert has his own circle, and I have mine. There's only one of his friends I've met more than once or twice, Archie Jones, a musician. I tried ringing Archie a couple of weeks ago but his flatmate told me he's sailing around the world. He's currently somewhere in the Pacific.'

Putting the photo down I locate a biro and jot the name and probable whereabouts of the musician in a new blue notebook. 'And there isn't anyone else you can think of?' After *Archie Jones, the Pacific* I scribble *ask for £200, drop to £150???* The cut of Gerry Williamson's taupe linen suit suggests the distinct possibility of a cash down payment.

'Well there's Harry Ablytt, the owner of the gallery which used to have exclusive rights to Rupert's work. I went to the gallery and introduced myself to Ablytt, but he claims not to have heard from my brother for ages. When I asked him if he was at all worried he merely said that Rupert was undoubtedly off "discovering himself", and that artists frequently do this sort of thing. Ablytt also represents Rupert's ex-wife, Anna, who's a painter, but he refused to give me her phone number or to tell me where she lives. However after some heated words on my part he did eventually agree to pass a letter on to her. I explained in this that the Colonel was asking about Rupert, and that I was becoming anxious myself, but all I got in reply was a two-line postcard saying she was sure my brother was fine and I had no need to fret. She didn't divulge her address.'

What's the military connection here? 'Uh, who is the Colonel . . .?'

He frowns slightly, as if irritated I need to ask. 'Why, the pater. He's eighty-four and had a major stroke ten years ago so he's almost completely gaga, I'm afraid. But every now and again he does remember Rupert and I have to come up with some lame excuse as to why his oldest son hasn't been to visit.' Irritation gives way to unease, 'It's not like Rupie you know, to let the old man down. Which means something must be wrong, Tor.' My client's eyes once again plunge into mine, 'Very, very, wrong.'

It's summer, July sliding into August and the days hot in the way only days in a real London summer can get hot. After parking in the quiet cul-de-sac I twist my shoulder-length hair into a knot then peel myself off the driving seat. From the outside Rupert Williamson's residence doesn't immediately suggest a need for concern. Gerry had said his brother's Victorian house was locked and vacant, but he hadn't told me the long lawn had been kept mown and the box hedge trimmed. As I walk up the central path I can see the sturdy plants in the border beds – ornamental grasses, Mexican orange blossoms, red and yellow nasturtiums – are thriving. Next to the front door, however, a sprawling Japanese maple isn't bearing up to the afternoon heat so well, its delicate leaves scorched redder than the brickwork behind.

I don't expect an answer when I ring the bell, so I'm not disappointed when I don't get one. Adjoining the house, to the left, is the double garage Gerry said his brother used as a studio, while to the right there's a six-foot-high wooden fence and gate. Walking past the bay window, with its drawn curtains, I push against the gate. It's locked. Glancing around I see an empty terracotta flower pot, which would probably provide me with just enough height to peer over the top . . .

'Fuck it!' The bottom's crawling with woodlice. I flick one off my hand and on to my cream voile skirt, at which point I promptly drop the pot.

'Can I help you?' A face peers at me through the lattice side fence. The face is female and elderly and no way could I describe the expression it's wearing as friendly.

Brushing off my skirt I rearrange my own features into what is meant to pass as a cheery smile, 'Hello there!' I chirp, 'I'm looking for Mr Williamson . . .'

Twenty minutes later I'm in a restaurant on the Kentish Town Road, positioned directly under a ceiling fan and casting a critical eye over what I've just written in my notebook: *Man comes (irregularly) to do garden.* It's surprising what intimate details people are prepared to confide in a complete stranger, as long as you get them on side. Unfortunately there was no chance of that happening with Rupert Williamson's neighbour, who'd made it quite clear that if she didn't approve of my language she approved even less of the fact that I'd broken Mr Williamson's pot. The only information I'd been able to wheedle out of her was that a gardener had been coming to mow the lawns and tend the plants.

Picking up the pen again I scrawl on the next line: *Who pays the gardener?* I'll tackle the other neighbours later, when there's a chance a few more will be home from work. In the meantime I down the remains of my orange juice, crunch on the last ice cube, and head out on to the mean streets – in the direction of the Kentish Town Public Library.

After a productive quarter of an hour in the stacks I'm back on the pavement, speaking to Gerry Williamson from a call box.

'Rosaline Jardinn?' he asks again.

I should have brought the mobile phone, there's not that much time left on my card. 'That's right. I've just looked up Rupert's address in the electoral register. No one is registered there this year, it simply says "no elector". But last year one Rosaline Jardinn was in residence.'

'Does the register say Rupert was living there as well?'

'No, it appears Rosaline Jardinn was alone. The year before that both Rupert and his wife, Anna, are listed. Maybe he rented the house out last year. I've checked the telephone directory but there are no Jardinns in sight. I was wondering if you knew who she was.'

A moment's silence is followed by a snort of laughter. 'How stupid of me! I'd completely forgotten that after Rupert and Anna stopped living together there was some mention of a girlfriend. Tor, it's extremely important you locate this woman, she has to know something.'

'I'll see what I can do,' I say in my best professional manner. Well, I'll give it a try.

I spend over an hour knocking on the doors of Rupert Williamson's neighbours, all of whom are anxious to point out that this is the sort of neighbourhood where people mind their own business. No, they haven't seen Mr Williamson lately. Yes, there was a woman living in the house last year, but no one thought to ask who she was. In reply to polite queries as to why I'm snooping I claim to be a long-lost friend of the family.

It's around seven-thirty when I get back home to Balham. I shove a frozen pizza in the oven then wander out to the patio with a weak g-and-t and the day's post. Sorting through the post takes about two seconds, bills on one side, the latest post-card from my lover, April, on the other. April says the Loire Valley is beautiful but baking and she's exhausted after a day spent tromping around semi-derelict *châteaux* with her parents. 'Love you lots,' her handwriting loops generously across the card. 'Miss you. How's does our garden grow?'

Considering we only moved in at the end of January, it's not growing too badly at all. The lemon verbena is in full flower and the evening's heavy with its scent. Down the far corner the weeping cherry, my first serious purchase, is flourishing and the jasmine and honeysuckle are already shooting sturdy ten-drils along the top of the fence. That's the good news. The bad news is that everything needs watering and there's a ban on hand-held hoses. If I'd known what this summer was going to be like I would have planted more carefully back in spring, putting in low-maintenance plants like the Mexican orange blossoms in Rupert Williamson's borders.

Half an hour later, as I lug the heavy watering can across the lawn, I can't help wondering who had planned those borders, Rupert Williamson or the mysterious Rosaline Jardinn? Because whoever it was had planned ahead; someone had expected that house to be empty for some time.

At ten o'clock the next morning I'm to be found in front of a very large oil painting of a very nude woman.

The assistant's tone is confidential, 'Splendid, isn't it?'

I wouldn't normally attract this level of attention in this sort of establishment, so can only assume my cherry silk suit, bought half price at a young designer's sale, is convincing. 'Yes indeed.' Although a mite overwhelming, I would have thought, for your average living-room wall.

Her smile is glossy, 'This work isn't actually for sale, but if you are interested the artist has an exhibition opening at our Holland Park gallery tonight, from seven to nine.'

'Really?' My own smile's in danger of taking on Cheshire-cat proportions. The artist in question is Anna Williamson, Rupert's ex, and the opportunity of seeing her this evening is both unexpected, and very welcome. The question now is whether my luck will hold out. 'You know I think I will go along, thank you for telling me. Right at the moment, however, I mustn't let myself be sidetracked. What I'm after today is ceramics, a large bowl, or maybe a plate, suitable for a conservatory. A friend of mine suggested you might have something by Rupert Williamson?' As I lie I think this is pretty convincing. But then, I'm a professional.

She's wearing a strand of pearls, which she now strokes as if in apology. 'I know Rupert Williamson's work, of course, all those brilliant sunflowers and poppies. But in the six months I've been here we haven't had anything by him. Are you particularly after a flower pattern? Because we do have three lovely bowls.' She leads the way into the adjoining room, 'The glazes are more delicate than Rupert Williamson's, but wouldn't these look glorious in a conservatory or sunroom?'

Absolutely, though I'd need some convincing about a five-hundred-pound price tag. The bowl closest to me is decorated with a sensual swirl of blue and pink: roses in a summer breeze. 'This is lovely,' I agree, 'however the conservatory is a sun trap and really demands stronger colours. I wonder if it would be possible to order a piece by Mr Williamson?'

Her voice regrets a lost commission. 'I don't know, you'd have to ask the owner, Mr Ablytt. Unfortunately he's on vacation for a fortnight. But you could enquire when he gets back.'

A fortnight? Oh shit. 'Oh dear, I was hoping to get something very soon – it's for a birthday present. Look, I hate to be a nuisance but do you think you could possibly give Mr Ablytt a ring and ask him how I might contact Mr Williamson? I'd be terribly grateful.'

Her laughter has an edge. 'If only it were that easy. Mr Ablytt is hiking somewhere in the Himalayas.' The door opens and she susses out the newcomer over my left shoulder. 'It's such a pity the Jardinn bowls aren't quite what you're after.'

The what bowls? I restrain myself from jumping up and down on the spot. 'Uh, *who* did you say those bowls were by?'

Her nod is half for me, half for her new customer. 'Rosaline Jardinn, that's with a double n. You won't see her work anywhere else, she sells only through us.'

'Really?' I'm gushing, but what the heck. 'Well those bowls are delightful and although they wouldn't suit the *conservatory* I *can* picture one in my study.' This wins back her full attention and I reward her with an enthusiastic grin. 'You know, I haven't even heard of Rosaline Jardinn before! Is she London-based?'

'I'm not sure,' her fingers clutch at the pearls. 'Mr Ablytt could tell you all about her, of course, but he's . . .'

'I know,' enthusiasm slides into disappointment, 'he's somewhere in the Himalayas.'

My afternoon is spent writing up a series of witness interviews for a local solicitor and it's almost five o'clock when I climb into Lucy, my elderly, blue Cortina, and drive across town to Holland Park. After finding a parking space a few doors from the gallery I dine on a surprisingly good risotto at a nearby pub, then present myself for the exhibition's seven o'clock opening.

'Hot, definitely hot.' This isn't a comment about the weather but the artwork and there's no doubting that the commentator's a critic. He and his entourage drift in the direction of a tray of Pimms, and I check my catalogue for the price of an etching that's caught my eye: '*Isabella weeps over the head of her lover, Lorenzo, buried in a pot of basil*'.

I manage not to whistle aloud, but only just – an Anna Williamson, even a small one, does not come cheap. Most of them don't come small either, the lady obviously enjoys working on a large scale and most of her canvasses are covered with billowing expanses of naked, female flesh. Her fans continue this theme in *fin de siècle* attire: throughout the room tanned buttocks peep from slashed harem pants and rouged breasts pop out of loosely laced basques. The artist's own emerald-green smock is, in contrast, high-necked and reaches down to her ankles. Her long red hair is pulled back in a knot and the bruised look around her eyes suggests an artistic temperament on the verge of a full-blown migraine. Which fits in with my plans rather nicely; this event is timetabled to finish at nine and

I'm hoping the star attraction will sensibly head straight home rather than go on to boogy elsewhere.

I've worked the party, chatting to as many people as possible, and have managed to establish that Ms Williamson's is a rapidly rising star and at least two articles are expected in the coming Sunday supplements. Dropping Rupert Williamson's name into the conversation however only draws a blank: no one seems to know what the ex-husband is up to these days.

'That man over there!' This is uttered, *sotto voce* into my right ear, by a pretty art student I introduced myself to earlier over a plate of crudités.

'Which man?' I whisper back.

'The one with the beard.' Her eyes are wide. 'Everybody's saying he's from the Tate!'

'Really?'

'Yes, apparently the Tate's interested in a painting she's working on at the moment. He's rather dishy, don't you think?'

I can't see it myself, but then I'm not a struggling student with a portfolio to flog. 'Well I know what you mean, although he's not exactly my type . . .' At which point my eyes alight on one of the most striking human beings I've ever seen in my life. Tall, with cropped, dark hair, wearing a long sky-blue dress; she searches across the room, catches sight of Anna Williamson, and smiles. It's a smile full of humour, full of promise, full of . . .

'I can't simply go up and introduce myself, can I?'

'Oh why not?' I hear myself gasp. 'Why not?'

Five minutes later the art student has engaged the buyer from the Tate in animated conversation and I'm surreptitiously eyeing the lady in blue as she gently stoops to listen to Rupert Williamson's ex-wife. Anna Williamson murmurs something and the woman's head sweeps back in a loud, happy laugh. 'But that's wonderful!' her voice is pleasantly deep. 'Absolutely wonderful!' She laughs again as a short man stands on sandalled toes in order to kiss both her cheeks.

'Rosaline!' He clings on to her hands, 'Rosaline Jardinn, how superb to see you here!'

At nine o'clock the next morning I'm parked around the corner from Anna Williamson's Muswell Hill residence. The previous evening I'd been sorely tempted to change my plans and tail the girlfriend rather than the wife, but Rosaline Jardinn had the look of a woman about to embark on some serious partying so, somewhat reluctantly, I turned my attention back to my original quarry. As soon as she started on a restrained round of good-byes I went out to sit in Lucy and watched as a small group, (including Ms Jardinn) escorted the artist out of the gallery and waved her into a waiting black cab. I followed from two cars behind. Now I'm wondering what reception I'll get.

Thrilled she isn't. 'Who?' she demands. Her eyes are still strained and, despite her relatively early night, it's evident she's tired.

'Cross,' I muster an ingratiating smile, 'Tor Cross. I was at your opening last night, which really was great fun, and I was *so* surprised to hear someone say you'd been married to Rupert Williamson. You see I've desperately been trying to purchase a bowl by him but I simply cannot find one anywhere. I know this is an imposition but I would be terribly grateful if you could tell me how to contact him. I want the bowl for my elderly mother, she's not been very well and . . .'

'How did you get my address?'

Thrusting my hands into my jean pockets I assume an apologetic lilt. 'I have to confess I wheedled it out of one of your friends. I explained that I'd been trying to get a bowl for my mother, it's her eightieth birthday soon, and . . .'

'That is complete crap,' the green eyes are narrow. 'None, and I mean none, of my friends would tell a stranger where I live.'

'I must have been very persuasive.' I give a nervous giggle, which at this stage of the proceedings isn't hard. 'Or maybe it was the Pimms.'

'Yeah, well I'm not in contact with Rupert anyway so I'm afraid I can't help you, Miss Cress.'

'Cross.' Taking a deep breath I decide to go the whole hog. 'One of the people I spoke to last night suggested Rosaline Jardinn might be able to put me in touch with Mr Williamson. Could you possibly tell me where Ms Jardinn lives?'

The door, which is in the process of shutting, comes to a halt, and the little colour she does have deserts her face completely. 'You can fuck off right now,' she hisses. 'I don't know who you are but as far as I'm concerned you can go straight to hell.' As the door slams I'm left to ponder exactly what it is I've said.

Five minutes later I'm parked halfway along the road. I've slipped off the red blouse and am now sporting a white T-shirt, green and black silk headscarf, and wrap-around sunglasses. There's a chance Anna skipped down the front steps in the time it took me to walk to the car and affect my transformation, but I doubt it. Her tousled red hair hadn't been brushed and my guess is she'll need that first cup of coffee before she goes anywhere. Assuming, of course, that she is going somewhere and my instincts are right.

They are, twenty minutes later she's locked the front door and is walking north, in the direction of Alexandra Park. I discreetly follow on foot. After a five-minute walk she crosses Priory Road and slowly climbs the front steps of a large, detached house. As she gets to the top the door opens and a tall figure with cropped hair welcomes her in.

This time I ring Gerry Williamson in his car yard, mobile phone to mobile phone. 'What excellent news, Tor!' He makes it sound as if this is case solved, 'I can't believe you've found this Jardinn woman in less than two days. And it was all so easy!'

Uh-huh. Sipping my iced tea I look out the open cafe window to where two women have stopped to talk to each other, fanning themselves with their hands. 'Gerry, Rosaline Jardinn might refuse to tell me anything about your brother. She might not be any more helpful than Anna Williamson.' The women on the pavement kiss, their breasts touching.

'But it's still brilliant you've located her. Look Tor, I've got some clients waiting to test drive a Rolls. I just want to say I feel it's vital you find out as much about this Rosaline Jardinn as you can. She lived in Rupert's house all last year, she must know what's happened to him. I want you to follow her, find out what places she goes to, who her friends are. Get some photos while you're at it.'

Photos? What does he think we'll be able to do with photos?

The problem with most of my clients is that they've read too many crime novels. 'Well I'll do what I can. I'll call on her this afternoon, but if she won't talk to me there are still other avenues to try. The gardener for example, if . . .'

'Must go, Tor. By the way there'll be a cheque for another two hundred in this afternoon's post. Remember now, I'm counting on you to come up with the goods on Miss Jardinn.'

In daylight she's even more fantastic than she was last night. 'Harry?' Arched eyebrows rising like new butterflies.

'That's right, Mr Ablytt.' I look up at her, a vigorous nod sending fake blond curls bouncing past my nose. The wig's horribly hot; my scalp itches and I can feel sweat trickling down my neck. 'I rang him from New York a few months ago and he absolutely promised to set up an interview with you. I gave him the dates I'd be over and everything!' On the whole I'm lousy with accents but I did spend a year in New York and like to think I can muster something believably Manhattan. 'I guess Mr Ablytt forgot, which is a real pity, Ms Jardinn, as there's such a lot of interest back home in England's women artists. I'd hate to have to leave you out of the article I'm writing. For *The New Yorker* you know.'

'Oh really?' Her smile is lazy, and faintly amused. 'I certainly wouldn't want to be left out by you, Ms . . .?'

'Stallman,' a name I heard somewhere, once upon a time, 'Cheryl Stallman.'

'Come in, Cheryl.' Cool fingertips, dry with clay, take my damp ones and I'm led over the threshold.

'So, what do you think?'

I don't know, I don't know what to think. Pulling my eyes away from the maze of pots spiralling crazily across the wood floor I realise I can't tell where the room ends and the garden begins. 'I think . . .'

'Yes, Cheryl?'

'That I've never seen anything like this before,' I say, quite truthfully. And then, quickly, 'But this isn't the States, I realise English gardens are a whole lot different.'

One of her silver earrings spins a shaft of light across a

whitewashed wall. 'This garden is, I believe, different from most. It has things in it you wouldn't believe. Ice?'

'Yes,' I watch as she pulls back a curtain of heavy foliage, revealing a small refrigerator. 'Yes, please.'

'In my art, and life, I'm attempting to blur boundaries. On the most basic level this means my bowls are almost plates, my plates bowls. Come,' she hands me a tall glass, 'let's go out into the garden proper.'

The garden is old, very old. 'How long have you lived in this house?' I ask, although I know it must be under a year.

'Me?' Her hand reaches out and caresses a leaf. 'Not long at all, I'm only the latest in a long line of gardeners, caretakers really. The woman who lived here before me was born in this house, and she was over ninety when she died. The back wall was badly damaged by the roots of the oak tree, so I simply had a wall of glass built around the trunk. I've let the garden into my house, along with the light I need for my work.'

Of course, why don't we all build our houses of glass? Why don't we all move barefoot across ancient lawns, our trailing hems stained green and gold?

'Cheryl?' She calls from the shadows.

'Yes, Rosaline?'

'You are remembering to take notes, aren't you?'

A notebook hangs limp from my hand. 'Oh yes,' I rummage in my shoulder bag for a biro. 'Um, I was particularly interested in what you were saying earlier.'

'Mmm?' Dark hair disappearing into shade, her face floats on the surface of a deep pond.

'Uh yes, you know, about blurring boundaries.'

'Exactly!' She springs in the direction of a bush heavy with old-fashioned roses. 'I'm obsessed with roses at the moment, the most cultivated, and yet the wildest, of flowers. Come closer, Cheryl.' She holds a pink bloom so I can smell its perfume. 'Pleasure . . .' As I bend forward I notice the bright bead of blood on the tip of a finger. 'And pain.' Her body bending to mine, her face close. 'The blurring of sensation.' Lips almost against my cheek, moving – aren't they? – towards my mouth.

I close my eyes, tilt my head, and a woman's voice calls from inside the house. 'Rosa?'

'Oh dear.'

Opening my eyes I find Rosaline Jardinn standing a good foot away, frowning down at me.

'Do you know I'd completely forgotten the time?' Taking my glass she tucks a hand firmly under my left elbow and marches me along the brick path. 'I am sorry about this, Shirley . . .'

'Cheryl,' I clutch at the wig as we push into a tangle of apple trees and what looks like an old chicken pen.

'Cheryl, of course. I'm afraid that's all the time I can give you this afternoon. I don't have a telephone, don't believe in 'em, but I'm here most days. Do feel free to call again.' Her hand fumbles under a mess of ivy and a gate swings open. 'Bye!' she calls, pushing me through.

Paradise is the other side of the wall and what I'm standing in is a back lane, in between a pile of strong-smelling rubbish bags and a large metal bin. Directly opposite a yellow skip is filled with broken chairs and building rubble. I find myself staring at the skip and wondering exactly what it was that had happened back there, in the garden. Had she been about to kiss me? Had I been about to let her?

Looking up at a blue, cloudless sky I blink tears. This is crazy: the scene with the roses, the woman, the house. The way I'm feeling. Shoving the notebook and pen in my bag I turn in the direction of the main road. Before I come to the corner, however, there's a narrow passage running between Rosaline's garden and her neighbour's wooden fence. Glancing into it I see a mess of broken bricks, old cigarette packets, smashed bottles, and without a second's hesitation I plunge in, creeping my way towards where the oak tree's branches form a canopy overhead. When I'm almost parallel with the tree I hear Rosaline's laughter float across the lawn.

A few feet away from me on the other side of the wall, Anna Williamson is less amused. 'I can't believe you let her in here. I warned you this morning she could turn up and you actually invite the bitch in!'

'There's no harm done,' Rosaline's voice is relaxed.

'Oh yes, and what if she comes back to quiz you on Rupert's whereabouts? What will you say then?'

'Poor Rupert, I knew him well. You know I sometimes wonder how he feels, pushing up my roses.'

'It's a bit late to get sentimental about it now.'

'Don't you ever feel a tinge of regret Anna? After all, you were married to him.'

'What concerns me isn't the past, but our future. She's a serious threat to that future, Rosa. She could destroy us.'

Now Rosaline's voice is concerned, and very close. 'Don't upset yourself sweetheart,' she murmurs. And then, 'I love you Anna, I love you so much.'

Silence follows, but I know that if I popped my head over the garden wall what I'd see would be two women kissing.

I'm not in a fit state to go back to the agency and instinctively I head south of the river. When I get back home I pour myself an orange juice, shakily slosh some brandy into it, then open the kitchen door and plonk myself down on the top step. So much for Paradise. What was it Gerry Williamson had said, that the police aren't interested unless you can produce a body? He'd suspected all along. He'd suspected that his brother had been murdered by those two women and yet he hadn't warned me. Instead he'd let me go into that garden alone. He'd let me kiss, well almost, a murderess. I can't wait to tell him what a creep he is.

I've left my case notebook in the office so I look up the number of Gerry's car yard in the *Yellow Pages*. It's past five and no one answers. Running my finger down the Williamsons in the residential listings I try to remember his home address; I remember wrong, however, and the voice that answers isn't Gerry's.

'Colonel Gerald Williamson,' it announces. The father, rather than the son.

'Oh, I am sorry,' I falter an apology. 'I've called the wrong number. I'm after your son.'

'After Rupie are you? Well it's a pity you didn't call at this time yesterday because he was here having tea.'

I see a rambling bush, heavy with roses, and remember Gerry

saying his father had a stroke some years back. 'No,' my voice catches, 'not Rupert. It's Gerry I need to speak to.'

'Oh him. Well, Miss . . .? I'm afraid my memory isn't what it should be, what was your name again?'

'Cross,' I offer.

'Well, Miss Cross, I haven't had anything to do with my youngest son for a long time now, and if you take my advice you won't either. A dishonest rogue, is Gerry.'

I'm watching myself in the mirror over the mantelpiece. Gaga was how Gerry had described his father. I'm not exactly sure what gaga is meant to sound like, but I don't think this is it. There's a flaw in the mirror's edge and my brown eyes boggle back at me.

'Mr, I mean Colonel, Williamson,' I tread carefully, each word a stepping stone, 'there seems to have been a misunderstanding. I was under the impression Rupert wasn't contactable, that he was, uh, out of the country on holiday. Or something. In fact it actually is Rupert I'm trying to locate.'

'Glad to hear it, Miss Cross! No, Rupie's definitely not on vacation. He lives in Muswell Hill, not far from here in fact, but I can't give you a number to ring as the lad can't abide telephones. You know what these artists are like. If you want his address you'll have to ring later, when my housekeeper, Mrs Harrison, is back. I'm blind, something I caught decades ago in the Sudan, and Mrs H keeps track of all the addresses. She's out having dinner with her sister tonight, but you could try ringing again tomorrow.'

'Thank you,' shifting sideways my everyday face stares at me. 'Thank you very much, Colonel Williamson.'

After putting the phone down I continue to study my reflection. I've got myself a tan without even trying. My lip gloss, and mascara, have run and my fringe is in desperate need of a trim. I think about these things for a couple of minutes and then three facts float to the surface. Fact one: from what Rupert Williamson's father says, his eldest son certainly isn't dead. Fact two, he also says his youngest son, my client, is a nasty piece of work. Fact three, the father himself is blind. Putting these facts together I come to the conclusion that I've been blind too. In short, I've been had.

For the first time in weeks there's the possibility of rain and as I stand on Rosaline Jardinn's doorstep I'm conscious of a slight chill in the morning air.

'Why, hello there.' Today she's wearing a man's shirt over clay-stained jeans and is clasping one of her own mugs. Gazing up at her I find that, despite knowing what I now think I know, I still find Rosaline Jardinn as sexy as hell. The lady gives a quizzical smile while I inwardly reel with implications that are post-feminist, post-lesbian, post-everything.

'It is Cheryl, isn't it?' she's saying. 'I hope you don't think I'm being rude, Cheryl, but you do look better as a brunette. That blond wig simply wasn't you.'

I attempt to pull myself together. 'My real name's Tor,' I reply, without the New York accent. 'Tor Cross.'

'I see.' She gestures with the mug. 'Before I invite you in for coffee, Tor Cross, I should do the responsible thing and ask why you're here. I am aware that you're not an art writer from New York, but you don't look like my idea of a *News of the World* hack either. Are you a representative of the tabloid press?' Her voice conveys genuine sadness at the thought.

I shake my head. 'Worse than that.'

Her eyebrows form two perfect arches. 'Oh? Surely not?'

'I'm a private detective, employed by Gerry.'

The arches fall into an apprehensive frown. 'Oh dear, that is worrying, although I'm not entirely sure what it means.'

'I suspect it means blackmail. I take my coffee white, by the way.'

Rosaline steps back and lets me in.

As we sit on the lawn the sky is cloudless again, a wash of pale blue. 'Do you garden?' she asks.

'Not on this scale. My mother did a lot of gardening and I've only recently realised how much I learned from her.'

Her eyes are fixed on something far away, beyond the rose bushes. 'So you know how important dead-heading is, plucking out the withered flowers so new ones can grow?'

An involuntary shiver goes through me. 'Yes, I do know but . . .'

'But what?' The grey eyes meet mine.

But flowers aren't flesh and blood, is what I want to say.

Her smile is gentle. 'It's not empathy I'm after, I understand that my experience is far removed from that of most people. What does surprise me, however, is the lack of sympathy. There are those who are willing to pity, yes. But sympathy is different.' Breaking the mood she nods in the direction of the oak. 'That lower branch, perfect for a swing don't you think?'

From where I'm sitting there are two trees, the reflection in the glass wall as substantial as the other. 'I guess so.' I shade my eyes with my hand, 'I'd prefer a brightly coloured hammock myself.'

'Of course, but I'm not thinking about us grown-ups, Tor. I'm thinking about a child.'

As she says this I catch a glimpse of heels swinging overhead, hear a trill of high laughter. A child, of course, the equation complete. Anna with the tired eyes, Anna pulling herself up Rosaline's front steps. 'She's pregnant,' I say.

'Rupert donated sperm for this purpose three years ago. Artificial insemination proved successful and the baby, a boy by the way, is due in December. A Christmas baby.'

There's an alarming innocence in the way this is said and I find myself glancing anxiously at the garden wall. It's high, but it won't be high enough. They'll bring ladders; they'll come swarming over the top and find a house built of glass. My chest is tight, 'You must make preparations! You can't keep this a secret for ever, and when it does become public . . .'

Her fingers, briefly, touch mine. 'That is, perhaps, inevitable, although I'm hoping it won't happen too soon. It would be terrible for Anna at the moment. And it's not only Anna and the baby I have to think about, there's also the Colonel. We would have gone ahead with this a long time ago, Anna and me, but we didn't want to hurt him. Eventually, however, we simply couldn't wait any longer. He's very excited at the thought of being a grandfather. A grandson! His housekeeper, Mrs Harrison, is an intelligent, and kind, woman and with her help we've managed to keep him blissfully unaware of the physical changes in his oldest son. Our chief fear to date has been the tabloid press; I should have known Gerry would be as great a threat – he's probably had suspicions for years.' She sighs, then shrugs. 'I was intending to put the Kentish Town house up for rent but I guess this means I'll have to sell it. Anna and I are making a fair amount these days – hopefully we'll be able to buy my dear brother off.'

I can tell she's not convinced, and neither am I. 'He'll bleed you dry, and then turn you over to the papers.'

Her palms are spread wide. 'What else can we do?'

There are a couple of solutions I can think of, but only one I'm willing to be involved with. 'You have no choice but to blackmail him back. The Colonel described your brother as a dishonest rogue. Do you know much about his business affairs?'

'Not really, though I've heard rumours about dodgy dealing.' Excited, she rises on to her knees. 'Tor, can I employ you to investigate?'

I smile in reply, she most certainly can. 'Tell me,' I have one last question. 'How does your relationship stand legally? I mean, have you and Anna actually got divorced?'

Her laughter skitters, echoes off glass. 'Divorced? Hell no,' she drawls. 'I am now what I've always dreamed of being. A happily married woman.'

MEG O'BRIEN

Kill the Woman and Child

'Come in, Outlaw. Over.' The low voice issued from a two-way radio attached to my belt. It was accompanied by a crackle of static.

Outlaw. The name, much as I despised it, seemed appropriate enough. My mom had labelled me Jessica when she was still in and out of the ether and Pop was on a drunk. It never even occurred to her that with a last name like James, I'd be known as Jesse by third grade. When I was twelve I hung out with boys, and I wanted to change my handle to Spike, or Bugs, or something equally amusing, but Mom wouldn't allow it. Just as well. In Rochester, New York, in my neighbourhood, changing your name was the sort of thing you did when getting married, or (same difference) on the way to jail.

I pulled the radio from my belt and punched the talk button. 'This is Outlaw. Come in, over.'

'Judas is heading in your direction. He's wearing a black leather windbreaker, work boots, brown cords...' I knew the rest of the description well enough: thirty-seven, six feet tall, light hair. A nasty scar running straight down the middle of his cheek. 'He's armed with a Wolfe 134 automatic rifle, and he knows we're here. Don't blow it this time.'

I clicked off without saying 'Over.' My mouth was too dry. I shifted the weight of my own rifle and raised it to shoulder level, peering through the sight and scanning the quiet street.

It was a small town, colonial in style like so many in New York State. An ordinary village, except that a child killer, a sniper – code name Judas – stalked its streets.

The temperature, I thought, must be in the nineties. The time was 2:07 pm. We were too far inland from Lake Ontario to get a breeze, but every now and then a truck rumbled by, raising dust in the air. My black sleeveless tee stuck to my back, and my long brown hair, tucked inside a fatigue cap, bled sweat on to my forehead.

I leaned my back against the brick siding of the town hall and tried to relax. Breathe in. Breathe out. Don't let your nerves take over.

The crackle again. 'Outlaw? He should reach you in less than ten seconds. He should be in your view. Over.'

I snaked a look around the building. I didn't see him anywhere. Nor did I hear any sounds. No birds, no dogs, and even the traffic had quit. I felt like the abandoned marshal in some Wild West movie. Was everybody hiding indoors, like in *High Noon*, that old Gary Cooper flick? And what would I do when Judas appeared? Would I step out, cool and brave as Coop, and shoot him dead? Or would I turn tail and run?

I had blown it yesterday. I couldn't fail again.

My hands shook. The rifle slipped from my grip. I caught it before it hit the ground.

I didn't want to do this. I hate guns. I hate killing. To me, heaven is a place where people leave people alone. But my job was to make sure Judas was killed. 'It shouldn't be that difficult,' they had said in the briefing. 'The man is a monster. He deserves to be killed.'

Keep telling yourself that, Jess. He deserves to be killed.

A sound, like that of a twig snapping. A grunt a short distance away. The hairs rose on the back of my neck. *Behind me.* I swung around. *Judas. Killer. Monster.* He stepped out from the shelter of a mom-and-pop grocery store less than thirty feet away, his weapon raised to shoot. I jerked back and felt my legs turn to liquid as bullets ricocheted above my head. From other areas I heard loud reports begin. Someone was covering me, drawing his fire their way. Maybe they'd get him first.

I closed my eyes, willing myself far away in Florida, the Caribbean, Duluth – anywhere but here.

At some point, the gunfire settled down. I took a deep breath and dared a look at the store again. A gun barrel glinted in the sunlight. It was pointed directly at me. I yanked my rifle up. Sweat blurred my eyes, and I had to pull back and hurriedly wipe them. I sighted into the sun again.

That quickly, Judas disappeared. Where the hell *was* he? One moment he was there, and the next –

Shit! Movement only ten feet away now – across the street by the bank. Judas? I couldn't be sure. Then something metallic clicked, so close that it almost stopped my heart. There was no doubt in my mind it was Judas. I whirled sideways and aimed my rifle as a projectile slammed into the ground at my feet, spraying pieces of asphalt everywhere. I wasn't thinking, suddenly, about how I hated killing. I pulled the trigger without thought, in a knee-jerk response to fear. The rifle bucked, slamming into my shoulder, almost knocking me down. The sound split my eardrums. I realised I hadn't put the automatic on, and I closed my eyes and squeezed the trigger over and over, not wanted to see the bullets strike their mark.

I heard a baby cry.

My eyes flew open, and with horror I saw that where Judas should have been, there stood instead a light-haired woman holding a baby. In my mind, a look of terror crossed her innocent face. (You understand, I tell this now from hindsight. It all happened simultaneously that day. The woman. The baby's cry. My finger squeezing the trigger.)

My bullets struck and the woman fell, clutching her child. They lay motionless in the dust.

I dropped the rifle as pain enveloped my heart. *I couldn't do anything right.* I heard Pop saying that over and over: 'You always do everything wrong, Jesse . . . never do anything right.' He'd say it in a drunken stupor most of the time, but that didn't change the fact that I believed every word. Even at thirty, I was still hearing it – a family recipe, handed down from one drunken Irish generation to the other: *You'll never amount to anything good.*

I stumbled the few feet across the street and stood above the woman and baby. Her chest, her face, the baby's entire body, were riddled with holes. Shaking with rage, I kicked the woman. She flopped a little, but otherwise, she didn't move. I kicked the baby. I stomped on his face. 'God damn you both,' I yelled.

Then, turning my back on the painted plywood target, I left the Davies School of Defense for Executive Bodyguards. I never wanted to see the goddamned place again.

I stopped in at a bar on the way home. Not Harrigan's, where the bartenders knew me and knew I'd been to a treatment programme recently. A dreary little joint called Jack's, somewhere along the river. It had rotting green window shades and was dense with smoke. Factory workers were drinking their lunch with sides of Polish sausages and pickled eggs.

I ordered a Genesee Screw – Genesee beer over sliced oranges, my old favourite from drinking days. I had to tell the bartender how to make it, and when I specified Genesee, he lifted a scraggly gray brow. Genesee is usually only ordered hereabouts by merchant marines, mass murderers, and embittered reporters like me.

When it came, I stared at it a while. While I stared, I remembered how I'd gotten into this mess.

Marcus Andrelli, head of an élite branch of the mob in Western New York, had offered me a job as his bodyguard. This is the New Mob, you understand – no drugs, prostitution, or ordinary street crime will ever tarnish its smooth white cuffs. A cabal of Harvard-type business grads, Marcus' group is dedicated to the proposition that all men are created to move money and land with the least amount of legalities and the highest level of profit possible.

I make no excuses for the fact that Marcus is my friend and sometime lover. The reasons are unclear, even to me, but have something to do – I suspect – with that old adage about moth to the flame. As for the offer of a job as bodyguard, being a reporter has its frustrations, and I guess Marcus noticed I had sort of burned out. I love writing (as Peter DeVries, I think, has said); what I can't stand is the paperwork. Marcus, on the other hand, offered $60,000 a year, a company Beamer, and travel to foreign countries.

You probably think that as a woman with very little cash in her pocket, a '68 car with bad karma, and a job I hate, I jumped at the chance.

Are you *crazy*? Me, Jesse James, work for (wait a minute

now, what's that euphemism?) the *organization*? Become an outlaw for *real*? My ingrained sense of guilt would never allow it.

Take the woman and baby, for instance. I will carry that moment of stupidity around with me all my life. The problem being: What if they'd been real? That, of course, was the whole point of the Davies exercise, and why it had played havoc with my nerves. As the kid of an alcoholic, I'd learned early on that more often than not, I fail.

So I could never work at a job that required I carry a gun. I opted instead for doing a little independent study at Davies School of Defense – research for a story on exotic vocations. I'd felt sure I could freelance it if the *Herald* didn't bite.

I pushed my cap back on my head and shivered as the air-conditioning finally had its way with my sunburned arms. I fiddled with the frosted glass of the Genesee Screw, but didn't drink. I kept seeing that target – that woman and child. The damned thing was like Swiss cheese. How had it gotten that way?

In the classes at Davies – before you go out on the exercise field – they teach you to stop shooting when you hear the baby's cry. It's the first clue you've blown it: an automatic wail issuing from a speaker high above the grounds once you hit the woman and child. The target is then picked up by an instructor and assessed as a kind of 'report card'. A new, unblemished hunk of plywood takes its place.

But the target I'd hit was already riddled with holes. My rifle hadn't been on automatic; a few splinters should have been the extent of the damage from me – provided I'd struck it at all. And I'd been the first student out on the field that day.

Someone practicing in the night, then? An instructor, say – and he'd forgotten to change the target before the day's run? Whoever, he was one mean son of a bitch. A crazy who didn't like women and kids at all. It gave me the creeps, and I wondered what kind of checks they ran on people before letting them teach at those schools.

I finally left the beer untouched and went in search of a phone. The wall around it was decorated with graffiti, and among its many offerings – the Salvation Army, Travelers' Aid,

1–800-HERPES2 – was an AA number. I ignored it, of course. Since drying out at St Avery's three months ago, I'd been seeing a New Age shrink in Pittsford named Samved. He and I had concluded there was nothing worse than imprinting a belief on one's consciousness like: *I am an alcoholic*. I mean, when you've already got a bad self-image, where do you go from there? I much prefer Samved's approach: *You have a problem with drinking on this plane, today. In reality, however, you are a perfect child of God. Children of God can be healed*.

I eyed my beer, back there on the bar. Wet my lips.

Uh-huh.

I clunked in a quarter and dialled Marcus Andrelli's private line.

Marcus, dressed in grey sweats and an old pair of white Converse running shoes, was still on the phone when I arrived. His black hair was damp and curling from a recent workout. His desk, a field of glass the size of a small hockey rink, was piled high with newspapers, *Wall Street Journals*, real-estate dailies and files on every major politician in the country. A computer blinked, a fax was busy spewing forth reams of paper, and two additional phones were ringing.

Behind Marcus, sheer blue curtains stretched over wall-to-wall glass. When the curtains are pulled back they reveal the entire city of Rochester beneath one's feet – and a fine place for the city of Rochester to be, if you ask me.

I paced, only half hearing a series of sentences involving words like *foreclosure ... bankrupt ... takeover*. I thought how much alike – and unalike – Marcus and I are. In his work, he manipulates and cons people, just like me. But I'm embarrassed when I do it, and immediately thereafter comes the guilt.

Marcus, on the other hand, considers his antics a skill. He learned to live with himself years ago, and hasn't always got a whole lot of patience with angst like mine. Why I burden him with it, I don't profess to know.

'Jess...' Marcus said as he hung up. He rose from his desk, a tall, well-exercised figure at forty-two, with hard, even features. His brown, nearly black eyes were tinged with caution most of the time, warranted or not. Marcus ordinarily doesn't turn that expression on me, for which I am glad. 'You look – '

'Dusty,' said an amused voice from the other end of the room.

I hadn't even seen Tark there. For a big hulk of a guy, he manages to kind of inconspicuously hang around. He was leaning against the back of a sofa, arms folded, legs crossed nonchalantly at the ankle.

Tark is Marcus's bodyguard and has been his friend since childhood. More Diogenes in latter days than Dillinger, Tark's fondest wish is to go on a backpacking trip in the Himalayas. He was hoping I'd take Marcus up on his offer of a job and sub for him while he was gone.

'Go ahead, laugh,' I grumbled. 'I'd like to see *you* out at that not so funny farm, crawling under barbed wire in one of those imported silk suits of yours.'

He grinned.

I turned to Marcus. 'I need a drink.'

His dark brow lifted almost as much as the bartender's at Jack's, but for different reasons. And even though he knew damn well what I meant, Marcus headed for the bar where he'd already fixed a pitcher of something cold and almost assuredly virgin. He poured me a glass.

'Try this,' he said.

I tasted the honey-laced pineapple crap and swore something unpleasant under my breath. Marcus could be damned aggravating when it came to helping me stay sober. Two Saturdays ago, for instance, I'd headed out to his cabin at Irondequoit, thinking it'd be a great day to sit on his yacht down on the water, drink a little, catch some rays. (I'd plotted the part about 'drinking a little' for three solid days in advance.)

Instead, there never was time, somehow, to sit on the *SeaStar* and fall from grace. We'd sanded and painted, scoured and scraped, and even ridden a fallen tree down an estuary of the bay, planning to use it for the mast of the Tancook Whaler that Marcus was building from scratch. I couldn't walk for days afterward, my muscles were that sore. I stayed sober, though. It wasn't until the weekend was over that I realised Marcus had planned it that way. Marcus Andrelli could be sneaky. Never saying a word, but ahead of me all the way.

'They've got all these targets,' I began now without preamble, pacing. The cap was jammed down over my eyes, and my hair was falling out of it in long sweaty strings. Despite the juice, I could taste grit in my mouth, feel it on my face, and I looked, I suppose, about as stunning as I ever do.

'One minute,' I complained, 'it's a genuine bad guy popping out at you. The next, it's Rebecca of Sunnybrook Farm. And the place is booby-trapped, fake bullets exploding all around, but you forget they're fake – you have to psych yourself up to kill or they wash you out, you *fail* . . .' I faltered over the word and turned away, picking up a small bronze figurine and staring at it blindly. 'You have to learn to think fast, because in real life there's no time to think. The problem is, I'm not fast.' I slammed the object down. 'I shot the woman and the goddamned baby.'

Marcus sat on the edge of his desk. 'You agonise too much. It was only a target, Jess.'

But Tark understood. 'The thing that's bothering Jess is what bothers me all the time: what if, in the heat of action, your instincts are wrong?' He stood with his broad back to the windows, hands stuck in the pockets of his expensive black summer-weight suit. His dark hair, tinged with gray, was short and brushed straight back, his features worked over but not otherwise bad. 'The thing you've got to remember, Jess, is that you haven't had the kind of training that others take before that particular exercise. I gave you – what? – six hours on a practice range, just so you could hold a weapon with some authority? You couldn't expect to do any better than you did.'

'Dammit, it doesn't matter. I made the wrong decision, I always do – '

'You always take on more than you should,' Marcus said impatiently. 'You throw yourself into hot water over and over, then ask yourself why you keep getting burned.'

I gulped down more juice and stared longingly at the bottles on the bar. A little rum in this stuff would taste real good. I sneaked a glance at Marcus. He seemed unconcerned, but that didn't fool me. If I reached for the rum he'd break my arm.

'Listen, I don't mean to make more of this than it is.' I managed a smile. 'I've got my story, after all. Hell, I've got a better story than I'd expected: SCREW-UP REPORTER SHOOTS WOMAN AND BABY. I can see the headlines now.'

Marcus and Tark didn't say anything. They just gave each other that look I'd come, lately, to know: *Jess is on the edge. How much longer can it be?* Any minute now Marcus would be saying, 'Jess, have you noticed how much you're swearing today?' (He worries about the old-fashioned Italian Catholic things like that. And for somebody who likes to be her own boss, this quaint, protective attitude toward women is perversely endearing to me.)

But I ranted on, unable to stop, I was so wired. 'What I can't get out of my mind is that shredded target. You'd think they were training the bad guys there, not the good ones.'

Tark murmured, 'Now there's a thought,' and turned to gaze out the window, looking thoughtful.

'Speaking of mercenaries,' Marcus said, 'will you be covering the Eastman bash tomorrow?'

'Ah, the definition of mercenary . . . corrupt, unprincipled, scheming . . . it fits our city's financial fathers to a T.'

The occasion tomorrow, according to the news releases, was a celebration of the remodelling of the George Eastman mansion. In actuality, the town's financial fathers had chosen this particular date because of the international peace talks taking place in the Thousand Islands this week. It was the perfect time to draw in foreign dignitaries, make business contacts 'round the globe.

'What about you, Marcus? You planning to cash in on this little opportunity too?'

'Got to keep ahead of the game,' he said, and shrugged.

The secret to Marcus Andrelli's success, in business and with people – always be ahead of the game.

He slid off the desk, put an arm behind my back, and drew me outside to a small terrace. I heard the apartment door close softly and knew that Tark had left us alone.

We stood looking out over Rochester: Marcus, who had made the leap from the wrong side of the tracks to owning maybe half of what he saw, and me – somewhere on the tracks themselves, wondering when, if ever, the train would come whooshing along and run me down.

Marcus said, 'We make choices in life, Jess. Year to year, moment to moment – once a path is set, a decision made, you can't go back and question everything. You could become paralysed that way.'

I pushed back my cap. 'Look, no offence, but Christ, Marcus – how can you live that way?'

'For me, there are no more choices. I can't change what I do.'

'Well, damn it all, anyway – '

He pushed a dusty tangle of hair from my face. 'Have you noticed you're swearing a lot lately?' my sometime lover said.

I had time on my hands after that, so I checked in at the *Herald* for the first time in a week, got yelled at by Charles Nicks, my editor, and ambushed by Becky Anderson – who had followed me here from the *Weston Free Press*. She did this to annoy me, I'm convinced. It's her Life Purpose to keep on reminding me that I'm not up to code in my dress, manners or style.

Charlie rubbed his bald little pate irritably with ink-stained fingers and yelled through his glass cubicle, 'Don't disappear on me again, James! I need you covering that Eastman crap tomorrow. You and Anderson. Keep an eye on that prince, that what's-'is-name. You know, the one those nuts tried to kill last month.'

Prince Rasir of Senadon. Only nineteen years old, an assassination attempt had been made against him in his own country less than fours weeks ago. Some hullabaloo over his wanting to enter into an arms agreement with the US. Not everyone in the South China Sea was happy about this state of affairs. He now travelled with an extra contingent of body-guards. I doubted there would be much action with all that muscle around. Some assignment. I started to grouse under my breath.

Becky interrupted. She smoothed a hand over her raw-silk skirt and said primly, 'Jesse, it would be nice if you'd dress tomorrow. Since we'll be there together, I mean.'

'Not to worry.' I dusted off my jeans while thumbing through papers in my IN box. 'I'll clean these up.'

She coughed delicately. 'Jesse.'

'Huh?'

'There will be visiting dignitaries there. I had in mind a dress and heels.'

I looked up. Becky's every shining blond hair, as always, was lacquered into place. Well, hell, she edits the Lifestyle section. She has to look neat for all those teas and Barbie Doll stuff.

I jammed my hands on my hips and stuck my chin out, narrowing my eyes to green slits. Daring her to say one more word about my clothes.

'Of course, if that's all you have . . .' she mumbled quickly.

I knew she'd back down. The woman has no balls.

When I got home to my apartment on Genesee Park Boulevard, Mrs Binty was on the front porch, rocking and shelling peas. She's been cooking lately for Mr Garson, across the street. He used to come over and help her prune the rose-bushes, but Mr Garson's been in mourning since his wife died three months ago. Now he even forgets to eat unless you put the idea in his mind. So Mrs Binty (my landlady) sits beneath her wisteria like some tiny little white-haired fairy-tale lady with an enamelled blue bowl on her lap, shelling away. She entices Mr Garson over with those fresh sweet peas like the old witch in 'Hansel and Gretel,' luring the children with bits of cake.

'I let your nice friend Grady North in,' she warbled as I stepped out of my '68 Campbell's soup can, a rusted red-and-white *Karmann Ghia*. 'He's been chipping off that old paint while he waits for you. That way, we can start redoing the window frames.'

Sure enough, there through the tree leaves was Grady North above me on the porch roof, chipping away. I sighed. Just what every girl needs to come home to on a hot summer day. A cop.

'It was only a plywood target,' I said after we'd gotten some iced tea and gone back out on the roof. 'But I felt those bullets hit *me*.' (Samved says if we listen to ourselves, we can know how much something's bothering us by how often we bring it up.) Grady and I sat with our backs against the windows, shaded from the evening sun by the branches of Mrs Binty's oak trees.

Difficult as ever, my friend the cop stretched out his long legs and opined: 'You will always have problems over moral issues so long as you insist on living half your life outside the law.'

I gave him a nasty look and noted that in a cotton preppy shirt, pleated khaki pants, and sneakers, he looked better, as usual, than me. Thank God for the paint chips in his sandy hair. They reduced his handsome quotient – despite his nice, tight ass – by at least ten degrees.

'Let's not get into the foibles of my personality,' I muttered.

'Everything you do, you do ass backwards.'

'Now you sound like my mother.'

'You know it's true. You look around, ask yourself what's legal, then do the exact opposite.'

'Usually, the opposite is best.'

'And I wonder just where you picked up an idea like that.'

'Leave Marcus out of this or I'm going inside.'

He swore under his breath.

'You're even testier than usual,' I observed. 'What's going on?'

He didn't answer directly, but broke a thin twig off the tree and bent it back and forth with one hand with so much nervous tension, it splintered in half. 'You covering the Eastman celebration tomorrow?'

'Yeah.'

'You heard any rumours?'

'About what?'

'Anything. Anything at all.'

'Sure. The president of IBM will be there with his three mistresses, one of whom has two heads. Tom Selleck may show . . . or was that Rex Reed? Hard to remember, there's so much shit floating around.'

'Never mind!' he exploded, getting to his feet. 'If you ever took two minutes to be serious – '

'Crimin*ee*. Take it easy, will you?'

My phone rang. I unwound my aching limbs and went in to answer it. It was the police commissioner's office, for Grady. He stood behind me, grabbing the phone before the words *It's for you* were even out of my mouth.

'Yeah? Yeah, okay. Right. Will do.' He paced back and forth, tugging at the phone line impatiently as he talked.

Grady's a detective in Homicide, but he works with the commissioner's office in planning security when important events take place. You wouldn't exactly say that Rochester is a hotbed of political ferment, but historically, it has been a center for activism. The major terminal for the Underground Railway in the north was here; it's the place of Susan B Anthony's birth and early feminist years; and during Vietnam the town was littered with marching priests and nuns – many of them my old teachers from Mercy High, in boots, miniskirts with fringe, and carrying guitars. (Mention this now and they look a little wistful . . . or simply blank.)

Aside from that, we're an important business town. Western Union was founded here, as was Eastman-Kodak, Bausch & Lomb, Xerox. And all of these companies, along with several others, were hosting the event this week at the George Eastman House.

'I'll be there,' Grady said. He slammed the phone down.

'What's wrong? What's going on?'

He rolled down his shirt sleeves and buttoned his cuffs. Despite an attempt to be casual, there was a look on his face I recognised – something that's only there when things have gone quite wrong. 'Goddamn foreign politicians,' he said angrily. 'They bring families and wander all over, let down their guard. I just wish they'd held this damn thing in Toronto.'

I couldn't get any more out of him. After he left I went over the list of VIPs I'd picked up at the *Herald*, the ones who would be at the Kodak Festival the next day. I could see Grady's problem with security. Aside from famous artists, photographers, and the usual sprinkling of politicians and business leaders, several heads of state from the peace talks had been invited. Further, it was summer; as Grady had said, they'd bring their families and combine the trip with a vacation. Rochester, with Lake Ontario and the Genesee River – lots of water, trees, flowers and clean blue sky – isn't a bad place at all to visit. If you catch us on a good day, in fact – one of the two or three between winter and summer – you might never want to go home.

The thought of trying to secure the Eastman grounds, however, with its hidden nooks and crannies, made me shudder.

I sipped my iced tea, going over and over the list. Memorising details to add to my notes the next day. Now and then I could hear the buzz of Mrs Binty's conversation with Mr Garson. There didn't seem to be much pizzazz in his tone. Strange, I thought, the way life stops for the survivor when someone dies. They cease functioning for a while.

Functionaries ...

The thought struck, but didn't go any further just then.

The George Eastman House has exhibits ranging from the first snapshot 100 years ago, to Lewis Carroll, Julia Margaret Cameron, and Ansel Adams today. The grounds are composed of stone walls and gardens, with high shrubs and trees. The mansion – fifty rooms or so – is Georgian, with mellowed brick, huge ivy-covered chimneys, and stone porches. Ordinarily, this is a quiet, peaceful place to wander and re-group.

Today, however, there was a black cloud of tension in the air. Grady North stalked by at one point – dressed for the occasion like a man on his way up, but obviously working – and I tried to get his attention. He glared and kept on stalking. I assumed he'd been working through the night setting up security. Besides the many Three-Piece Suits that looked like executive security types, there was a sprinkling of cops throughout the grounds. Grady had them arrayed in spiffy dress blues, their black shoes polished to a glassy sheen. They managed to look impressive rather than unnerving, sort of like the British Royal Guard.

I was standing with Becky Anderson beside a bed of periwinkle and herbs. It stated just that on the little metal sign stuck in the ground: PERIWINKLE AND HERBS. In deference to Becky's sensibilities, I had worn my white cotton slacks, a red silk blouse, and flats. I had even combed my hair. There were sweat stains already beneath the armpits of the blouse, but looking at Becky, I didn't feel too bad. It had rained during the night, and the ground was still damp. Becky's high white heels had been sinking up to the hilt since we arrived, unintentionally aerating the grass. Following behind her, I had tried not to laugh, but she'd caught me.

'You've always intimidated me,' she said now.

I didn't hear her at first. I was busy watching the wife of

Rasir, the young Prince of Senadon. No more than a girl herself, she was chasing after her three-year-old son. Her long teal-blue dress, shot through with gold thread, was coming undone in the chase. She grabbed at it with one hand while the other hid a bubbling laugh. A tall nun in white habit – à la Mother Teresa – had been taken by surprise as the ruler's son snatched her long white skirt in passing. The nun pushed with frantic modesty to keep her skirt down. She wasn't quick enough. The kid's pass revealed bare legs above white socks with tennis shoes. The ruler's wife caught up with her child at last and, giggling, swooped him high off the ground. The nun jammed her hands into her full sleeves irritably and turned away.

Even Becky laughed, and that's when I realised what she had just said: 'You've always intimidated me.'

I faced her and said belatedly, 'I intimidate *you*?'

She flushed. 'You seem so sure of yourself. The way you dress and act, like you couldn't care less what people think.'

I should have felt good. I'd never known my nemesis felt that way about me. Underneath all the bravado, I was intimidated by *her*.

For a brief moment I wanted to tell her so. Then I was distracted by the sight of Marcus talking with one of the country's top political photographers, along with a man I recognised from the papers as a vice-president from Xerox, and the mayor. Nobody ever said Marcus doesn't mingle well.

He was looking sharp: three-piece summer grey suit, white shirt, blue tie. A slight breeze lifted his black hair as he stood with one hand in a pocket, the other punctuating his conversation. He seemed attentive to the group, but never once stopped scanning the crowd. On one pass he saw me. Becky caught the message that passed between us and cast me a scathing look.

'I'll see you in a while,' I said. 'I have to talk to someone.'

Her mouth thinned out. 'We're supposed to be covering the prince.'

'Jeez! Becky – ' I bit my tongue. 'You go. I'll be with you in a minute, okay?'

She aerated the ground some more and flounced away.

I wandered off to a side garden, where there were fewer

people milling around than out front. After a few minutes, Marcus joined me. We stood a few feet apart and gazed in different directions, talking in low, casual tones as if commenting on the weather or the state of periwinkles in July. (Maintaining a low profile in public, we call it.) Marcus still surveyed the grounds.

'You look unusually vigilant,' I noted.

'With good reason.' He glanced at his watch. 'When are you leaving?'

'Leaving here? After the fireworks, I guess. Whenever this shindig is over. Why?'

'It seems your friend Grady North has been more than usually busy since last night. Beefing up security, bringing in out-of-town help.'

'I noticed. What do you think's going on?'

'Tark has been hanging out with the bodyguard contingent. Apparently, there's been an assassination threat.'

I had a sinking feeling. 'Don't tell me. Rasir.' Christ, I'd just sent Becky Anderson off alone to cover the story of the year.

Marcus nodded. 'Could be a false alarm, of course. A scare to throw a monkey wrench into his Washington trip.'

Rasir's country, Senadon, was one of the largest and richest island countries south of China. Rasir was said to be nervous about the recent unrest there. He was scheduled to fly to Washington after the peace talks in the Thousand Islands, to sign an alliance that would arm his country and help him to build its first army. A small opposing faction in the South China Sea was said to have been behind the attempt on Rasir's life last month.

I looked around at the Eastman grounds, thinking that I'd been stupid to disregard the likelihood of another attempt here. It was true that Rasir was protected now by a virtual wall of bodyguards – a fact I'd confirmed upon arriving. Yet, access to these grounds was relatively easy. And there were over 300 guests milling about; a large turnaround crowd. People kept coming and going.

I could see why our friends in Toronto had passed up the chance to hold this little clambake over there.

'I wonder why Grady doesn't just shut the whole thing down. Send everybody home.'

Marcus began to speak but paused as his eyes lit on a cop who had just entered the West Garden. The cop's glance slid over us, then away.

'From a purely pragmatic viewpoint,' Marcus said quietly, 'North is faced with a sticky diplomatic problem. There's a lot of potential wealth here today, and more at stake than the life of one prince from one small country. I'd hate to be in his shoes.'

He was right. Half the people here were from Fortune 500 companies, their hopeful fingers in the government tills of other lands. Grady's orders from high up almost certainly would have been to bring in all the help he needed – but to handle things.

Marcus was still looking at the cop. 'There's something...' He shook his head. 'Let's walk.'

When we were beyond the crowd, on the other side of a high stand of shrubs, he faced me and folded his arms. His chin went up in that cocky don't-argue-with-me manner I knew so well.

'I've arranged for Tark to take you home.'

'Excuse me?'

'Don't argue, Jess. I don't want you hurt.'

'Marcus, it's my job to cover the prince. I can't walk out on that now. Besides, I won't be hurt –'

'If there's trouble around, you find it. Jess, you look to be hurt.'

Now, that really did hurt. It was good for another ten minutes of dialogue, in fact. I revved up for it – but then I remembered a lesson from crafty old Samved on passive resistance: *Don't be afraid to go with the programme now and then. If nothing else, it quells suspicion.*

I didn't give in too easily. I appeared to think about it. Then I shrugged. 'Where is Tark?'

'By the refreshment tent, waiting for you.'

'I have to use the rest room. I'll meet him there.'

A pause while Marcus considered the efficacy of leaving me on my own. Finally he nodded, although his mouth held a slight worried smile. The small white scar beneath his left eye stood out in relief; a sign of tension. He tilted my chin up with one finger. 'Thank you, Jess. I know how you loathe being taken care of.'

I gave him a warm look. I even met his eyes. 'By anyone but you,' I said.

I swung my tote to my shoulder and headed in the direction of the rest rooms, which were near the refreshment tent. Once out of Marcus's sight, however, I turned without a qualm the opposite way.

There's another thing my guru/shrink is wont to say (paraphrasing Shelley): *Obedience is the bane of all genius. It makes slaves of men.*

That's what I love about Samved. He's got a quote for everything.

The thing is (and aside from the fact that Marcus had become too damned protective of late), I needed a story. More particularly, I needed something different from all the rest. Charlie Nicks had been on my back about being out of the office too much, and I'd been fired from one too many jobs in the past few years. 'You just don't know how to follow orders,' was the most common complaint. It was true. So to make up for that failing, I try harder. And when I come up with something brilliant, some story they can't possibly turn down, I buy myself another week, another month, before I'm out the door.

The key word, however, is *brilliant*. Things have to have a twist – something my fellow scribes don't click into, at least until the story's out on the wires under my name. And it had occurred to me, listening to Marcus, that there just might be one hell of a twist going on here today.

Casting back in memory, I dredged up everything I'd read about the chain of command in Senadon. The man who would replace Rasir, should he die, was his brother. From all reports, they thought alike. He would presumably carry out Rasir's quest for arms.

An assassination, therefore, would do nothing to stop an alliance. It might, in fact, hasten one. It seemed to me the opposing faction would realise that eventually, and realise, too, that the alternative way to bring a country – or a political talk – to a halt is to see to it the functionaries stop functioning.

Which is exactly what might happen if Rasir were thrown into mourning.

I have to admit I didn't think this up out of a clear blue sky. It occurred to me only because I'd been haunted since the night before by the image of Mrs Binty's friend, Mr Garson – and the malaise he'd suffered since his wife died. For three solid months now, the man had barely been able to tie his own shoes.

How, then, would a nineteen-year-old boy, albeit prince, cope with the death of that bubbly young girl and their toddler son?

It took me less than five minutes to locate the princess again. She and her child were in the East Garden, watching a puppet show from the last row behind a small group of mothers and kids. Two foreign-looking bodyguard types, in black suits, stood behind them. I remembered that they had been on the periphery earlier, when the princess was chasing her son. The cop I'd seen in the West Garden was here now, too, clearly keeping an eye on things.

The princess still seemed unconcerned, however. I realised that she must not have been told about this latest threat. The prince, possibly to keep any danger from touching her and the child, was as far away as he could be – involved in talks with various business leaders at the front of the mansion. I'd left Becky Anderson to keep an eye on him there, which was either the smartest or dumbest thing I'd ever done in my life. Becky might wind up with the hottest story of her fluff-filled career, while I'd be out of a job.

I'd never seen anyone so jumpy as Rasir. His complexion was pale, and when I saw him he was rubbing constantly at a small mole on his homely, boyish face, looking about nervously as he waited for the blow to fall.

I wandered behind the audience at the puppet show a few minutes, but then I worried about being seen by Marcus or Tark and carted off to someplace safe and banal. There was a natural grouping of shrubs and trees along one wall, and I eased back into it. I could still see most of the garden through a screen of delicate vines. Twenty minutes later, when nothing had happened, I began to feel stupid lurking in the shrubs that way. The air was hotter and thicker than mustard in hell, and

I half expected to look sideways and see, peering back through the greenery, a fellow wretch from the *National Enquirer*.

Bored, I stretched prone on the ground, cleared another space to see, and propped my chin on my hands. All sorts of organisms rose from the ground to attack my nose. I swallowed a sneeze. Birds chirped and insects buzzed. From the front lawn came the strains of the Navy Band as it played Sousa marches and light pop. Wiping my eyes clear of sweat (I hate summer; have I said that yet?), I focused on the young princess –

And then I saw that nun again. The one who'd been so angry at having her skirts hiked up by the royals' son. On such a hot day, in that habit, why was she even hanging around? Was she a glutton for punishment? A secret exhibitionist? Was she hoping for another thrill?

One way or another, something about her was off.

The puppet show continued, and the nun made a slow circuit of the garden. She appeared to read from a small black book. Now and then she'd stoop to touch a flower. And although I'll admit to a suspicious nature, it seemed to me, after watching her at this for a while, that she was in fact checking out the young mother and her son.

Interestingly, the cop had a close eye on the good sister too. As did the black-suited bodyguards.

It was one of those times, when the nun bent to read a tag on a rosebush, that her sleeve caught on a thorn and was pulled back. She was about ten feet away from me then, and I saw a gleam of chunky gold on her wrist. She pulled the sleeve down quickly, but not before I saw that the gold was a watch.

A gold watch? I thought curiously. On a nun? Times had changed.

But well, come on . . . vow of poverty or not, if nuns could wear miniskirts in the seventies, why not gold watches in the nineties? Think of it: yuppism, alive and well and living in a convent in Rochester, New York.

While I was mulling all this over, the puppet show ended. The audience of children and mothers began to wander from the garden to the front of the mansion. The sky was growing dark; it was nearly nine pm.

The nun, approaching from the left, began to walk slowly

towards the princess – who, with her son, followed by their bodyguards, was trailing the rest of the crowd. As the princess picked up her pace, the nun did too. The distance between them closed, and the nun's hand reached into the deep folds of her habit. She seemed to pat something, as if reassuring herself it was there.

My own hand, which had curled around a narrow branch of shrubbery, tightened. My skin prickled. I had never carried a gun in my life before last week, but the first, most important lesson at the Davies School had been: Be aware of your weapon at all times. Know where it is, be sure it's in good order and accessible. Time after time I had made that patting gesture myself – out of nerves, more than anything.

The nun, of course, could have been patting a rosary. Or maybe she had a pastrami sandwich tucked away in there.

At that instant, a loud boom sounded – almost stopping my heart. But the princess laughed and picked up her child, pointing to the sky as it bloomed with red and gold. The fireworks had begun. Her son squealed with delight, then buried his head in her shoulder – frightened, no doubt, by the rapid noises that followed.

I looked up at the fireworks, too, an automatic reaction ... and when I looked back into the growing gloom, I saw with a start that the bodyguards were gone. So was the cop. Christ, they had left the princess and her son alone.

Further, the young mother's journey towards the front of the house had been effectively cut off by the nun. The princess looked startled at the nun's hastening approach. She took a step back, an anxious question (I thought) in her eyes. It was so much like my experience the day before at the Davies School, with the innocent woman, the expression of alarm, the child –

The nun reached into her habit again, and I moved.

I stumbled to my feet, my legs stiff and protesting. Shoving the vines aside, I tore across the grass. As the nun – whose back was to me – took another step towards the princess, I reached her and grabbed her by the shoulder.

She turned, her dark eyes flaring with anger.

'It's Saturday. Confession time,' I said.

The hand came out of the nun's habit, and in it was a gun.

The young mother screamed. Her son began to cry. She clutched him tighter and backed away.

I held my hands up, palm out. 'Don't shoot. Take it easy.' I was scared out of my wits. My legs were weak, and my jaw felt like it was wired; it barely moved. I edged around, trying to position myself between the two royals and the nun.

The nun raised her weapon, pointing it at me.

'Look, don't do this,' I pleaded. And again, it was like Davies – in slow motion, everything happening at once. 'I've got a friend on his way – a cop – he's armed –'

I can't even begin to explain the chaos that followed. The fireworks were exploding above us in rapid bursts of light. One of them whistled, like those old bombs in World War II movies. The garden flickered with white, then dark, and from the shadows behind the nun came a cool, familiar voice.

'Well, what have we here?'

It was Marcus. Tark moved in beside him, yanking his Magnum from its holster. The nun whirled to face them, and as she did, Marcus grabbed her arm and, with a quick, hard twist, relieved her of her weapon.

'Get Jess out of here,' he ordered Tark, holding the nun at bay. 'Get her out ... now.'

Meanwhile, the cop from earlier came racing across the garden, revolver drawn. He came to a halt several feet away, legs spread. 'Drop your weapons!' he yelled nervously. 'Stand back!'

There was an explosion then from the front of the mansion, unlike that of the fireworks. It rocked the ground beneath our feet. Screams and the crash of breaking glass. It sounded as if the whole George Eastman House had been bombed.

The princess, squeezing her baby to her breast, cried, 'My husband!'

We all froze, like a da Vinci tableau, to stare in that direction. Then the princess made a move as if to run to the front of the mansion. Marcus grabbed her. He thrust her at the cop, who was still in firing stance, yelled, 'Watch her!' and took off running towards the sound of the screams.

Tark glanced at the young cop, who seemed frozen by the

events except for a tremor in the hands that held his gun. The poor guy looked like he'd never been faced with having to shoot anyone before. 'Christ,' Tark muttered, 'rookies.' He shoved his Magnum into my hand. 'Take care of things.' He ran after Marcus. I stood there with the heavy weapon hanging like an unpleasant fish from the end of my hand.

My stomach coiled. 'Get out of here, Princess.' I jerked my head in the direction of the museum buildings behind the mansion, where I thought she'd be safe. 'Go, *now.*'

'Wait.' That from the cop, whose hand was moving on his revolver.

And while he was focused on us, the nun reached into her full white sleeve and pulled out a second weapon, its silver casing no more than a wink in the darkening night. In one smooth movement she brought it up, aimed at the cop, and shot. Blood spurted from the cop's neck. He fell. Almost without thinking, I raised Tark's Magnum and gripped it with both hands. The nun's pistol was levelled at me now.

'Police!' the nun yelled. 'Drop it!'

Police?

I wavered, confused.

The cop, still on the ground, grabbed up his fallen revolver and shot the nun, who staggered back, dropping her weapon, her hand flying to her shoulder. Fireworks went off like strobe lights, and in their flash I saw that blood had spattered the cop's uniform and brown shoes.

Brown shoes – Jesus, God, I thought inanely, *the cop has brown shoes.*

But then it was dark once more, and I wasn't sure what I had seen.

'Shoot him!' the nun cried, reaching for, but unable to grasp, her weapon.

But the nun was not a nun. She was someone claiming to be a cop – while the cop had turned his revolver on me.

My finger closed on the trigger of Tark's Magnum as I vacillated half seconds between the nun and the cop, then back to the nun again. I broke into a cold sweat. *Christ Almighty, help*, I prayed. *Don't let me fail this time.* My own reasoning voice came back, clear as a bell: *The nun is a terrorist, Jess, the nun is lying ... shoot the nun, shoot the nun. Shoot -*

So I goddamned shot the cop.

That was last week, and things have quietened down a bit since then. Even the weather's cooled off, and I'm sitting out here on the roof of Mrs Binty's porch, in an evening breeze off Lake Ontario, trying to put my thoughts on paper.

I guess the first thing to clear up is that I made the right decision for a change – although, either way, things would've worked out okay.

The 'cop' was a hired assassin, and no wonder he was nervous: the princess was his first paying job. He had slipped on to the grounds and gone unnoticed during Grady's last-minute pull-in of out-of-town help.

'Rasir's enemies in Senadon,' Grady told me, 'knew they'd never get to him. He's too heavily guarded. They hired the assassin to stall the alliance by killing his wife and child.'

The Garson Directive, it shall be known as henceforth.

Which leaves us with the 'nun'. She, it turns out, was one of Grady's undercover cops. I could have been in deep shit, getting in her way. But talk about a twist (and saving ass), what Grady didn't know was that in going through an anti-terrorist course at Davies, the undercover 'nun' met up with a genuine terrorist who was training there secretly at night. Practising on the 'good-guy' targets to overcome any qualms about shooting into crowds. Hence the well-ventilated target of the woman and child.

Anyway, the nun and the terrorist fell in love (how's that for a movie title?) and the nun turned. While Grady had put her on the Eastman grounds that day to protect Rasir's family, the young woman's actual agenda was to kill the princess and her child.

Her terrorist friend took out the princess's bodyguards during the first boom of fireworks that night, when the rest of us were distracted. Their bodies were found later in a maintenance shack on the Eastman grounds.

So like I said, I could've shot either the nun or the cop; both were the bad guys that day. But the cop was the one left pointing a gun – and I wouldn't be alive now if I'd gone the other way.

Samved claims I was being guided 'from another plane', given bits and pieces of information to process that helped me make a right decision in the end. But the only thing I can remember processing is the fact that Grady North, being the worst stickler for the rules I've ever known, would not in a million years allow a real cop – on that kind of high-level duty – to wear brown shoes.

I'd appreciate it if you wouldn't tell anyone I even mentioned that. Things are bad enough without the tabloids printing some scuzzy story about how I killed a guy over his Thom McCanns.

The city offered me a medal of 'valour' for saving the lives of the princess and her son. (The prince was fine; the bomb a mere distraction. A few windows had to be replaced, but other than that, little harm was done.) I balked and made humble noises about the medal, but then I thought: *What the hell – how else would I ever get pinned?*

Besides, it'll look good on a résumé someday. With my record for being fired from jobs, that's not a minor consideration.

While the crowd applauded and the press took pictures and I stood looking like an idiot in a white suit and Becky Anderson's borrowed new heels, I couldn't help but think how easy it is to con people about these things. Because no matter how I try, I can't get beyond the fact that what I did that day resembled nothing like valour at all.

Sure, I saved the princess – and for that I'll be eternally glad. But I had my own agenda when that gun was in my hand. Most people do, when they kill. For me it was the fear of screwing up again, and according to the 'experts', that all goes back to Pop.

I remember him saying once: 'Jesse, girl, you ... your mother ... you're too much a burden on the heart.' This was one night when he was stewed to the gills (otherwise I'd never tell this; you have to understand, Pop was a peace-loving guy at heart, but when the drink was on him, he tended towards morose). Anyway, he was sitting there in his overstuffed chair, still in the tired coveralls he always wore to climb down into those hot, gassy vats at Kodak, although he'd been fired the night before. He was horribly drunk, and holding a gun to his temple. I was ten at the time, and I remember throwing up right there on the living room rug, and then crying until he stopped and put it down.

The world exacts a high price from men who would be poets, who dream of tossing words like silver birds into the sky and wind up shovelling food into the mouths of dependents instead.

Later he said: 'Jesse, girl, you couldn't even let me die in peace.' He said it heavily, with none of the usual twinkle in his eye, and I've always understood, no matter what anyone since has said – counsellors, gurus, or well-meaning friends – that I'd screwed up yet again.

So the circle of guilt goes round and round. Someday, when the prisons are too full to put any more people in them, the courts will assign all miscreants an Irish Catholic father to instil perpetual remorse for their sins. As for me, I grew up with mine, and the only mystery, so far as I can see, is that I haven't yet succumbed this week to an overwhelming desire for a Genesee Screw.

PAM MASON

The Handsome Cabin Boy

Father's church overlooks the sea. All winter long the wind blasts sea salt against the windows, and now they are clouded and will never again be clean and clear. Anyone could come up here, unseen, except for a flicker of shadow against the blind glass.

Father's wife would help him, but she cannot. She sits in the vicarage, listening to the sea drown out the pale singing, waiting for him, like the sailor's wife who knows that one day the sea will widow her.

'Brethren!' father cries, but he is quite alone. The sea water has corroded away the big iron gates and is eating at the brickwork, taking away the faces of the stone saints, wiping out the names of the dead. Every year, the sea sweeps away sheep and cattle and eldest sons. One day it will come for father. At night, he dreams that the church and house, so close to the cliff edge, are sliding, slowly, with a terrible noise, into the sea. He wakes in a sweat, sure he has been screaming. But father cannot cry aloud to save himself. Father cannot be saved. Father sold his soul to the Devil long ago. And now the Devil has come for him.

When he was twenty-two years old, father went to America to minister to the souls of the Red Indians. Father had heard much about America, had heard that Satan was strong there. But father fought the Devil in the East End of London, a place once thought beyond redemption, and he plucked many souls out of that inferno. So he was confident of success in the New World.

Father watched England slipping away from him without anxiety. 'Take care, my love!' his fiancée called, but her voice was so thin and the engines so loud that father heard nothing.

The Mersey dissolved into the Irish Sea without father being aware of it.

Father opened the door of his cabin, and cried out when he saw a figure there, half-hidden in the darkness. A boy. He turned towards father, came closer, head bowed. 'I am here to serve you,' he said. He raised his head and stared at father. And father saw that he was beautiful.

Father was reminded of the black-haired queen in a pantomime he had seen when he was five years old, so cruel, so powerful, so far beyond all human control, that at the first sight of her he had screamed and begged and fought to be taken home again. This lad might have been that queen's son – or daughter, for he was as lovely as a girl. Father stared at the lad. Then remembered his manners, his Christian faith (breathing a prayer to the son of God) and said, 'What is your name, my lad?'

'Jack Hardy, sir,' the lad said in his sweet, dark voice.

'Hardy,' father said, shaking slightly. He clasped his hands together tight, and asked the boy to unpack. He had intended to chat to whichever servant he was given, to lecture him on the moral hazards sailors face. But he looked at the boy, bent over the trunk, and could not speak.

At night, the steerage passengers sing sad, slow songs about love and betrayal. Father watches the lights of the ship glitter on the water.

And the Irish Sea becomes the Atlantic Ocean.

Miss Rochester takes father's arm as a sister might, and together they parade around the first-class deck. She speaks of chastity and temperance. Father believes men can curb their desires just as women do, and says so.

Miss Rochester informs father that women do not have carnal desires, and father blushes.

They touch the Oscar Wilde case delicately. Miss Rochester expresses the usual mixture of abhorrence and puzzlement. Father does not illuminate her ignorance: indeed, he shares it. 'A man must be a man,' he says, and clears his throat, and goes red. And finds himself staring at the cabin boy, whose eyes glow in the twilight, like a cat's.

Far out across the Atlantic, thousands of miles from land, the engines stop dead. Nothing will revive them. The ship drifts on through the darkness, and the passengers huddle around the rails and chatter into the enormous silence.

'I want to learn to read, sir,' says the cabin boy. 'I want you to teach me.' And his face is so frank and innocent, expecting no evil. 'Do you, indeed,' says father, his flesh creeping because the lad is so close to him. He frowns with an intense aversion, something that might tempt a man on to gross acts of violence, or worse. In the East End, father saw harlots with the faces of angels: he knows full well that the Devil adopts many cunning disguises in his hunt for Christian souls to violate.

But what harm could a boy do to father?

'I hesitate to force myself on you in this way, sir,' said the lad, 'but I know you minister to the poor, you bring them to God, you help them to better themselves. If I could read and write, sir, my prospects would improve beyond all bounds.' The boy tossed his ragged curls out of his eyes, showing off his slender neck. The Devil made father want to wind those curls around his fingers, to press those full, bright lips against his own.

Father felt sick.

'Very well,' he said, since he could not in all conscience refuse. 'It would be no sin!' he joked grimly, and the lad smiled, and father remembered that all sinners say that.

'It is not given to many,' he said, as if to reassure himself, 'no, it is not given to many.'

'What, sir?' said the lad, eyes wide, hands behind his back, sweet and clean as the baby Jesus.

'To teach,' said father, as if in reply to a challenge, 'to show the young the Way.'

'To be vigilant against the Devil,' the boy breathed.

'Yes,' said father, feeling Satan as a third presence in the room.

The engines could not be repaired. No one could say when help would come. The weather grew freakishly hot, and the ship moaned as the sun warmed it, deck and hull, all the way down to the filthy water in the bilges. Father could not resist staring at the women, their necks and forearms exposed, and the Devil sent him dreams of the girls in third-class, languishing half naked, their legs long and bare.

Miss Rochester buzzed and buzzed in father's ear until he longed to slap her into silence.

And every day the cabin boy sat beside him, very close, since the desk was so small. And the boy's soft cheek touched his own so briefly, as they bent over the Bible, and his eyes glowed and then he looked away, and father sighed but could not bring himself to stand up and go, vile though it was. 'You are so very clever,' father sighed, closing his eyes, struggling against the Devil who possessed his body but not his soul, not yet.

The lad blushed at the praise, and said, 'You are such a fine teacher, sir.' He grinned suddenly, looked at father, and seemed to be about to embrace him. With a tremendous effort, father wrenched the Devil out of his body, hurled Him, metaphorically, into the burning sea. He stood up and flapped the Bible shut.

'Sir?' the boy said, smiling, then frowning as one of the sailors called his name.

Father hears the cabin boy joking with his mates.

The Devil pours jealousy into father's heart.

And now the cabin boy is playing cards with the other crewmen, and losing, and they speak to him gently, like fathers and uncles, and pat his back, and the cabin boy laughs, throws back his head, enjoying his laughter from head to toe, lost in it. And the Devil makes father think he would kill to please the lad so. And the cabin boy looks at father, and Satan is inside the sockets of the lad's skull, and his eyes are terrible.

And now father and the cabin boy are at the desk again, and the boy's arm, round and full as a lady's, rests against the sleeve of father's coat, and father feels himself burning.

There is a mirror in father's cabin, five inches square. His face just fits into it. Now he looks, and sees, not a servant of the Lord, but Lucifer in the guise of a young man, proud and cold with evil.

And he puts his hands to his face and digs in his nails as if he wants to tear out his own eyes. He riffles through the pages of his Bible, but for all his clumsy-fingered searching, cannot find the passage he so desperately needs.

The cabin boy, being a servant of the Devil, is quick-witted and soon learns to read fluently and write a reasonable hand. And then, his face all fierce tenderness, like a young wife with her first-born, he says to father, 'Please, I beg you sir, teach me more.'

'You know quite enough for a lad of your station already! More than enough!' father cries.

'I don't want to remain in my station!' says the cabin boy. 'I left home to rise above the dreariness in which I found myself. I want to travel the whole world over, I want to learn and learn and work and work, and, oh, earn such heaps of money, sir! And come home a hero, and never be poor and drab and low again.'

Father cannot speak. The cabin boy looks at him, afraid, hopeful, as if about to make some great confession. Then his eyes fall, and he sighs, and says, 'I had a – a sister at home, sir, and they put her into service, and she was so unhappy! Do this, do that, all day long, forever, until you're too old to work any more. I don't want any daughter of mine to have such a life as that.'

'This is blasphemy!' cries father, slamming his hand down on the Bible, making the boy jump. 'You are opposing God's will!'

The cabin boy says, 'But sir, I want to serve God by improving myself.'

And now the Devil takes complete possession of father. He

can no longer fight. He sits beside the boy, almost suffocated with love. 'How old are you, my lad?' he says.

And the cabin boy sits straight and says 'Sixteen, sir!' so emphatically that father knows he is lying.

Father takes the lad in his arms as lightly as if he believed his bones to be made of strands of glass, and lays his head on the lad's shoulder, and breathes in the sweet scent of him, and groans. He thinks he will die of ecstasy.

Quickly he lets go.

The cabin boy is reluctant to leave, he wants a kind word from father, but father is silent. Father will not look at the cabin boy now, will never again look at him with eyes of kindness. Father will never look kindly upon anyone again.

'Our Father, which art in . . .' he mutters when he is alone, tumbling the words into senselessness. 'Forever and ever and ever . . . Oh God!'

And the engines were still silent. Father told the steward that he was ill, that he must not be disturbed by anyone, most especially not by the cabin boy. He locked himself into his cabin for three days, and lay, unsleeping, on his bunk.

On the fourth day, at dawn, he came out on deck. And there sat the cabin boy, cross-legged, facing east, as if he worshipped the sun. Father studied him from a distance, desire hammering in him. The air stirred the boy's hair, he parted his lips and sighed and lifted his lovely face in pagan surrender. 'Yes!' father whispered, 'Yes!' But he fled away from the sight of the boy, and, not knowing where he was going, stumbled past red ropes and along dark gangways and down into the hot, close hold where the third-class passengers waited.

They were singing. It was a jolly, rousing song, so far removed from his present state of mind that he itched to get away from the sound of it. But he hesitated and caught a few words.

It's of a pretty female, as you shall understand
She had a mind for roving, into a foreign land
Attired in sailor's clothing, she boldly did appear . . .

Some breeze coming down the gangways washed the rest of the verse away. Father came closer, anxious to hear what came next.

> *Her cheeks appeared as roses, with her locks all in a curl*
> *The sailors oft-times smiled and said, He looks just like a girl!*
> *But eating captain's biscuit her colour did destroy,*
> *And the waist did swell of pretty Nell, The Handsome Cabin Boy.*

Father did not need to hear any more.

'I am the Devil!' father raved as he staggered back to his cabin. 'I am the Devil! Beware, beware!'

But the only one who heard was the cabin boy, and he came running – awkwardly, like a woman. 'Sir, sir, sir, please wait, please stop, are you all right sir? I've been so worried about you!'

'Follow me. Come! Now!' father ordered.

'Sir?' said the cabin boy, trailing after him. There was no one else about, no voices, no footsteps, only the cabin boy and father and the Devil.

'Sir?' the cabin boy repeated, watching father lock them both into the cabin, and put the key into a drawer, and lock that, and put the drawer key into a deep pocket, and pat it, as if he was just putting his watch away. The boy was bewildered, but did not object. 'Sir, have I failed you, have I offended you somehow without meaning to, have I done you any harm?'

'Oh yes, you have harmed me, you have harmed me badly!' said father, taking off his belt. The cabin boy, afraid at last, leapt back, expecting a beating. He scrabbled at the door, could not escape, looked wildly at the window, which faced only the sea, and bit his lip, as if about to burst into tears.

Father laughed.

'Sir!' cried the boy, tears spilling down his face.

'You're a girl, aren't you!' father said, grabbing his arms, pinning them to his sides, pulling him close. 'You're a damned little whore of a girl!'

'No!' cried the cabin boy, turning his face away.

But father's big red hands soon uncovered all the evidence he needed.

In the excruciating sweetness of what followed, father somehow failed to hear the girl calling to God to help her.

Next day the engines started up again.

In the brief remainder of the voyage, father and the girl did it several more times. Father did not much enjoy it, but could not help himself. Each time they did it, he promised himself: I will never do that again. But it was beyond all his powers to stop.

As for the girl, she complained less and less each time, though something seemed to go out of her. She could have protested to the Captain or even Miss Rochester, anyway, if she had really wanted to. But she did not.

At the end of the voyage, Father gave her five guineas and a copy of the Bible, and she took the gifts and curtseyed and went away. Father put lust out of his mind, sought repentance and the forgiveness of God. But God was gone now. As for the girl, he assumed she had merely sunk into the scum of New York, but in fact she had worked her way back to Liverpool, to give birth to me, to start our difficult life together.

And every time my mother tells me this story, father's part in it grows less violent, until in the end he almost becomes her hero of romance. And some days she looks out across the Mersey, out to sea, shading her eyes with her hand, waiting for him.

Father's mission went badly. The Indians closed their hearts against Jesus. A friend of father's from his Oxford days caught cholera and died in agony. Another young man went mad and shot several braves, one or two fatally. And then there was the young nun who fell for the chief of a tribe and wanted to marry him and had to be committed to an asylum.

Father came home to a wife who bled monthly but was quite barren, and to a parish whose people worshipped God in public but the sea in their hearts.

And on Sunday, when he is walking down the aisle, he stops and stares at me, this stranger in his parish, but says nothing. And then I am part of the crowd who say farewell to him as they leave the church. And he looks at me, and still says nothing, but his eyes are like the dead things that wash up on the beach in winter.

He preaches and preaches against the Devil, but he does not recognise me.

And I finger the knife concealed in my skirts, and I smile, and wait.

MARY WINGS

Hot Prowl

5.12 p.m. February 19, 1992, 124 Bonnieview Drive, San Francisco.

I had been watching my tape and scribbling down numbers to the steady bubbling of the crockpot brewing dinner in the kitchen when I heard it. A cross between a smash and a thud against the steady pattern of rain. I went into the living room where he jumped as I entered. The remote slipped from my palm as I froze.

'Why did you have to be home?' he growled. He had a semi-automatic gun in his right hand.

He made a rush for me, pulling a ski-cap over his face. The cap had been waiting on top of his head, it glistened with waterdrops as he pulled it down. His face would only be a flash of pink in my memory, a speaking blur. But I would never forget his voice. It turned out he talked a lot.

He slammed me up against the wall and I heard my nose crack on the plaster.

'I don't want any trouble,' I reassured him when I could breathe, my lips pressed against the wall. I didn't want him to know I was in pain. He swung me around by one shoulder. I looked up the barrel of his gun, to the ski-mask behind it.

'Into the kitchen,' his mouth was a mobile circle, issuing commands. I did as I was told. He was a mezzo-alto and he pointed the muzzle straight at me. Like a magic wand the gun moved me into the kitchen towards a corner of the room where the pantry door was firmly shut.

He was a medium-sized white man between twenty and thirty, I figured. Some brown hair was sticking out from the eyehole in his cap. I quickly turned my eyes away from his face. I didn't want to die.

He was hopping on his feet like a fighter getting ready for the ring, like a man on drugs.

'This is great,' the ski-mask said as his eyes pored over the contents of my living room, the Beta Cam camera with enhanced chip. The AMPEX audio mixer. He had made his haul for the week. I was the only problem, me and the rain outside which had begun to pour. It hadn't rained in a long time and I hadn't thought about my gun in a long time. It was sitting in my drawer. What was I supposed to do, wear it around the house. Sit down to my dinner with a shoulder holster?

I hadn't thought about men with guns for a while. I was glad I hadn't thought about them. Now it was going to start all over again. The ski-mask's eyes blinked; I realised I'd been staring at him, the only two fleshy spots that moved in the ski-cap, two holes, organs of intelligence guiding a predator.

I could see in the hallway that he'd taped one of the small panes of glass on the front door and broken it. He must have reached around and let himself in. The rain picked up, it was coming in sheets now.

'Now, look, I'm just going to lock you up in the pantry, lady. I don't want no trouble. You really made my day here,' his eyes twitched over all the black plastic and shining knobs still visible from the living room. 'So let's just keep calm.'

'Don't rip the cords out of the wall of that deck there. It's hell getting replacements,' I advised him, my heart pounding.

'Sure, thanks,' he said ripping the cord off one of the tele-phones instead, yanking it out of the wall and coming towards me. I was shaking, violently.

'Sit the fuck down, lady,' he growled. I sat down on the hard kitchen chair and stared at his dirty tan suede jacket, dark grease stains at all the skin contact points, the collar, the sagging pocket from which he had drawn the gun. It was at my eye level.

'First I'm going to get you all settled down here,' he explained. I moved my eyes away from his mouth, the lower lip that curled over the knitted material. I looked down at the semi-automatic. It wasn't going to be easy tying me up and keeping the gun in his hand. I considered making a move but the little red dot in front of the hammer told me the safety was off.

'Close your eyes,' he commanded, putting the barrel against my head. I felt the cold metal through my thin hair. My bowels moved. He reached behind him for the knob of the pantry door. It turned but the door was stuck. He crouched down behind me and started tying my hands with the cord.

'Okay, you just be good here, I won't put you in the closet. If you don't interfere with my business here this will all work out fine. I've had enough trouble today.' I felt his fingers on my arms pulling the telephone cord tighter. I winced.

'Listen, I ain't going to rape you. I'm not a sicko,' he reassured me. 'Even though you're pretty cute.' His sweaty palms tangled with mine as he fumbled.

Swell, I thought, and with his knot-tying expertise in a minute we'd be holding hands.

'And all that technical stuff in there is really going to help me out here,' he explained from behind me. 'If that goddamn fucking rain doesn't hold me up.'

'Ouch!' I yelled, as he'd pulled my arm back hurting the healing scar on my chest.

'Sorry,' he mumbled, looking up at the blurry black and white images flashing on the monitor. We heard a clap of thunder outside. Rain was pounding on the skylight in drumbeats. The big branches of a pine tree waved above us.

'What's all this camera stuff?' he asked. 'What are you some kinda movie director or something?'

'I teach video. San Francisco State.'

'Video, well excuse me, lady. I just go to the movies. Now what kinda movies you make?'

'Nothing you've ever seen,' I said.

'What, you think the only time I been out at night is driving a cab or something?'

'No, I wish you had seen it. That's all I mean. If I'd made a big film you would have seen it. And then I would have a production company and all this equipment wouldn't be in my house, and my house would have a security system and you wouldn't be here stealing it.'

'Yeah, I guess you're right about that. Things are tough all over. But you should know I've seen a lot of films in my time,' he picked up the gun and waved it in the air. 'Now how about you and me watching one of your movies.'

'What?'

'I mean, let's take this stuff with all the numbers off and watch something else.'

He looked at a box on top of the television 'That a movie you made?'

'Yes,' I said, my heart sinking.

'You and me can just relax in a chair and watch a movie and wait till this rain lets up.' I watched as he popped the tape in and worked the controls until the titles came on.

'How come those numbers are still there?' I was glad he was focusing on those numbers.

'They're for editing purposes later; see I'll probably cut out some bits and put them further up, in the next section. You'll see,' I said in the tones of my instructor voice. Well, I thought, the better he knows me, the longer I spend with him, the less likely it is that he'll shoot me.

An image came on the screen. The camera followed the back of a fat woman lumbering down the street. Her black knitted pants were much too tight; rolls of flesh jiggled as she walked. The camera was close up on her posterior now, moving in front of her we rounded her huge belly. A sports sack tied around her waist looked like a colostomy bag.

'No wonder you don't make any big movies,' he said. 'Who wants to look at a fat cow like that?'

The camera moved slowly upwards and her right hand came up from below hip level, across those mounds of flesh and we, the camera, the burglar and myself, all looked down the barrel of her Smith and Wesson revolver.

5.15 p.m. February 19, 1992. Police Officer Laura Deleuse:

It hadn't rained for a while in San Francisco. The first rain always brings up oil on the streets, car skids, petty fist fights. It made the air cleaner anyway and gangs tended to stay inside.

The car was idling and I was in a bad mood. Kevin and I weren't speaking and we got this reporter on a ride-along. Interested in female cops. Special feature article for a Filipino weekly. I'd already introduced her to my sergeant who still spoke Tagalog and a black female lieutenant. Now we were in the car waiting for my partner Kevin.

'So what's the difference between burglary and robbery?' she asked folding her legs gracefully in the back seat. She'd worn a two-piece suit for the occasion; it wasn't going to do for the rain, but then she had to stay in the car anyway. That was the agreement.

What was Kevin doing in the locker room? I wondered. I thought maybe he was waiting till the rain let up. So me and the reporter could get acquainted and fog up the windshield a little. Her eyes had a nice sparkle but I wasn't in any kind of mood.

Kevin was angry because I didn't go to the memorial service of his ex-partner last weekend. I had problems of my own. I'd been to enough funerals lately but Kevin wasn't into understanding. Or letting go. Now we couldn't fix it because we had this reporter in the car.

'Burglary. Okay so you want to know about burglary as opposed to robbery?' I asked her and my words took on the easy rhythm of the random raindrops landing on the hood of the car. I watched her get out her steno notebook.

The reporter asked me about robbers and burglars I'd arrested, about their character. I sighed and held myself back. Public relations and all that.

'Your robber and your burglar are basically two different kinds of people. Your burglar isn't into contact. He's secretive, furtive. He wants the goods and the last thing he wants is you,' I said.

'What? Oh. I'm saying "he" because I have never run across a female burglar. Well, except kids. Kids are used to squeeze in small places. And women work the bars to sell the goods. Fifteen, twenty dollars for equipment that's worth ten times that. Car stereos go right over the bar.'

'Robbery's something else. Robbery is committed against a person,' I sighed. Why didn't she just read the penal code. I'd be glad to send it to her. Why didn't Kevin hurry up? 'Burglary is breaking and entering. Someone who enters a structure, any kind of structure. Be that your home, or your trailer, tent, aircraft or other vessel with the intent to steal.'

Kevin got in the car and we just nodded to each other. He introduced himself to the reporter. He could just be heard over the rain.

We started driving up Mission Street just past Army where a produce store owner was quickly taking *piñatas* down from the awning. The red crêpe paper skirt of a mermaid was nearly soaked. My eyes flicked over the storefronts and the bar doors open despite the rain.

In between the slapping sounds of the windshield wipers the reporter asked me what happens if someone burgles an occupied house. I hesitated. Why didn't Kevin do some of this work? I looked over at him. He was stony faced. Eventually he took out a toothpick to use between his teeth. Thanks Kevin.

'What if there's somebody home during a burglary?' she asked, an edge to her voice. We weren't making her job easier, I thought. I started to feel more sympathetic towards her.

'I'd say 99 per cent of burglars never encounter a human being. They're not stupid people. But if they're unlucky and somebody's home, it's called a "hot prowl". You'd have to be pretty stupid to burglarise an inhabited dwelling. All you have to do is ring the doorbell. Or you know those phone calls when you answer and somebody hangs up?'

The reporter shuddered. She didn't need to write that down. The radio started squawking. We listened to it for a while. I pulled over to a little Lebanese grocery store where Kevin always got a pack of cigarettes and a hard-boiled egg.

'Hey, pick up some coffee beans for me, would you?' I slipped

Kevin a five dollar bill. I put the car into park and watched him run quickly into the store through the rain.

'Have you been on any burglary calls when someone's been home?' the reporter was asking me. Kevin was loitering in the grocery, making the owner nervous.

'No,' I said. 'But a lot of people will come home when their house has been worked over by professionals and they'll find their personal possessions all over the floor and big kitchen knife out on the counter. That's because if you do happen to come home and the burglar has a situation on his hands he can use the knife as a weapon against you.'

'It's a big thing among burglars not to bring a weapon,' I continued, slowing my words so she could relax a little while scribbling. 'Ups the degree of burglary. From second to first. Longer prison sentence. He's a career junkie and wants as much time on the outside as possible.

'The last thing he wants is contact. If you come home and you got a hot prowl on your hands you'd better believe he's got that knife ready. But I'll tell you,' I leaned back and looked at her. She looked back. Something unusual in those eyes. 'There's more than one person who's opened their front door, saw this stranger running at them full speed with their butcher's knife in his hand and then ran right by them and straight out the door.'

The reporter's face lit up. They love this kind of detail. I always wonder why people like the seamy side of life. Curiosity? Like healthy animals circling slowly around sick ones, not touching it, just looking. Or was it just her job?

I thought about mine. I was tired of patrolling the Ingleside trying to hold back the tide of crime. It was like shovelling shit into the wind.

I would be a blip on the street forever, I thought. Not married to a cop, no cop brother, father, and not even Irish.

Kevin got back in the car. He started peeling an egg; the smell permeated the interior, as he knew it would. I hated it when he ate eggs in the car.

'Burglars aren't social,' I told the reporter with a sidelong glance at Kevin. 'They got a career to protect. Of course, that's not the case with your basic jumpy sociopath. They're not what you'd call your career burglar.

'Your basic sociopath isn't concerned about the finer points of law or the point of his life. He's got an IQ the level of room temperature. He's just waiting to go inside; let's hope he doesn't get you in the process.'

5.25 p.m. February 19, 1992, 124 Bonnieview Drive, San Francisco.

Blam! The fat woman in the video unloaded the weapon at the screen. The burglar pushed the power button on the monitor. Her image shrunk to a pinpoint and was gone. But the burglar was pacing back and forth, agitated.

'What kinda stuff you messin' around with here lady?' I looked up at his eyes and mouth, the moving holes within the black ski-mask.

'I dunno,' I said. I had wanted to get away from sexualising guns. The feminine gun in the little beaded handbag, the eyes with the eyeshadow and long lashes behind the sights. But eyelashes wouldn't matter to me anymore. What mattered was guns. And mine was sitting in a drawer. The ski-mask took a long look at me. I looked away.

'I don't like it, I don't like it one bit,' his voice rose. His hands were twitching at his sides. I didn't know if he meant the video or the fat woman or my trying to de-sexualise guns. I felt like he could read my mind.

His gun was back in his right pocket. Then suddenly his hand was up high in the air, I was watching it come down, hearing it crack across my cheek, my neck seemed to crack with it.

'You got any guns here, lady?'

'No,' I said. 'No, I swear.' I looked away from the mask. It could tell I was lying, I was sure.

He considered my answer while looking at his hands. They were shaking. His knees seemed to be trembling and he reached behind him to steady himself on the kitchen table.

'I'm not lying to you,' I said. I could hardly speak. I was hyperventilating. It would be better to talk a bit, get my voice back. I would try to be more normal, I thought with the one part of my brain that wasn't thinking about dying. 'There's about forty dollars cash in my purse, the equipment, no jewellery worth mentioning.'

'Good, that's good,' he said, but he didn't feel good. The burglar reached his hand into his left pocket and pulled out a vial with brown powder in it. He unscrewed the cap and tapped some of the powder on to his finger, put his finger up to the fleshy hole in the middle of the mask and snorted. I had to do something here. I couldn't just sit in the chair anymore, I thought. I would just die in this chair. I watched him take the drug. I had no idea if it would be an advantage that he was stoned.

But his hands stopped twitching and he stopped dancing on the balls of his feet. He sat down, leaning into the back of the chair, waiting for the drug to take effect. His profile with the ski-mask made him look like a pawn in a chess set. We listened to the rain pounding on the skylight together.

'Where you from?' the ski-mask asked.

'Philly.'

'Hey, me too,' his words had trouble escaping his lips. I knew he'd had too much. Whatever that brown powder was, he hadn't learn to control intake.

'Go to the Italian Market?' I asked.

'Yeah. Where the peaches come in tissue wrappers and they yell at you if you touch them,' the long globe of his hand bobbed up and down in slow motion, his words coming separately, like beads on a string.

Then he heard the bubbling. The crockpot lid was jiggling with escaping steam. All his frantic energy seemed to return, as if he'd never taken the drug. He sprang out of the chair. It wasn't heroin, I thought, discouraged. It would be something else, something synthetic, angel dust.

'Hey, what's cookin'?'

He looked over to where the crockpot was gently gurgling. Then the mask looked up, squinting into the skylight.

'I could just make myself at home here,' he sat down and put his long lanky legs on the kitchen table, moving aside my Minnie and Mickey Mouse salt and pepper set with his engineer's boots.

I could see the tread pattern and little bits of soil and pine needles stuck to the bottom of them.

Those damn pine needles, I thought; I'd been sweeping them out of the house all week. Pine needles. Would that be the last thought I'd ever have? Sweeping pine needles. It wasn't a bad thought.

Agatha would be arriving in twenty minutes for dinner. I strained my head to look behind my back, turning my wrist to try to see my watch. He noticed.

Suddenly the crockpot didn't look so good to him.

'Expectin' company?' He picked the gun up and pointed it at me.

He pulled the hammer back.

'No,' I lied, 'I mean, not for awhile.'

He threw the semi-automatic on the table and it spun past Minnie's clownish high heel. The muzzle was pointing straight at my chest. He picked up a cookbook from the kitchen table. 'Oilless Diet,' he read and opened the cover. 'Yeuch.'

The phone in the living room rang. The pupils in the ski-mask fixed on me as we listened to my own message on the tape. 'This is Naomi Grielli. Thanks for calling, I'm fine now, but can't come to the phone. Please leave a message . . .'

The burglar and I both stopped and listened to the voice after the beep. It was Agatha. She was cancelling dinner. Her car had broken down in the East Bay. She couldn't make it across the bridge in time. And she knew me well enough to know not to come too late.'

'I hope you didn't put the okra in yet,' she advised. 'It really turns into mush if you cook it so long. And I won't be able to bring the garam masala. That's the only thing that saves those parsnips,' she sighed into the tape. 'Do your best with cumin and garlic. I'll call later tonight.'

The burglar released the hammer of the semi-automatic and put it back on the table. It was still raining hard outside.

The eyehole of the ski-mask winked at me. 'Maybe I'll stay for dinner.'

5.25 p.m. February 19, 1992. Police Officer Laura Deleuse:

The three of us watched shoppers going in and out of the Safeway. A little kid was selling candy bars in front of the automatic doors. Kevin got out of the car to buy one.

'Jewellery. Some burglars have that kind of sparkle in their eye,' I continued. 'We're not talking about your cat thief, Robert Wagner kinda guy. Black turtleneck pirouetting over rooftops. We're talking junkies who have to bring in fifteen hundred a week. What they have to do to get it is not a pretty picture. Although some of them know their way around the better antiques. Only take rugs over a hundred years old.'

'Do many get caught?'

'Not a high closure rate on any of your professionals. You figure for every four times they're arrested they've done maybe two hundred, three hundred burglaries.' Kevin got back in the car. He had the candy bar but he put it away and I knew why. It would be difficult to eat it without offering it to both me and the reporter. Kevin had manners. 'Sacred Heart High School Peanut Butter Melt Away,' the wrapper had said.

5.40 p.m. February 19, 1992, 124 Bonnieview Drive, San Francisco:

The telephone cord was loose. He hadn't tied my hands together very well. I could wiggle my fingers up into my palms under the cord. I could probably just slip the whole thing off. I looked over at the burglar. He was reading the diet book again. He'd forgotten his plan about putting me in the pantry.

He threw the cookbook on the table. It barely missed the semi-automatic. His motor responses were clearly affected by the drug.

The safety was off on the semi-automatic. But there was something weird about that gun, the way it spun past Minnie Mouse's shoe.

He went over to the crockpot and took off the lid, leaning back quickly when the steam seeped through his mask.

'Smells good,' he said.

'It's okra, tofu, seaweed and parsnips.'

'You shittin' me,' he said. He stuck a wooden spoon that was lying next to the crockpot and scooped some of the steaming food into his mouth.

'Fuck!' the mask screamed and leaning over the sink, cooling his burnt tongue with tap water.

I froze. My fingers had loosened the telephone cord behind my back so that I could easily slide the nylon up and down.

'Shut the fuck up, stupid bitch,' the mask mumbled even though I hadn't said anything. 'Too bad for you Agatha ain't coming for dinner. Maybe it's too bad for me too, ha, ha, ha. You ain't bad lookin' though.'

He went to the cupboard and got himself one of my Fiestaware plates, a bright aqua, and a soup spoon. He ladled some of the hot food on to the plate and laid it steaming on the table. The white and brown mush steamed on the bright aqua circle. He stood and watched it.

The gun lay next to the food, the muzzle was aiming at the plate, at him, at his crotch which was just at table height.

5.45 p.m. February 19, 1992. Police Officer Laura Deleuse:

'What about your war stories?' I asked Kevin in front of the reporter. He shrugged. He was being just peachy tonight. I matched his stony silence and all three of us listened to the rain for awhile.

The radio came on and we listened and then it went off. Kevin didn't do anything with his candy bar. He knew better than to smoke in the car.

5.45 pm. February 19, 1992, 124 Bonnieview Drive, San Francisco:

'You got anything good in that pantry?' the burglar asked. I didn't answer.

He walked towards me and I quickly slid my fingers back under the cord. The cord still appeared to be around my wrists. His gun was on the table. He was walking past me; I could feel his dirty suede jacket brush my arm when he stopped. He looked down at my shirt where my one right breast seemed to pull the material away from the flatter left hand side.

'Hey, you ain't got no tit,' he said.

'You think that's news to me?'

'Stop shittin' me. And hey, you quit looking at my gun.' He backed away quickly, picking up his gun suddenly and never taking his eyes off my face. The little semi-automatic flopped into his palm.

'Is that your gun?' I asked, and his hesitation told me almost everything I needed to know.

'Well it's my gun now, lady,' he said, waving it a few times in front of my face. Without meaning to, he gave me a good look at the thing. A good enough look to see that there was no magazine, no clip in the handle. That was almost good news. Then came the bad. He walked behind me into the pantry, he grabbed the knob and pulled at it. The door was warped from the moisture and stuck in its frame. But with a hard pull he got it open and the room was filled with an odour sweeter than any market in Tunisia.

'SHEEEEEEEIIIIIIT!' He screamed and my heart sank. 'PAYDAY BABY!' he leaned back out of the pantry and gave me a big hug, that horrible dirty suede covering my blouse like skin of a sick animal, pulling the scars across my chest.

5.45 p.m. February 19, 1992. Police Officer Laura Deleuse:

'Stop here, I want to make a phone call,' Kevin said. It was a hard night for him, I could tell. He needed to talk, but that was his problem. The rain had let up and he was on the street, moving his eyes all around while he spoke to somebody on the end of the line.

The reporter waited until he picked up the horn of the pay phone to ask me.

'Have you arrived at any homicide scenes?' she asked.

'No,' I lied. I didn't want to tell her. We sat in the silence, watching Kevin on the phone, his weight on one foot and then the other. Kevin was going to try and get me to do all the relating tonight, I thought stubbornly. Homicide. I looked at the reporter. She was biting her lip. It was a nice lip and I didn't think she should be biting it, but I didn't want to be the only one filling up the air space in the car either.

'Would you like to work homicide?' she asked.

'Sure,' I said. But it wasn't likely. Homicide inspector? Not in my lifetime. In my twelve years on the force there have only been two appointments for inspectors and neither was for homicide. The chief has to appoint you specifically to homicide.

And I had a lieutenant who didn't like me. For some reason he thought I was a hippie and I just couldn't shake it.

All that plus a vindictive mayoral administration where heads had a way of rolling easily along the corridors of the Hall of Justice. Patronage and revenge. No, I'd never make Homicide Inspector.

At least inspectors are governed by a civil service exam now. It used to be that all the inspectors were grandfathered in by the chief. Appointed.

I thought about the night I first met up with those dinosaurs. They usually came from cop families and couldn't make the lieutenants or even sergeant's exam. So there were some bone-head homicide inspectors with only a police lineage to recommend them. Yes, I'd met those goons.

It involved this prostitute who worked Capp Street. Her street name was Streak because she had this white streak of hair just in one spot. She was young and the rest of her hair was dark. Made a very pretty impression.

Usually someone loses the pigment in their hair when they sustain a blow to the head. At least, that's what it usually means in someone that young. Concussion, she'd gotten hit with a heavy object, something like that.

Apparently she'd picked up this cabdriver and he'd taken her to his flophouse room. We received the call and when we came on the scene we found her head on the floor with a bullet in the middle of her forehead, just under that silver streak. Her face was covered with powder and there was a lot of blood and scalp and grey matter on the floor underneath all her long hair.

The cabbie was shrugging his shoulders and saying he didn't know what had happened. He also twitched a lot and hadn't shaved in a few days. Streak had been scraping the bottom of the barrel.

We called over the inspectors who were on night duty. A great crowd of dinosaurs, they'd all been dining at one of their favourite Irish places when dispatch reached them.

Irish juice has run deep in the department since the first officers hit the street in 1849 in long button-down coats. These boys didn't get where they were by being born yesterday. They were born a hundred years ago.

So they've gotten the call and they came into the flophouse room. Still a few after-dinner cigars stuck in their mouths, totally AB, alcohol breath, and generally continuing to have a good time.

Saw the girl, saw the cabdriver and immediately identified with him. He told his story in the best-boy style, shrugging his shoulders. Those expendable trashy women, you just never know what self-destructive thing they'll do next. They all had a good headshake about that's the way it goes sometimes.

I couldn't believe it. I saw the cocaine on the mirror on top of the refrigerator. Never got put in the report. The cabbie's story was that it had happened when he went out to the store; he came back and found her dead on the floor. I didn't see any beer, or brown paper bag or anything lying around that indicated that he'd made a trip. The cigarette he was smoking was one from a pack that was half full and his hands shook like he'd be lucky to hold on to the steering wheel another six months.

Those goons didn't even ask. They just clucked their heads and walked out, engaging in some little pissing on the tree contest about gunshot wounds to the head and who'd seen the most grey matter.

Fucking well-juiced dinosaurs. Patronage jobs. Most of them are retired now. Thank God. New blood is slowly coming in. Still it won't be mine.

So who leaves a prostitute alone in a room, anyway? Why would he bring her up there? Since when don't cabbies park in bus stops and run in to your local convenience store for whatever. Yeah, sure, tell me he went out to get a condom.

No, the way I figured it, they had some kind of fight. She either tried to steal the gun, or he tried to use it against her, or she was ripping off his drugs. Or he'd been pimping her and she was holding out his percentage.

Somebody was trying to rip something off from somebody and she got shot in the head. And those goons never even bothered to find out.

What bothered me so much about it, yeah, the young woman in her prime and all that, but what was her future anyway? What bothered me was the cabbie. He's still out there somewhere, driving around, picking up whores and carrying a gun with less to keep him from shooting it. Those homicide inspectors gave him a pat on the back.

Long forgotten by everyone but me. Would I tell our back seat cub reporter?

I looked back at her, nyloned knees crossed, she was looking over her notes carefully. Shorthand. Maybe she floated up from the typing pool. It couldn't have been too easy for her either, getting ahead in a male world.

'We usually stop for dinner around eight,' I said.

We'd go out to dinner with the reporter and if we were lucky nothing would happen tonight. Then I would go home at about 2 am to my house whose floor joists were being eaten away by termites.

When I wake up in the morning I'll have coffee with my room-mate who has just gotten thrush. It was the first symptom he'd had since he'd been diagnosed HIV positive one year ago.

It was also something I didn't feel like Kevin needed to hear.

5.50 p.m. February 19, 1992, 124 Bonnieview Drive, San Francisco.

The burglar was still exclaiming his good fortune and I was breathing heavily from the sudden pain I'd felt, including a sinking heart.

In the pantry, hanging upside down were three five-foot tall, limp but verdant plants. An arrangement of long, thin bright green leaves, pungent, with long powdered flowers on the ends, pointing at the floor. The burglar had discovered the best sensimilla harvest I'd ever had.

Resin was coating the hairs on his arms as he embraced the

plants, adding aroma to the skin of his jacket. I breathed in deeply, just as he did.

'Where are the fuckin' garbage bags, lady?' he said.

'Third drawer under the sink.'

He got out a roll and quickly tore off a few bags, one ripped down the middle; he swore at it.

He worked quickly, putting the gun in his pocket, cutting down the plants, one by one. He got up on a chair, trying to break off the green stalks but they resisted. Then he put the branches across his legs, forcing them to bend. The gun bounced against his hip, almost falling out of his pocket. I watched him frantically trying to control those plants, making them behave. The white garbage bags were punctured by the sinewy green stalks.

He kicked one of the bags across the floor towards the kitchen door. Then another. He followed the last one punching the sack with the toe of his foot. His toe came in contact with the wall through the bag. That must hurt, I thought. He seemed to get angrier. He kept on kicking until I saw the wall begin to give way underneath his shoe until he punched a good sized hole into the sheetrock.

Then he got down on his hands and knees and stared into the hole. There was something very wrong with him.

I don't want to die, I thought. I didn't want to be thinking about not wanting to die. I wanted to get his gun.

He scuttled into the pantry for the last few bags running past me, the gun hanging heavily in the dirty suede pocket where he'd forgotten about it. The handle of the gun loomed out of his pocket, almost touching me at shoulder level.

I made my move, whipped hands from behind, beeline for the weapon, palm around the handle.

He scarcely noticed that my hands were untied, in front of me and taking the gun in his pocket. I stood up and stepped back, my finger finding the trigger. He smiled nervously. Guns make all the difference.

'Hey, lady, guess what!' the ski-mask was grinning as he hoisted a bag of pot over his shoulder.

'Yeah, I know what,' I put his ski-mask head right between

the sights. 'The safety is still off and my finger is on the trigger and you have a big bag with my pot in it.'

'It ain't loaded,' the mask smiled and laughed at his joke.

'No, wait a minute. You don't really know that, do you. You don't know that because it's not your gun.'

'Yeah but there's no magazine in the thing – '

'There could be a bullet, one last bullet in the chamber.' I moved the gun slightly out in front of me. Abdomen height. I remembered the position. Close in.

'Do you know how many police officers have wounded themselves, gun professionals shot themselves with semi-automatics? It's because there's no way to tell if there's a bullet in the chamber. Now you may have taken the magazine out, but are you absolutely sure there isn't one left in the chamber? And are you willing to bet your life on it?'

I looked at his eyes and it told me all I wanted to know. I was right. He hadn't checked the chamber. I took a deliberate step away from him, never moving the gun off him.

'Sure I know there's no bullet in the chamber, man, I loaded it myself,' the mask grinned, but his hands were trembling, the plastic sack with all the pot in it shuddered.

Suddenly he turned and lunged towards me, but I took a step back faster and was out of his reach, pulling the hammer back. He heard the metal click. His hesitation meant I had him.

'You do that again, I'll shoot,' I promised. 'And I know how.' I tried to keep my hands steady. If I had a bullet I had only one. I couldn't waste that last bullet. 'You stole this gun, didn't you? You probably stole it this morning,' I saw in his eyes that my words were true. 'I could smell that it had been used recently. And certainly someone didn't use it on you or you wouldn't be here. So you just took it off of whoever and took out the magazine and thought that was that. Didn't you?'

'I didn't think nothing,' the mask said sullenly.

'Sit down.'

He glared at me.

'Sit the fuck down or I'll shoot you I swear. I don't have that much to lose,' I found myself saying. But neither, I thought, did he, if he had actually shot someone earlier in the day.

My lips became small and tight and I looked at him without

blinking and I said, 'If you try for this gun I'm going to pull this trigger.' I thought about my chest, about my illness. I thought about the scalpel of the surgeon that cut off my breast, about jury trials and pulling the trigger. 'You sit the fuck down,' I growled.

He pulled a chair up to the kitchen table. My intended dinner was already cool on the plate in front of him. The parsnips had turned into grey mush, the okra had burst open spilling its bitter seeds throughout, the slimy leaves entwining with long black strings of hiziki seaweed.

Those horrible stupid diets, the terrifying fear that the chemo wouldn't work. That moment when they took off the dressings and I looked down at my own body and couldn't believe what had happened to it, the weeks after the operation when the wound was so big I thought it could never heal ... But it did. And I did. And I wasn't going to eat okra parsnip seaweed tofu meals anymore. He was.

'Eat.' I said.

'What? This?'

'Eat?'

'Fuck no man,' he whined but I yelled louder, 'Eat.' I was getting hysterical, and I didn't want him to think I was losing control. But the threat of my losing control would help him obey me, obey the possibility of that one bullet still being left in the chamber.

He lifted up the spoon and dove it into the mass and a lump of tofu shuddered its way into the utensil, covered with okra seeds. It came towards his mouth and fell inside. I saw his lips quiver and tears sprung to his eyes, the ski-mask moved above his face and he grabbed his stomach. He was going to vomit.

I moved to where the other telephone was, keeping him carefully in the sights, but he was so busy trying not to puke he didn't notice at first. 911 was easy enough to dial. I said my address. I said to come immediately. I said 'gun' and hung up.

I looked back at the burglar. He'd finished vomiting. His mask moved slowly from side to side, like he was adjusting his neck but then he was on to the balls of his feet and flying at me through the air.

The filthy suede flapped at his sides like the wings of a sick bat, his arm outstretched, aiming to push the gun away, but he wasn't fast enough.

I didn't even think about whether there was a bullet in the chamber. There wasn't time. I stepped back and pulled the trigger.

5.55 p.m. February 19, 1992. Police Officer Laura Deleuse:

It had stopped raining and it was getting dark. Then the call came over the radio.

'In the Ingleside. A priority. 459. Hot Prowl. Roll Call 3 Henry 3. 124 Bonnieview Drive.'

That was us. The address was near the top of Diamond Heights. The reporter was trying to appear calm, but she was clinging on to the handholds in the back seat and something like a smile played across her lips.

Arrived at 6.02, way up in the hills. Hate those kind of calls. People with hillside houses and expensive, easily fenceable goods. Two TVs and one for the kids. Everybody with their own computer. A high-end Macintosh for Dad. Throw in a few VCRs, some jewellery and some cash. And an attitude that doesn't make the job easier. They have the kind of life where they feel like bad things shouldn't happen to them.

When I arrive there that's the kind of mood they're in. Pissed off at me for not doing my job, for not protecting them from what's just happened. Even when they have French doors because the little panes of glass are so pretty and easy to break into. Houses way off the street, front doors hidden down paths of gnarling vines with rose blossoms and fragrant night blooming jasmine.

I told the reporter to stay in the car, since Kevin wasn't saying much to either one of us. She looked gravely disappointed, but what did she expect?

I walked down a long flagstone pathway under the trellises that arched above me loaded with old, well-established vines. Small, security-useless fairy lights lit the flagstone steps leading down to the redwood shingled house. A big pine tree loomed above the roof and spilled wet needles down all along the path. Everybody up in the hills emulated this Snow White and the

Seven Dwarfs kind of architecture and landscape, but it wouldn't be a fairy tale when we got there. The 911 call that came in had mentioned a gun.

Kevin and I pulled our weapons out as we stood on either side of the pretty French door. He gave me a look that I knew and it fixed a lot of things that were wrong with the night.

I won't let it get in the way, his look said and I knew for the next moments he would be totally on my side.

Someone had knocked out one of the panes after taping it. Someone who was probably still inside.

The wind played with the copper patina'd tubes of a wind chime. Kevin put his hand through the broken pane, reached up and turned the knob.

In the hallway we heard a regular swishing sound. We crept along the wall and aimed our weapons into the kitchen. A forty year-old white woman was diligently sweeping her floor. At her feet lay a man in a ski-mask. He was bleeding. She was careful not to let the bristles of the broom touch the gathering pool of blood underneath his hips.

'Oh, you're here!' she said, smiling nervously, leaning the broom up against the wall.

I thought about how I would write it up in the report.

We'd entered with our guns drawn, but holstered them immediately.

A man in a ski-mask lay wounded and unconscious on the floor. He needed an ambulance. A semi-automatic Walther lay on the kitchen table.

I took a good look around the place; there was a lot of fancy camera equipment and televisions. A familiar pungent odour was in the air, mixed with gunpowder. A kitchen chair was circled with telephone cord. A gooey grey mound of food on an aqua plate was sitting on the table.

A pantry door was ajar. Inside, strings were handing down from the ceiling. Somebody had kicked a hole in the wall in the kitchen and a lot of white plastic bags with escaping vegetation were littering the floor, along with some pine needles she'd been trying to sweep up.

The woman was about five foot six inches tall, about forty years of age and was holding a broom in her hand. She didn't look healthy and she identified herself as Ms Grielli. I picked up the weapon from the kitchen table with my handkerchief. There was no magazine in it; the chamber was empty.

The burglar's head was resting on a white plastic bag filled with marijuana and there were other plastic bags piled by the kitchen door. He had a spoon clutched in his hand. He had a fairly strong pulse. She'd hit him in the upper thigh.

Kevin went to call an ambulance and support; I leaned down and carefully pulled the ski-mask off his head. I recognized him. I'd seen that face before. Another revolving door customer of the city jail. He had a rap sheet as long as his dick and I'd had the unfortunate opportunity to see that too.

Ms Grielli claimed he was an armed intruder and had tied her to a chair. I saw no reason to dispute this.

He would be charged with first degree burglary, possession of narcotics, and possible kidnapping. I couldn't wait to meet him again in court.

Ms Grielli claimed that the intruder had entered the premises with intent to burgle and upon seeing her, drew the gun. According to her statement she managed to get it away from him as he burgled her apartment. She knew it didn't have a clip in the handle but was aware of the possibility that there might be a bullet left in the chamber.

She claims to have gotten the gun from his pocket and then called 911. He attacked her and she shot him.

'And then I just stood there and didn't know what to do,' she said with a quick little laugh. 'So I started sweeping,' she picked up the broom and put it back in the pantry and closed the door. The floor wasn't clean yet.

She showed me a World War II Browning semi-automatic in a locked box with current registration, supporting her story that she was familiar with the workings of semi-automatic pistols. She said she had been mugged in her driveway in October 1987. The armed robber in that case had never been apprehended.

After I took my report I saw no reason to take Ms Grielli into custody. I found no evidence which contradicted her story.

I spent some time talking to her. She didn't appear to be terribly shaken, just nervous. In fact, she seemed proud of having disarmed the man and shot him. It was a gutsy thing to do, the odds were against her but she beat them.

Ms Grielli appeared to have some health difficulties. She had that burned-out radiation look; hair that was only fuzz covering her head. I hoped she kept beating the odds.

Officers Chu and Scappichio arrived on the scene and escorted the prisoner to the ambulance and to San Francisco General Hospital.

The suspect will be arraigned one week from now, held on charges of burglary 459, kidnapping and possession of narcotics. End of report.

'Got a friend you can call to come over tonight?' I asked Ms Grielli. She was looking better, the colour was coming back into her face.

'Yes,' she said. 'I think I'll have my friend Agatha, or George, my neighbour come over and spend the night,' she indicated a house next door. I could see the lights burning inside. A few curious neighbours would probably be outside.

'Want me to go over there with you?' I asked.

'No,' she said, 'I'm just fine now, I really am.' I believed her.

Kevin was outside, waiting for me just in front of her door. I walked to the door and on second thought returned to the kitchen where she was leaning into the sink, pouring the grey congealed contents of a crockpot down the garbage disposal.

'And Ms Grielli – ' she turned around. She was smiling as she threw the gelatinous matter away. 'They might want to come to your house for questioning,' I said. 'So you'd better give your floor a good vacuuming,' I nodded towards the pantry. She looked at the closed door and her eyes slid back across the floor where pine needles and other vegetation littered the black and white linoleum.

'No problem,' she said quietly. We stood there for a moment in the silence and then she flipped a switch of the garbage disposal. We both watched as the gooey grey matter disappeared into the city's sewer system. She was a nice lady, but maybe she needed cooking lessons.

7 p.m. February 19, 1992, Patrol Car, San Francisco. Police Officer Laura Deleuse:

I got back into the patrol car. The reporter leaned forward over the seat rest and asked quietly, 'Officer Deleuse, tell me what happened in there,' she said. 'I mean all those white garbage bags coming out of the house. I saw the other officers put them in their car.'

'Narcotics,' I said. 'Marijuana.'

'Was that what the burglar was trying to get? What happened to the woman? Was she shot?' The woman sounded almost hopeful.

'She disarmed a thief and shot him. Haven't seen many of those.'

'She did!' the reporter crowed and took out her steno book.

'Listen,' I said, 'It's dinnertime and for a half hour I'm off duty.'

'Sure, sure,' the reporter said. 'Sorry.' She tucked her steno book back into a neat little leather handbag. The clasp closed with a click.

I thought about all the ways people needed drugs. Chemotherapy patients. My room-mate whose insurance wouldn't cover his AZT. Junkies that don't have a life anymore and don't think twice about taking a few people along with them.

I looked at the reporter. I could see in the street light that she was prematurely grey. I thought about the prostitute, Streak, the cabbie and the detectives who didn't see the cocaine on the refrigerator, the detectives who didn't care. I hoped I was a different kind of cop.

Kevin was finished with the radio. He was in a better mood and I was glad. He was talking to the reporter about a restaurant review he'd read in the *Chronicle* last week. Patricia Unterman, the restaurant critic had recommended the curries of a Thai restaurant right here in the Ingleside district.

Kevin liked green curry. The reporter preferred Pad Thai noodles.

I looked forward to little potatoes and coconut sauce and hoped that nothing else would happen tonight.

ROSIE SCOTT

Senseless Violets

It happens like this. A tall, robot-faced punk wearing a tartan tam-o'-shanter stabs a man in the street. The man staggers, grunting in a way which makes my senses leap, it's as if he had been waiting for this knife for a long time. The blade is driven right up to the hilt in his slight chest. The wicker basket he is carrying falls, scattering groceries and a pair of leather gloves, the brown fingers curling grotesquely on the pavement. The man falls heavily against some stone steps and lies like a huge twisted bird, startlingly dead. Later on in my dream I can see the body lying motionless under a ragged blanket, one shoe poking out with ghastly coyness. Someone has picked up the basket and repacked the contents – it waits beside its owner like a dog.

As soon as I wake I know it's Angel and his seedy diary. I shouldn't have read it, sure, but it was still lucky I did because it was even more psychotic than I had ever suspected. The dream hits me again when I'm sitting at the table eating peaches out of a tin for breakfast. It gives me a thump of anxiety in the chest. It's as if some repressed forbidden longing has activated a switch and the reels have begun to turn silently, projecting troubling figures on a tiny screen in my brain.

In my sea-green studio with its morning shadows, the radio murmuring in the corner, my cigarette smoke hanging in the air, Angel's presence has suddenly become electric. I know for sure I have to get rid of him today, he is like an evil black bird circling over me. I hadn't ever thought consciously that I was in any danger. I've tolerated him for so long because in lots of ways we do suit each other, we're like Siamese twins.

For instance, he is the only visitor I've had for years who let me know that I was a freak the minute he set eyes on me. I am so tired of sycophantic people from the art world coming and murmuring at me. They murmur, their eyes averted reverentially as if I were some living icon. And here I am like a huge pale subaquatic monster sitting at the bottom of a greeny-dark pond, snuffling for the few particles of light slowly filtering down to me.

('Miss Rathbone, I was wondering how you see to paint?')

Visitors just ignore the whole bizarre set-up and pretend we're sitting in a drawing-room and that I'm a trim, bright-eyed matron. They all say such nice things and keep their faces so wonderfully smooth and untroubled and delighted with everything. I still remember the day Angel came – his startling orange hair close against his skull, making him look deformed. We looked at each other in instant, amused recognition. I liked that. He instinctively knew me. He could see all the grotesque desires which still drive my old bones. With one glance that inhuman adolescent could see that I am an old person in whom the natural ageing of the impulse, the dignity of resignation, is completely absent.

Later on as I got to know him well, it was always amusing to watch his struggle between utter contempt and an almost hysterical desire to be my disciple, my friend, manage me, slime in on my creative energy, muscle in on my fame and somehow, anyhow go down with me to posterity. His presence brought a strong meaty whiff of the streets into my closed-in old world, there was something dangerous about him, which was at least alive. Like a hunting beast, with his rodent face and deformed skull. He really needed me for something else as well. I had been feeling that strongly recently – that was why I finally read his diary which he left in his desk.

It's as if he has started to feed off my flesh like a reptile. I can almost feel his pointed little teeth. He's so small and pale and reptilian with his orange death's head skull and flat insect eyes. The only genuine carnality about Angel is the dab of crusted spittle on his lips. Once recently he touched me by mistake and I suddenly imagined us in bed together. It was horrific. My huge wrinkled body, elderly smell and Angel, small and sinister, grotesquely excited, burrowing in my flesh like a maggot.

The worst of it is that he seems to guess my fantasies, which he mostly finds contemptible. He somehow meshes in with them, feeds them. Here I am, a gross old baggage, lying in bed at night feeling a hollowness because I haven't got a man in bed with me. At my age. Me, imagining the young body and soft curls on my mouth, the clean musky smell. Even I know there is only a thin line between Angel and me and the pit. I probably didn't even need to read the diary to know that.

And then of course, straight after I met him we worked together on what proved to be my most famous series. Angel even named it – *Senseless Violets* his title was. My dream is actually a replica of some of those paintings. It caught the selfsame quality I had been trying to express in the series – that graceless, clumsy, almost sensual way men move in their slow motion dance of violence. That sensuousness as they move in for the kill. I've probably carried those muddy images round for years, long before I met Angel, but it was his unwholesome adolescent presence which triggered them off. I see now of course that it would have been better to ignore the urge. Six months of working like a dog, sleepless nights – feeling blank and stressed and twitchy all the time. Of course Angel helped in every way he could. The paintings, I see in hindsight, must have been meat and drink to his disordered soul.

I'm too sheltered now, that's the problem. That's why Angel's crudity was such a breath of fresh air. I've been living here for so long in this house that I'm like a foetus pickled in formulin. Immersed in my environment, peering wistfully out. It's possible Angel is the only breath of reality I've had for years. Once, quite recently a clutch of Polynesian kids came to my door by mistake. I could see they were quite terrified of me when I opened the door. They could even smell me, they stood there, poised like little gazelles, their nostrils delicate, sniffing the wind. They were lovely. I savagely wanted them to stay just for a while. I told them their friend didn't live here and asked them if they wanted something to eat. It was dumb, but I actually had some dates in my hands at the time – they looked in absolute horror at the blackish mass I offered. I really wanted them to stay, I even called out to Angel to bring them something to eat, but they made a bolt for it, right in front of my eyes. They were silly with terror. They ran down the path past my funny garden with the old iron sculpture. It was banging and scraping desolately as it does when there's a southerly. Angel came to the door looking petulant for some reason.

It was such a wounding insight into how I really looked to some people. I did one of the first self-portraits I have done for fifteen years as a result of that – of an enormous woman blocking out a doorway, looking down on some children, a mound of dates like worms in her hands. The painting was slanted down to the children's perspective, there was a brown spiky nettle at the corner of the house. I liked it very much, but a lot of my friends were horrified. They thought it was a grim view of myself. They said I must have bad dreams. Angel thought it was a bit overboard, he said I was grotesque, sure, but not quite so unwholesome as the picture suggested. He has that ludicrous cool way of speaking which almost makes me laugh in his face sometimes. He takes himself so seriously, always calculating the most advantageous response to anything. Sometimes he calls me Dorry and it always sounds like a threat.

But this morning I'm not exactly frightened. I know he's due to come in soon and I want to finish it all in one chop, I've had enough of this bizarre game we've played for so long. Going through my morning routine – cleaning up, getting the canvas ready, dawdling around smoking roll-your-owns, I feel sharp as a fox, I've got all my wits about me. I know instinctively how to deal with him – it's almost like dealing with myself.

When he does come in, it's almost an anticlimax, my head has been buzzing so much. It's as if I have conjured him up out of my imagination. He walks so softly in his white sand shoes, my creation. I see how super-ambitious he is under his studied manner, all that nonsensical chic.

'Hello Angel,' I say, leaping straight into the breach. 'I'm going to paint you this morning. I had a dream about you. You were murdering someone.'

He is quite quiet and I sit there watching him attentively, my cigarette smoke wreathing around my head as he stands poised. I feel all-powerful, huge, absolutely still.

'What do you mean?' he whispers.

'You know, Angel.' I'm not at all afraid of him. It's as if our whole association, the great festering swamp the two of us have been dabbling in for a year is to be drained with one brutal cut. We've looked at a few things together, Angel and me, and now I'm itching to tell him to go.

He says softly, he is recovered almost instantly, 'Have you been reading my diary? I thought I'd left it here. Were you reading about the performance art? Snuff movies, you name it. Hacking grotesque old women to death. Body art maybe. They video it you know.'

He knows all is lost, I can tell he is wishing, wishing he could say something else to me, his partner in crime, his real mother. Such courageous bravado nearly makes me lose my head.

'Sure I have. The trouble with you Angel is that you're quite ordinary. You're straight out of the "Professionals". You know, the wizened little psychotic who's been doing all the bizarre killings. He's nearly always caught in the last frame. You know. Before the credits start coming up. You're on nearly every week.'

Of course, I'm going too far but he's really irritating me, it's good to be drawing blood, piercing his sour skin.

He says, 'I've never liked you much, that's true. Why do you think I hang round you all the time?'

For the first time in our association I hear a whine in his voice. He sounds quite young and pathetic.

'Don't be dramatic. Come on, we've leached on each other quite long enough. You're not coming here again.'

I guess I knew how it would go, right from the minute I woke up.

'I hope you have more bad dreams, Dorry,' he says so softly I have to lean forward. I don't want to miss anything he says. His voice is so soft in the dusk and sea-green room. The cats are watching us steadily with their wicked eyes. I can see he is still rigid with the desire to somehow win me back and keep his power, even though he knows deep down he's lost it. He's still not ready to go out into the wide wide world, poor Angel.

'Body art,' I say, insultingly, smiling a bit. It's just to help him out.

He laughs, suddenly, giving up. He is quite genuinely amused, I'll give him that.

'All right, all right. I'm going. But I'm coming back.'

It's only a friendly admonition. Angel, the murderous dream, my huge black bird, moves out of my sight.

Settling in with my paintbrushes and the cordial smell of canvas in my nostrils I feel relaxed, uplifted, easy. I even talk to the cats who shift uneasily at my voice. It's still hours till my first cup of tea.

SARA PARETSKY

The Man Who Loved Life

Simon Peter Dresser looked down at the long rows of tables. Pride made his heart grow in his chest, pressing against his throat so that he could hardly respond to the bishop sitting on his right. If only his daddy could see him now, bishops deferring to him, politicians courting him and hundreds of people looking up to where he sat at the center of the head table, admiration glowing from their faces.

His daddy had snorted when Simon told him he'd been asked to head the Illinois group. That was in 1975, two years after the baby murderers had persuaded the family haters on the Supreme Court to give women all over America abortion on demand.

Leave politics to the politicians, the old man had said. You got enough to do looking after your family. Then he died before Simon's picture appeared in *Newsweek*. Died before Simon got the invitation to address the House of Bishops. He'd have seen then that Simon truly was a rock, the rock on which a whole nation of Christians was building its hope of bringing morality back to America. Yes, Simon Peter, on this rock I will build my church. His daddy picked him to be the rock because he was the oldest and the younger ones had to obey him just like he had to obey his daddy. But sometimes the old man had his doubts. If only he could've lived to see this night.

Simon's heart started thudding faster and louder as he thought of the praise that lay ahead for him. Although the steak was cut thick and cooked the way he liked it, just a little pink showing, he could hardly taste it for excitement. But he politely handed sour cream to the bishop and glanced at Louise to make sure she was talking to the state representative on her left. He'd tried to impress on her before they left home how important it was to pay attention to the man, how much Simon needed him to carry out his programme for Illinois, that she couldn't do her usual trick of staring at her plate all through dinner.

When she saw him looking at her she flushed and put down her fork and blurted something to her dinner partner. Simon shook his head a little, but nothing could really dampen his exultation. And it wasn't fair to her, not really, she wasn't at home with crowds and speeches as he was. She seldom came with him to public events. She didn't like to leave the children, even now that Tommy was eight and could get along without her.

He turned back to the bishop and delivered a short lecture on tactics in response to a comment the prelate had made with the sour cream.

'Of course it's largely a social problem,' the bishop said when Simon finished. 'The breakdown of the family. Parents unwilling to assume any moral authority. Very few with your kind of family-centred life. But you don't need me to tell you that.'

'It's a question of respect,' Simon said. 'Children don't respect their parents and their parents don't do anything to force them to. It was different when you and I were boys. You take my old man. You said yes-sir when you spoke to him or he made sure you never forgot a second time.'

The bishop smiled in polite agreement and told a long tale about the demoralized state of modern seminary training. Simon took another roll and explained that his daddy had been tough. Tough, but fair. He'd sometimes felt hurt when he was little, but now he thanked God he had a father like that, one who knew right from wrong and wouldn't put up with any crap. No-sir, you thought you were being slick, putting one over the old man, but he was always a jump ahead of you. And he had a hand as strong as a board. He wasn't afraid to use it, not even when you got to be as big as him. Bigger.

The bishop nodded and shared an anecdote about the man he'd first served under as a priest.

Simon pursed his lips and shook his head at the right places. That time he'd gone out drinking with his buddies, he'd been eighteen, getting ready to start at St Xavier's (stay with the Jesuits, his daddy said; they don't snivel every time some JD comes to them with a hard-luck story.) He'd thought he was old enough to do what he wanted on Saturday night.

Don't be a sissy, for Christ's sake. He was pretty sure it was Jimmy who had put it into words, Jimmy who was going into the army along with Bobby Lee Andrews. That was when being a soldier meant something, not like now, when all the soft liberals in Congress encouraged kids to burn their own country's flag. So he and Jimmy and Bobby went out with Carl and Joe. One last get-together for the team before they went their separate ways. The other guys were always on him, how he was scared of his old man. They didn't recognize it was respect, not fear. You respect the man who's strong enough to know right from wrong and teach it to you.

But just that one time he couldn't take their hassling any more. He got weak, soft, caved in and went out with them. And then, two in the morning, giggling drunk, trying to sneak in through the back door. His mother had left the back door open. She knew he was up to something so she snuck down and unlocked it. She was always soft, always weak, trying to subvert his daddy's strength. His father made rules and she tried to break them, but she couldn't. No-sir, not any more than her children. If she was fifteen dollars shy in the grocery money his daddy knew: he added all the bills against her household allowance. Don't tell me you lost a receipt, Marie, because I sure as hell don't believe you. Where'd that money go to, anyway? And she'd snuffle around and cry and try to lie, but his daddy always could tell.

It was disgusting watching her cry, it made him sick even to this day when he thought about it. He'd told Louise that back in the first year they were married. Don't ever cry in front of your children, he warned her. At least, I'd better not ever hear of you doing it.

'The trouble is,' he said to the bishop, 'too many men just are too lazy or too scared to buck all these libbers and liberals and take on their role as head of the family. They'd just as soon the government or the schools or someone did it for them. That's why you get all these girls going into the abortuaries and letting someone murder their babies. Their daddies or their husbands are just too damned – excuse me, Your Grace – too darned lazy to control them.'

The bishop smiled again. He was used to hearing people swear and used to hearing them apologise for it.

Simon's glow of satisfaction extended to his well-run family. None of his five daughters ever talked back to Simon. None of them had ever even tried, except Sandra. She was the oldest; maybe she thought that gave her special status, but he'd sure as hell beaten that nonsense out of her.

He didn't believe it when she was born. When the nurse came out and told him it was a girl he knew she'd made a mistake, confused him with one of the other men waiting for news. His daddy'd been so disappointed. Disappointed but pleased at the same time: it proved he was a bigger man than Simon would ever be. Then it had taken three more tries before they got their first boy and he was a skinny little runt, took after Louise's family. And then his daddy died before they got their second boy. They named him Tom for his grandpa, and he looked like him, a big, muscly boy, but it was too late; his daddy never saw Simon had finally gotten himself a real little man.

He realised he'd missed the bishop's next remark, but it didn't matter: he'd had the same conversation a hundred times; he could respond without thinking. Not like the first time he'd talked to a bishop. Really talked, face to face, not just a hand-shake after a special service. He'd been so nervous his voice had come out in a little squeak, that high squeak he'd hated because it was how he always ended up sounding if he tried to argue with his daddy. But now he could see the bishops were men just like him, with the same kind of problems running their dioceses he had running his organisation. Except now that he was head of the thing for the whole country it was probably more like being pope. Of course he never said any of this to the bishops, but it did give him a little edge over the man on his right. Just a suffragen, an assistant. Maybe twenty parishes under his care. Not like being responsible for the whole country.

The waitress filled Simon's coffee cup. He took cream and sugar from the bishop and used them generously. When he turned to offer them to Louise he saw she'd already been given some by the state representative. She shouldn't use so much sugar; she'd never really gotten her figure back after Tommy was born. But he wasn't going to spoil his big night by worrying about her problems.

As the bishop finished his dessert Simon's heart started its happy thudding once more. The bishop deliberately folded his napkin in three across the diagonal and put it on the table so it was exactly parallel with his plate. He waited for the master of ceremonies to inform the diners that they would have grace after dinner, then slowly stood and offered the benediction.

Simon fixed a pleased but humble look under his beard. He leaned over to the bishop when he sat down and made a jovial little comment. The bishop nodded and chuckled and everyone on the floor could see that Simon was on equal, maybe even superior terms, with a bishop.

The master of ceremonies told everyone how happy he was they could be here to honour Simon. A staunch fighter for the unborn. Untold thousands of lives saved because of him. Wouldn't rest until babies were safe all over America. Special tribute tonight. But first they'd prepared a slideshow: *The Fight to Protect the Unborn.*

The lights in the ballroom were dimmed and a screen unfolded on the stage behind the head table. Simon and the bishop turned their chairs around so they could see. After a second's hesitation, in which she looked questioningly first at Simon, then the state representative, Louise scooted around as well.

Simon had seen portions of the slide show before, sections that were used at fund-raising events and which showed him shaking hands with the President after their historic March for Life in the nation's capital. But they'd put that part together with a series taken at demonstrations and other important events around the country and added a soundtrack. The whole show had been completed in time for tonight's dinner. They'd use it in the future to educate high school students and church groups on how to fight for Life, but it was being unveiled tonight just for him.

Their logo flashed on the screen while solemn but cheerful music played behind it. The dove of the Holy Spirit spreading its wings over the curled form of a helpless foetus. Then his own voice, his well-practised tenor that he'd spent four years in college studying speech to perfect, to get rid of that shameful squeak. It was a clip from the talk he'd made in Washington, the warm tones vibrating with emotion as he told the gathered hosts that no one in America could be free until every unborn life in America was held sacred.

While they played the speech pictures flashed on the screen showing the mass of Pro-Life marchers carrying banners, holding up crosses to which they'd nailed cut-outs of murdered babies, all the marchers looking ardently at Simon, some with tears of shared passion in their eyes. Even now, six years later, listening to his own words his throat tightened again with rage felt on behalf of those million-and-a-half babies murdered every year. Hands as big as his father's coming down to choke the life out of them. Even when he'd been eighteen, old enough to go to college, he hadn't been big enough to stand up to the old man, so how could a poor helpless little baby in the womb that didn't have any hands at all stand up for itself?

The show went on to display pictures of Pro-Life activists marching outside death camps. Cheers came from the audience when the photo of a fire-bombed death chamber was flashed on the screen. They'd have to take that one out when they showed it to the high school students, but it proved that the helpless could gain power if they banded together.

The screen zoomed in close to the face of a girl going into one of the camps as she passed a line of peaceful picketers trying to get her to change her mind. Her face was soft, weak, scared.

Simon's fists clenched in his lap. Something about the girl made him think of his own mother. When his father beat him her face had that same expression, frightened but withdrawn, a bystander at the torment of her own baby. Don't do it, Thomas, she would beg, tears streaming down her face. He couldn't stand to hear her crying, as if she was the one being punished, and all the candy hearts she gave him later never really soothed him. He never let Louise cry. She'd done it the first time he'd had to give Sandra a whipping for talking back to him, she'd come to him sobbing as if being weak and scared was any way to stop him teaching his children right from wrong. He'd made it real clear she was never to do it again.

Then the girl in the picture was shown changing her mind. The Pro-Life counsellor was able to persuade her to put Life above her own selfish desires to control her body. The audience cheered again as the girl walked off with the counsellor to a Pro-Life clinic, funded with donations of tens of thousands of little people just like them who cared enough for Life to donate a few dollars every week.

Simon's fists relaxed and his mind wandered off to the remarks he'd make when his turn came. He'd worked on them all week, while flying to Toronto to protest the suspension of a policeman who wouldn't stand guard outside a death camp, while meeting in Springfield with key legislators on a number of bills to protect the unborn. He wanted to sound spontaneous, but authoritative, a leader people could rely on to make the right decisions.

Next to him Louise sucked in her breath, a little half-conscious sound of consternation. He glanced at her, then to the screen where she was staring. The picture showed a small band of picketers that faithfully came every Saturday to an abortuary in De Kalb. The soundtrack talked about how a few faithful could fight death and selfishness just as much as a big group could: the key was commitment. The Pro-Life counsellor was exhorting a girl in a lime-green parka as she headed up the path to the death chamber entrance.

Each shot moved closer to her face, the face pinched with a fear and weakness which Simon knew without seeing by the colour of the parka, by the way the fine brown hair parted over the bowed white neck. His bowels were softening and turning over and his throat so dry he could only trust himself to whisper.

'You did this,' he hissed to Louise under the flow of the soundtrack. She shook her head dumbly. 'You knew about this. You knew about this and never told me.' She only shook her head again. Tears spurted from her eyes and she turned to grab her napkin to blot them out, turned so fast that she jarred the table and knocked a glass of water down the state representative's back.

The accident made her throat work as she tried to swallow the tears that kept spilling. She tried wiping her face, then the legislator's back. The state representative was gracious about it, helping mop the front of her dress, laughing off the damp patch on his back, but Simon was sure he would be chuckling about him with other colleagues before the week was over: why should we listen to Simon? He can't even control his own wife.

Simon grabbed Louise's left arm and pulled her head down close to his mouth. 'You go off to the ladies room,' he ordered in that same voiceless hiss. 'You leave now and don't come back until I'm through with my speech, you hear?'

Dumbly she pulled her arm away, apologising through her tears to the state representative, dropping her handbag, spilling lipstick and Kleenex on the man's lap. The legislator patted her on the shoulder, tried to make out that he didn't mind, that it was an accident and he didn't need her to dry his back or pay to have his suit cleaned. She gave the man a fixed little smile and stumbled from the stage. If she'd practised for a month she couldn't have done more to humiliate him.

The bishop leaned over and asked with unctuous concern if Louise was all right. Simon managed a twisted smile. 'She's fine. Just needs to go to the ladies.'

But he could kill her for this. Kill her for destroying him at his moment of triumph, for working hand in glove with the old man to get him. He really thought he'd die. That night he came home drunk from being out with his buddies and his daddy stood waiting by the refrigerator with a baseball bat.

You tell me one reason why I shouldn't use this on you, Simon Peter. The rock. The old man spat at him. The sand. I'm like a man who built his house on the sand. And Simon tried talking to him, tried making his voice come out big and booming to say he was a man, he could go out with his buddies if he wanted, but the only thing that came out was that terrible little squeak and then the old man was hitting him, hitting him so hard he ended up curled on the floor, peeing in his pants. He was lying on the floor all wet and bleeding and sobbing while his mother stood crying at the top of the stairs, her tiny voice pleading for him from the far distance.

And all the while a face like Sandra's – white, scared – stared at him from the screen. 'One of our failures,' the soundtrack intoned. 'We didn't have the resources to give this girl the help she needed to choose Life. But with your support we'll be able to help other girls like this one, so that truly every life in this great land of ours will be held sacred.'

VAL McDERMID

A Traditional Christmas

Last night, I dreamed I went to Amberley. Snow had fallen, deep and crisp and even, garlanding the trees like tinsel sparkling in the sunlight as we swept through the tall iron gates and up the drive. Diana was driving, her gloved hands assured on the wheel in spite of the hazards of an imperfectly cleared surface. We rounded the coppice, and there was the house, perfect as a photograph, the sun seeming to breathe life into the golden Cotswold stone. Amberley House, one of the little jobs Vanbrugh knocked off once he'd learned the trade with Blenheim Palace.

Diana stopped in front of the portico and blared the horn. She turned to me, eyes twinkling, smile bewitching as ever. 'Christmas begins here,' she said. As if on cue, the front door opened and Edmund stood framed in the doorway, flanked by his and Diana's mother, and his wife Jane, all smiling as gaily as day trippers.

I woke then, rigid with shock, pop-eyed in the dark. It was one of those dreams so vivid that when you waken, you can't quite believe it hasn't just happened. But I knew it was a dream. A nightmare, rather. For Edmund, 6th Baron Amberley of Anglezarke had been dead for three months. I should know. I found the body.

Beside me, Diana was still asleep. I wanted to burrow into her side, seeking comfort from the horrors of memory, but I couldn't bring myself to be so selfish. A proper night's sleep was still a luxury for her, and the next couple of weeks weren't exactly going to be restful. I slipped out of bed and went through to the kitchen to make a cup of camomile tea.

I huddled over the gas fire and forced myself to think back to Christmas. It was the fourth year that Diana and I had made the trip back to her ancestral home to celebrate. As our first Christmas together had approached, I'd worried about what we were going to do. In relationships like ours, there isn't a standard formula. The only thing I was sure about was that I wanted us to spend it together. I knew that meant visiting my parents was out. As long as they never have to confront the physical evidence of my lesbianism, they can handle it. Bringing any woman home to their tenement flat in Glasgow for Christmas would be uncomfortable. Bringing the daughter of a baron would be impossible.

When I'd nervously broached the subject, Diana had looked astonished, her eyebrows raised, her mouth twitching in a half-smile. 'I assumed you'd want to come to Amberley with me,' she'd said. 'They're expecting you to.'

'Are you sure?'

Diana grabbed me in a bear-hug. 'Of course I'm sure. Don't you want to spend Christmas with me?'

'Stupid question,' I grunted. 'I thought maybe we could celebrate on our own, just the two of us. Romantic, intimate, that sort of thing.'

Diana looked uncertain. 'Can't we be romantic at Amberley? I can't imagine Christmas anywhere else. It's so . . . so traditional. So English.'

My turn for the raised eyebrows. 'Sure I'll fit in?'

'You know my mother thinks the world of you. She insists on you coming. She's fanatical about tradition, especially Christmas. You'll love it,' she promised.

And I did. Unlikely as it is, this Scottish working class lesbian feminist homeopath fell head over heels for the whole English country house package. I loved driving down with Diana on Christmas Eve, leaving the motorway traffic behind, slipping through narrow lanes with their tall hedgerows, driving through the chocolate box village of Amberley, fairy lights strung round the green, and finally, cruising past the Dower House where her mother lived, and on up the drive. I loved the sherry and mince pies with the neighbours, even the ones who wanted to regale me with their ailments. I loved the elaborate Christmas Eve meal Diana's mother cooked, I loved the brisk walk through the woods to the village church for the midnight service. I loved most of all the way they simply absorbed me into their ritual without distance.

Christmas Day was champagne breakfast, stockings crammed with childish toys and expensive goodies from all the Sloane Ranger shops, church again, then presents proper. The gargantuan feast of Christmas dinner, with free range turkey from the estate's home farm. Then a dozen close family friends arrived to pull crackers, wear silly hats and masks, drink like tomorrow was another life and play every ridiculous party game from Sardines to Charades. I'm glad no one's ever video-taped the evening and threatened to send a copy to the women's alternative health cooperative where I practise. I'd have to pay the blackmail.

Diana and I lead a classless life in London; almost no one knows her background. It's not that she's embarrassed. It's just that she knows from bitter experience how many barriers it builds for her. But at Amberley, we left behind my homeopathy and her Legal Aid practice and for a few days, we lived in a time warp that Charles Dickens would have revelled in.

On Boxing Day night, we always trooped down to the village hall for the dance. It was then that Edmund came into his own. His huntin', shootin' and fishin' persona slipped from him like the masks we'd worn the night before when he picked up his alto sax and stepped on to the stage to lead the twelve-piece Amber Band. Most of his fellow members were professional session musicians, but the drummer doubled as a labourer on Amberley Farm and the keyboard player was the village postman. I'm no connoisseur, but I reckoned the Amber Band was one of the best live outfits I'd ever heard. They played everything from Duke Ellington to Glen Miller, including Miles Davis and John Coltrane pieces, all arranged by Edmund. And of course, they played some of Edmund's own compositions, strange haunting slow-dancing pieces that somehow achieved the seemingly impossible marriage between the English countryside and jazz.

There was nothing different to mark out last Christmas as a watershed gig. Edmund led the band with his usual verve. Diana and I danced with each other half the night, and took it in turns to dance with her mother the rest of the time. Evangeline ('call me Evie') still danced with a vivacity and flair that made me understand why Diana's father had fallen for her. As usual, Jane sat stolidly at the table nursing a gin and tonic that she made last the whole night. 'I don't dance,' she'd said stiffly to me when I'd asked her up on my first visit. It was a rebuff that brooked no argument. Later, I asked Diana if Jane had knocked me back because I was a dyke.

Diana roared with laughter. 'Good God, no,' she spluttered. 'Jane doesn't even dance with Edmund. She's tone deaf and has no sense of rhythm.'

'Bit of a handicap, being married to Edmund,' I said.

Diana shrugged. 'It would be if music was the only thing he did. But the Amber band only does a few gigs a year. The rest of the time he's running the estate and Jane loves being the country squire's wife.'

In the intervening years, that was the one thing that had changed. Word of mouth had increased the demand for the Amber Band's services. By last Christmas, the band were playing at least one gig a week. They'd moved up from playing village halls and hunt balls on to the student union circuit.

Last Christmas, I'd gone for a walk with Diana's mother on the afternoon of Christmas Eve. As we'd emerged from the back door, I noticed a three-ton van parked over by the stables. Along the side, in tall letters of gold and black, it said, 'Amber Band; bringing jazz to the people.' 'Wow,' I said. 'That looks serious.'

Evie laughed. 'It keeps Edmund happy. His father was obsessed with breaking the British record for the largest salmon, which, believe me, was a far more inconvenient interest than Edmund's. All Jane has to put up with is a lack of Edmund's company two or three nights a week at most. Going alone to a dinner party is a far lighter cross to bear than being dragged off to fishing lodges in the middle of nowhere to be bitten to death by midges.'

'Doesn't he find it hard, trying to run the estate as well?' I asked idly as we struck out across the park towards the coppice.

Evie's lips pursed momentarily, but her voice betrayed no irritation. 'He's taken a man on part-time to take care of the day-to-day business. Edmund keeps his hands firmly on the reins, but Lewis has taken on the burden of much of the routine work.'

'It can't be easy, making an estate like this pay these days.'

Evie smiled. 'Edmund's very good at it. He understands the importance of tradition, but he's not afraid to try new things. I'm very lucky with my children, Jo. They've turned out better than any mother could have hoped.'

I accepted the implied compliment in silence.

The happy family idyll crashed around everyone's ears the day after Boxing Day. Edmund had seemed quieter than usual over lunch, but I put that down to the hangover that, if there were any justice in the world, he should be suffering. As Evie poured out the coffee, he cleared his throat and said abruptly, 'I've got something to say to you all.'

Diana and I exchanged questioning looks. I noticed Jane's face freeze, her fingers clutching the handle of her coffee cup. Evie finished what she was doing and sat down. 'We're all listening, Edmund,' she said gently.

'As you're all aware, Amber Band had become increasingly successful. A few weeks ago, I was approached by a representative of a major record company. They would like us to sign a deal with them and to make some recordings. They would also like to help us move our touring venues up a gear or two. I've discussed this with the band, and we're all agreed that we would be crazy to turn our backs on this opportunity.' Edmund paused and looked around apprehensively.

'Congratulations, bro,' Diana said. I could hear the nervousness in her voice, though I wasn't sure why she was so apprehensive. I sat silent, waiting for the other shoe to drop.

'Go on,' Evie said in a voice so unemotional it sent a chill to my heart.

'Obviously, this is something that has implications for Amberley. I can't have a career as a musician and continue to be responsible for all of this. Also, we need to increase the income from the estate in order to make sure that whatever happens to my career, there will be enough money available to allow Ma to carry on as she has always done. So I have made a decision to hand over the running of the house and the estate to a management company who will run the house as a residential conference centre and manage the land in broad accordance with the principles I've already established,' Edmund said in a rush.

Jane's face flushed dark red. 'How dare you?' she hissed. 'You can't turn this place into some bloody talking shop. The house will be full of ghastly sales reps. Our lives won't be our own.'

Edmund looked down at the table. 'We won't be here,' he said softly. 'It makes more sense if we move out. I thought we could take a house in London.' He looked up beseechingly at Jane, a look so naked it was embarrassing to witness it.

'This is extraordinary,' Evie said, finding her voice at last. 'Hundreds of years of tradition, and you want to smash it into pieces to indulge some *hobby*?'

Edmund took a deep breath. 'Ma, it's not a hobby. It's the only time I feel properly alive. Look, this is not a matter for discussion. I've made my mind up. The house and the estate are mine absolutely to do with as I see fit, and these are my plans. There's no point in argument. The papers are all drawn up and I'm going to town tomorrow to sign. The other chaps from the village have given up their jobs, we're all set.'

Jane stood up. 'You bastard,' she yelled. 'You inconsiderate bastard. Why didn't you discuss this with me?'

Edmund held his hands out to her. 'I knew you'd be opposed to it. And you know how hard I find it to say no to you. Jane, I need to do this. It'll be fine, I promise you. We'll find somewhere lovely to live in London, near your friends.'

Wordlessly, Jane picked up her coffee cup and hurled it at Edmund. It caught him in the middle of the forehead. He barely flinched as the hot liquid poured down his face, turning his sweater brown. 'You insensitive pig,' she said in a low voice. 'Hadn't you noticed I haven't had a period for two months? I'm pregnant, Edmund, you bastard. I'm two months pregnant and you want to turn my life upside down?' Then she ran from the room, slamming the heavy door behind her, no mean feat in itself.

In the stunned silence that followed Jane's bombshell, no one moved. Then Edmund, his face seeming to disintegrate, pushed his chair back with a screech and hurried wordlessly after his wife. I turned to look at Diana. The sight of her stricken face was like a blow to the chest. I barely registered Evie sighing, 'How sharper than a serpent's tooth,' before she too left the room. Before the door closed behind her, I was out of my chair, Diana pressed close to me.

Dinner that evening was the first meal I'd eaten at Amberley in an atmosphere of strain. Hardly a word was spoken, and I suspect I wasn't alone in feeling relief when Edmund rose abruptly before coffee and announced he was going down to the village to rehearse. 'Don't wait up,' he said tersely.

Jane went upstairs as soon as the meal was over. Evie sat down with us to watch a film, but half an hour into it, she rose and said, 'I'm sorry, I'm not concentrating. Your brother has given me rather too much to think about. I'm going back to the Dower House.'

Diana and I walked to the door with her mother. We stood under the portico, watching the dark figure against the snow. The air was heavy, the sky lowering. 'Feels like a storm brewing,' Diana remarked. 'Not even the weather's pleased with Edmund.'

We watched the rest of the film, then decided to go up to bed. As we walked through the hall, I went to switch off the lights on the Christmas tree. 'Leave them,' Diana said. 'Edmund will turn them off when he comes in. It's tradition – last to bed does the tree.' She smiled reminiscently. 'The number of times I've come back from parties in the early hours and seen the tree shining down the drive.'

About an hour later, the storm broke. We were reading in bed when a clap of thunder as loud as a bomb blast crashed over the house. Then a rattle of machine gun fire against the window. We clutched each other in surprise, though heaven knows, we've never needed an excuse. Diana slipped out of bed and pulled back one of the heavy damask curtains so we could watch the hail pelt the window and the bolts of lightning flash across the sky. It raged for nearly half an hour. Diana and I played the game of counting the gap between the thunderclaps and lightning flashes, which told us the storm seemed to be circling Amberley itself, moving off only to come back and blast us again with lightning and hail.

Eventually, it moved off to the west, occasional flashes lighting up the distant hills. Somehow, it seemed the right time to make love. As we lay together afterwards, revelling in the luxury of satiated sensuality, the lights suddenly went out. 'Damn,' Diana drawled. 'Bloody storm's got the electrics on the blink.' She stirred. 'I'd better go down and check the fuse box.'

I grabbed her. 'Leave it,' I urged. 'Edmund can do it when he comes in. We're all warm and sleepy. Besides, I might get lonely.'

Diana chuckled and snuggled back down in my arms. Moments later, the lights came back on again. 'See?' I said. 'No need. Probably a problem at the local sub-station because of the weather.'

I woke up just after seven the following morning, full of the joys of spring. We were due to go back to London after lunch, so I decided to sneak out for an early morning walk in the copse. I dressed without waking Diana and slipped out of the silent house.

The path from the house to the copse was well trodden. There had been no fresh snow since Christmas Eve, and the path was well used, since it was a short cut to both the Dower House and the village. There were even mountain bike tracks among the scattered boot prints. The trees, an elderly mixture of beech, birch, alder, oak and ash, still held their tracery of snow on the tops of their branches, though following the storm, a mild thaw had set in, and as I moved into the wood, I felt drops of melting snow on my head.

In the middle of the copse, there's a clearing fringed with silver birch trees. When she was little, Diana was convinced this was the place where the fairies came to recharge their magic. There was no magic in the clearing that morning. As soon as I emerged from the trees, I saw Edmund's body, sprawled under a single silver birch tree by the path on the far side.

For a moment, I was frozen with shock. Then I rushed forward and crouched down beside him. I didn't need to feel for a pulse. He was clearly long dead, his right hand blackened and burned.

I can't remember the next hours. Apparently, I went to the Dower House and roused Evie. I blurted out what I'd seen and she called the police. I have a vague recollection of her staggering slightly as I broke the news, but I was in shock, and I can't remember what she said. Diana arrived soon afterwards. When her mother told her what had happened, she stared numbly at me for a moment then tears poured down her face. None of us seemed eager to be the one to break the news to Jane. Eventually, as if by mutual consent, we waited until the police arrived. We merited two uniform constables, plus two plain clothes detectives. In the words of Noel Coward, Detective Sergeant Maggie Staniforth would not have fooled a drunken child of two and a half. As soon as Evie introduced me as 'my daughter's partner,' DS Staniforth thawed visibly. I didn't much care at that point. I was too numbed even to take in what they were saying. It sounded like the distant mutter of bees in a herb garden.

DS Staniforth set off with her team to examine the body, while Diana and I, after a muttered discussion in the corner, informed Evie that we would go and tell Jane. We found her in the kitchen, drinking a mug of coffee. 'I don't suppose you've seen my husband,' she said in tones of utter contempt when we walked in. 'He didn't even have the courage to come home last night.'

Diana sat down next to Jane and flashed me a look of panic. I stepped forward. 'I'm sorry, Jane, but there's been an accident.' In moments of crisis, why is it we always reach for the nearest cliché?

Jane looked at me as if I were speaking Swahili. 'An accident?' she asked, in a macabre echo of Dame Edith Evans' 'A handbag?'

'Edmund's dead,' Diana blurted out. 'He was struck by lightning. In the wood. Coming home from the village.'

As she spoke, a wave of nausea surged through me. I thought I was going to faint. I grabbed the edge of the table. Diana's words robbed the muscles in my legs of their strength and I lurched into the nearest chair. Up until that point, I'd been too dazed with shock to realise the conclusion everyone but me had come to.

Jane looked blankly at Diana. 'I'm so sorry,' Diana said, the tears starting again, flowing down her cheeks.

'I'm not,' Jane said. 'He can't stop my child growing up in Amberley now.'

Diana turned white. 'You bitch,' she said wonderingly.

At least I knew then what I had to do.

Maggie Staniforth arrived shortly after to interview me. 'It's just a formality,' she said. 'It's obvious what happened. He was walking home in the storm and he was struck by lightning as he passed underneath the birch tree.'

I took a deep breath. 'I'm afraid not,' I said. 'Edmund was murdered.'

Her eyebrows rose. 'You're still in shock. I'm afraid there are no suspicious circumstances.'

'Maybe not to you,' I said. 'But I know different.'

Credit where it's due, she heard me out. But the sceptical look never left her eyes. 'That's all very well,' she said eventually, 'But if what you're saying is true, there's no way of proving it.'

I shrugged. 'Why don't you look for fingerprints? Either in the plug of the Christmas tree lights, or on the main fuse box. When he was electrocuted, the lights fused. At the time, Diana and I thought it was a glitch in the mains supply, but we know better now. Jane would have had to rewire the plug and the socket to cover her tracks. And she must have gone down to the cellar to repair the fuse, or turn the circuit breaker back on. She wouldn't have touched either of those in the usual run of things. I doubt she'd even have any reason to know where the fuse box is. Try it,' I urged.

And that's how Evie came to be charged with the murder of her son. If I'd thought things through, if I'd waited till my brain was out of shock, I'd have realised that Jane would never have risked her baby by loading Edmund over the cross bar of his mountain bike and wheeling him out to the copse. And if I'd realised it was Diana's mother who killed Edmund, I doubt very much if I'd have shared my esoteric knowledge with Detective Sergeant Staniforth. It's funny business, New Age medicine. When I attended a seminar on the healing powers of plants given by a Native American medicine man, I never thought it would prove a murder.

Maybe Evie will get lucky. Maybe she'll get a jury reluctant to convict in a case that rests on the inexplicable fact that lightning never strikes birch trees.

KITTY FITZGERALD

At Loubles

SELINE'S JOURNAL SCRIBED BY MINCIO, CHANTED BY ARVACA,
LAGOOSE 1ST TOWNSHIP. FIRST EXTRACT.

I got news today that Inso is following us. There needs to be
a record of events. It began almost a year ago. Ragacine
returned to the autumn site under the cover of darkness. His
face was badly cut and bruised, his legs and feet torn and
blistered. His breath came out in gasps, his eyelids trembled,
his whole body shook in unison with mine. My daughter,
dead, he said. Sixteen years old, just beginning on her life.
She deserved a better death, a dignified death, honour and
respect. My thoughts froze. It was unthinkable. Ragacine
insisted in stealthy whispers that he and I leave the site that
night. He had fought and wounded Inso, the cause of my
daughter's death, but not fatally. Inso being the son of Marcos
our tribe leader would undoubtedly return with a story of
his own and demand our silence and some sort of revenge
for being caught out. No amount of pleading on our part
would save Ragacine. There was too much history involved.
We left within an hour of his return. I cried for three days.

Saura entered the square at dawn. It was deserted but she knew
that she was being watched. She felt them; smelled them; their
curiosity was almost tangible. It was going to be another scorch-
ing day, the sort of day which caused tongues to wag and
tempers to fray.

The fountain in the centre of the square was dry and dusty,

Saura sipped reluctantly from her water bottle, just enough to wet her cracked lips. She had walked most of the night, a distance of twenty miles, from Miramor. Miramor had yielded few new threads to add to the details already gathered but what she had learned had convinced her she was on the right track. 'Try Loubles' they'd suggested.

Saura found a wooden bench in the shade. It hugged one corner of the square as if claiming a longer heritage than the surrounding walls which Saura guessed had spanned three or more centuries. She lay back and closed her eyes. Her plum-coloured hair brushed the stone path. At that moment, as if to the call of a silent bell, shutters began clattering open all around the square. Saura smiled to herself. The day had begun.

Esra the Scribe and Cora the Chanter were first to enter the square. On their heels came elderly men and women on their way to the fish quay to make barter on the night's fishing haul. Esra and Cora wore the bright pink and turquoise calico robes common to the region. Esra licked his wrinkled lips as he stood watching Saura. He found a decayed tooth – one of his few remaining ones – and dug his tongue into the cavity unable to resist the painful pleasure of the sensation. He was too old to care about propriety, it was doubtful that he ever had. Cora clicked her tongue in irritation as he unceremoniously pushed Saura off the bench and began to lay out the tools of his trade: wooden pen holders, feather quills, dyes and inks in various colours, wax candles, matches and rulers. The bench had belonged to his kin for generations.

Cora, ample, large-boned and taller by a good foot than her father helped Saura to her feet. With a shrug of understanding which well-seasoned travellers obtain she grinned at Cora and gestured her thanks. Cora laughed suddenly, pleased at her father's aggravation and the stranger's equanimity. It was a loud unfettered sound which echoed around the walls of the square and bounced back repeatedly.

'Tea!' Esra barked without glancing at either woman. Cora continued to chortle quietly as she laid out the charcoal burner and the makings of the tea. Saura watched the proceedings silently sitting on her haunches with her back against the wall. She was rewarded with the first freshly made cup a few minutes later. Esra grunted. Cora laughed again, deliberately irritating the old man.

As the first of the barterers returned from the quay with their glistening baskets of fish a small queue began to form in front of Esra's bench. He called for Cora to join him so that the day's work could begin. Saura watched on, fascinated. She had been able to study scribes and chanters for the first time when she had reached the Lagoose regions. In the northern wooded lands where she came from they relied wholly on an oral tradition. Here in Loubles, as in Miramor and Lagoose, scribes were paid to write down whatever people wanted written: wills, testimonials, letters, replies to central government, proposals of marriage, threats of revenge and so on. Cora's role as chanter was to listen to the essence of what was required and transform it into flowing and often flowery messages. She also composed songs, for a slightly larger fee. Money never exchanged hands. The services were paid for with fruit, vegetables, weavings, pots and even live animals, which they in turn exchanged for their needs. As a system it seemed to work remarkably well.

Saura had been travelling, pursuing, hunting for nearly a year. During that time, of necessity, she had learned most of the basic symbols of the written language. She pulled out her tattered jottings and joined the queue behind three sisters who were happily chattering about the form of marriage proposal they should make to three brothers who ran a small fishing boat and made a decent living. They finally decided on a song. As Cora worked out the rudiments of verse and tune Saura memorised her notes. One thing a scribe refused to deal with was the jottings of another of his trade. It was said to bring ill luck to the occupation.

SELINE'S JOURNAL SCRIBED BY MINCIO, CHANTED BY ARVACA, LAGOOSE IST TOWNSHIP, JANUARY. SECOND EXTRACT.

The first week of our journey southward we travelled by night and hid and slept by day. My dreams were filled with morbid, bleeding images, my body ached with sobbing, my eyes stung continuously, they were swollen and tender to the touch. Ragacine was kind and gentle, rarely speaking so as not to disturb my mourning. He forages for food, always maintains a good supply of water and rubs away my aches and pains with the juice of olives. His eyes are haunted though, the sockets are deeply hollowed. I'm afraid he will overtax himself. I am determined to get strong again quickly.

I think of Inso and I shiver. It is an uncontrollable shiver, as if ice has set on my back bone suddenly. I helped to raise him, suckled him occasionally when his mother Clarience was unwell. It was my first partner, Brience, who taught him to swim. It was my father, Lauryon, who taught him to carve his fertility masks. What a bright-eyed son of fortune he was, silvery white hair from birth, a face creased with laughter lines. Everyone agreed that he was a child to be proud of. My daughter was a year younger ... I can't bear to speak her name ... and as playmates they were inseparable. Had he not taken a vow of celibacy at his thirteenth birth day I am certain that he and she would have chosen to be mates. A vow of celibacy indeed! How could he do that to her? A major crime in our society and particularly so for a celibate. Rape. The very word is a curse. And then to murder to cover his tracks! Inso is not the only one pursuing us. Ragacine will only sleep while I'm on watch. I fear he will collapse before we reach the South East border.

Esra had clearly take a dislike to Saura. Whether it was due to her invasion of his bench or her obvious empathy with Cora was unclear. He was truculent and unhelpful as Saura tried to ease information from him. She had the seal of approval from the Scribe and Chanters Guild, given to those in pursuit of criminals, but still Esra evaded her questions. He insisted that she repeat over and over again the story she'd gained so far. Cora clicked her tongue and made tea. Chanters were not allowed to challenge the decisions of the scribe, such were the rules of the guild whose governing body was dominated by scribes. Still Cora continued to listen and observe Saura's body language with great intensity. It was as if something were at stake between the two women.

Saura sighed deeply. She was aware that a crowd had developed behind her, all impatient for their turn. Unless she moved on soon they could become hostile to a stranger hogging their scribe. She gave Esra a look that vowed she would return and moved away from his bench. It would be siesta time in under an hour. Saura decided to eat and rest in the hope that Esra would be more forthcoming after a sleep.

As she moved slowly out of the square and followed the path to the beach Inso moved with her. He kept plenty of distance between them, not wanting Saura to catch sight of him, knowing that she would be enraged to see him shadowing her so closely. Cora, however, had noted his presence and his interest in Saura. She had little doubt what it meant. Knowing, as she did, some of the traditions of the northern tribes. Esra rapped her hand with his rule to bring her attention back to work. Cora spat on the ground by his feet and glared at him. Esra swallowed uncomfortably, tasting fragments of his breakfast. Cora was not obedient in the way a daughter should be but he knew there was little he could do about it, apart from pretending to be in control.

SELINE'S JOURNAL SCRIBED BY MINCIO, CHANTED BY ARVACA, LAGOOSE 1ST TOWNSHIP, MARCH. THIRD EXTRACT

Brience, my partner, died just before our daughter's thirteenth birthday. He was killed in a hunting accident and Ragacine carried the body back to our summer site singlehandedly. A journey of six miles. He was kind and caring and helped me through that difficult time. Many frowned on our friendship because he was so much younger than me, including my daughter who was cold to him at first. Eventually we were reluctantly allowed to marry. But Marcos was never reconciled to it. Brience had been his best friend. Inso also stopped calling round. I ignored all of the gossip and disapproval, in fact I think it drew us closer together.

Ragacine was delegated to hunting parties more regularly than anyone else. He never complained. Often he would return so exhausted that we didn't make love for weeks at a time. I didn't mind, I just loved to lie close to him and listen to his soft voice. Sometimes he came back covered in bruises and cuts and told me how one or other of the men had started a fight with him because they were jealous of our relationship. Before long most of my women friends stopped gossiping with me. I knew they envied me so I swallowed my pride and concentrated all my energy on Ragacine and my daughter. She was by this time a beautiful fifteen year old, bright, alert, demanding. Only Ragacine could quieten her down. He'd pull her on to his lap and whisper things in her ear and she'd look at me with those huge dark eyes inherited from Brience and I'd have no idea what she was thinking.

That summer she took the lead in a campaign to allow women to join the scout and hunting parties. The tribe had far more females than males and she argued logically and forcibly for a break with tradition. Ragacine and I supported her at the Annual Gathering as did many others and the day was won. Still my heart lost its normal rhythm when she set off on her first trip. Ragacine comforted me and told me tales about tribes of women in the East who did all the hunting while their men stayed at home to cook and care for the children. She came back proud and glowing, a success.

Clarienca came to see me that evening. I hadn't spoken intimately to her for months and months. She looked drawn and anxious. We chattered superficially about the crops and the clay yield; about our children; about the dreams we'd had, until eventually she got to the point of her visit. Ragacine. I became enraged. I wouldn't listen to her nasty insinuations. Ragacine arrived back in the middle of the row. He had a huge wound on his head, blood dripped through his fingers as he pressed on the jagged cut. I didn't need to ask what had happened. Clarienca's face said it all. Marcos had done it. While his wife had tried to destroy my trust in Ragacine, Marcos had attacked him.

I knew what was behind it all. Ragacine and I had discussed

it in depth. The position of tribe leader was up for selection again and Marcos was worried that Ragacine, who had the support of a lot of the young bloods, would be a serious challenge to him. Politics and power can kill friendship in an hour, Brience had often said.

So. I've continued to ask myself, could it have been pre-planned that Inso attack my daughter and provoke Ragacine? Would anyone stoop that low? And yet here we are in exile, with a daughter dead and unburied and hotly pursued. You make of it what you will.

Ragacine has grown his hair long and removed his facial hair. We wear the pink and purple robes of the Southern Nomad. He looks younger and more beautiful than ever.

I can feel Inso and our other hunter getting closer. I know the traditions of our people well. I helped to form some of our rules and certainly Brience was central to the development of our criminal laws. If a male is accused then a female is put in defence of the case and a male in prosecution. It has worked well. Inso is stalking us and so are you sister. I must know you. I have pondered it long and hard and yet I can't be sure just who would have been given this task. Sister, whoever you are, I appeal to you to gather your defence well. Ragacine is a good man, it is Inso you must watch out for. I know my scribed words are confused and patchy but I am doing my best to provide you with all the background information you need. Listen well, judge fairly.

Saura bought fruit and cheese and headed for a small cave she'd noticed earlier. It was quiet and deserted. She hoped that Inso wouldn't dare pursue her there. Saura knew that the rules dictated that they must keep out of one another's sight and at all costs have no communication, but it was foolish to pretend they were not aware of each other. Seline's hatred and sus-picions of Inso, detailed in her scribings, had sunk deep, yet she smiled to herself as she followed the old mule track down to the beach. It was rocky, loose stones tumbled down the hillside. She knew the precise moment he gave up following her from the sound of the rocks. He would sit throughout the siesta in the full blast of the sun in case she returned to the town and moved on. He could only know fragments of what she knew, could only suspect her next step. As prosecutor he had no legal access, that was the rule. He relied on corrupt or drunken scribes to share their knowledge.

Saura settled in the shade of the cave. It was cool and damp, a welcome relief from the blistering sun. She lay on her stomach munching the fruit and cheese, savouring the juices and flavours. The hollowness which had been with her since the start of the investigation was beginning to heal as she got closer to its conclusion. Although the weight of responsibility she carried would never lessen. In under a month she would return home for the Annual Gathering to bear witness and influence its decisions. Lives were at stake and Saura knew that her evidence and plea would be crucial to any judgement made. She had volunteered for the task against Marcos and Clarienca's wishes, against their vociferous protests. She had won only by the eloquence of her speech and by appearing far more confident than she was.

Saura was convinced that at Loubles things would reach a climax. Esra had the last part of Seline's tale. Of that she was certain. Seline and Ragacine were close by, she could feel them, and she knew they wouldn't be wearing the pink and purple robes of the Southern Nomad. Saura fell asleep listening to the sound of the sea dragging at the pebbles on the beach.

SELINE'S JOURNAL SCRIBED BY DILCANO, CHANTED BY JOANCLARA, MIRAMOR NORTHSIDE, MAY. FOURTH EXTRACT.

The travelling is beginning to tell on us. Fugitives cannot relax and we are on top of one another all the time. Ragacine's temper has surprised me. I can sympathise but I don't like it when he turns on me and wishes he'd never set eyes on me. Why do people always hurt those closest to them? I am filled with loss and I fear now that I will lose him if I don't hold my tongue. I keep thinking back to Brience, how we grew like two trees side by side, sharing the sun and rain and never attempting to overshadow one another. His strength had been internal, enduring, not the outward display of so many men. What a waste.

Sister, I fear it is stupid to spend my scribing time telling you these things but I know you will be a young woman, that is the way of things. If I can make you see the power of emotions, the effect they can have on judgement, maybe it will help you understand. I know I wasn't really aware of these things when I was younger and maybe we can only learn them through experience. Anyway ... Marcos' friendship for Brience cannot help but taint his view of Ragacine. His and Clarienca's love for Inso would cloud the most objective mind. Ragacine's youth and vitality, his flaunting of his sexuality never endeared him to the older members of the tribe. It was intended that I take an older man for my second partner. You must take *all* these things into account as you gather your case.

I miss my home, my daughter, the clarity of our way of life, the cool of the northern winds. Ragacine does not want me to do any more scribing. He wants us to disappear, leave no more trace. But there will be more sister although they may be brief. I keep wondering if we've eaten or danced together or maybe worked in clay on the banks of Typora or Stapelena. Did we like one another? Did we smile and laugh together?

While Saura slept Inso came closer. He was confused, wondering if he should move on without her or stay on her trail. He'd noticed a change in her over the last few days. She seemed calmer, more at ease with herself, as if she had resolved certain things. Inso had been all set to leave Loubles and continue South after his first sight of the place. No one could hide in such a small, inward looking community. But Saura thought differently, he could tell.

He gazed at her small body, tight-limbed and supple. The sun gave her hair a ruby glow. He felt himself becoming aroused and fought with it. He hated himself when he couldn't control it. He should confess his failures and refute his vow of celibacy but if he did, he believed his esteem among the tribe would drop and never be regained. It was a common fault amongst the young males of the tribe, this fear of honesty.

Saura opened her eyes suddenly. Inso met her look for an instant then loped off back up the hillside. Saura spat on the ground to get rid of the taste of salt in her mouth. She stretched and gazed out over the sea. It was time to turn the screws on Esra.

Cora smiled as Saura approached the bench and indicated with her eyes the balcony up on Saura's right. Saura nodded imperceptibly. She knew that Inso was there, hiding in the shadows. Cora offered hot tea as Esra spat and turned his back on them. The afternoon queue had not yet begun forming, but it was only a matter of minutes. Saura drank the tea back in one gulp, handed the cup to Cora and swept all of Esra's tools from the table. She held them over the charcoal burner. They were mostly made of delicately carved wood and would burn in seconds. Esra gasped and took a fit of coughing as he lurched towards Saura. She stood her ground. Cora waited and watched.

A small crowd was beginning to form as Esra got control of his spluttering. They began mumbling, making unintelligible comments about what was going on. Saura dropped her hand closer to the burner. She could feel the heat prickling the back of her hand and sensed Inso move closer. Esra was calculating the loss of his tools against the cost of his pride. It took several seconds. The tools won. He promised Saura a full accounting at the end of the day's trade. A collective sigh escaped the crowd. They were slightly disappointed that the drama had ended so quickly but pleased that business continued as usual.

SELINE'S JOURNAL SCRIBED BY DILCANO, CHANTED BY JOANCLARA, MIRAMOR NORTHSIDE, JULY. FIFTH EXTRACT.

I am pregnant. I'm certain that it's a sign that all will end favourably. I've tried to persuade Ragacine that we should not start the journey back home and throw ourselves at the mercy of the Gathering. You know sister how pregnancy and childbirth are highly regarded amongst our people. If we were to return voluntarily and I were to plead for mercy I'm sure all would be well. After all, Ragacine's only real crime was striking Inso to protect my daughter. Then I should be able to give her a dignified burial and lay her soul to rest properly. Ragacine won't listen. He insists that we move on immediately. I can't bear to see him so bitter. I understand now that he's never had any faith in our system of justice, that he never will have. I am making this record without his knowledge or approval.

Sister you must look inside the facts, turn them outside in. I am depending on you. At times Ragacine seems like a stranger, someone I have never known. He is short tempered, demanding, even with a glint of cruelty in his eyes. This is not the man you should judge, he has been altered by circumstance, he is haunted, nearly trapped.

Inso fell against the balcony wall with shock. There, just a few feet from Saura, stood Ragacine. His face was partially hidden by a fisherman's cowl but Inso knew him. He saw Ragacine flinch then stiffen as he recognised Saura. She was at that moment unaware of him. She was immersed in conversation with the chanter. Inso wanted to fly down from the balcony and confront Ragacine. All his being struggled against that impulse. Seline had to be found also, that was the rule. He would have to follow him.

Saura must have sensed something in the air because she suddenly began to turn towards Ragacine. At that moment the square was flooded with hungry fishermen returning home after a hard haul. In an instant Ragacine was lost among them as they scattered in all directions. Inso cursed himself repeatedly for his slowness. When he glanced back at Saura she was staring at him as if her mind were firing questions in his direction. He knew his whole body would be signalling failure.

Saura turned back to Cora. She knew she had missed something vital and that Inso had too.

'Come back and eat with us,' Cora said. 'Esra is more relaxed over food.'

Esra mumbled as he packed away his tools and Saura took

it as a sign of approval. It would be comforting to eat a proper meal after so much scavenging.

Inso was left squatting in an orange grove opposite Cora's house as Saura followed the chanter and her father indoors. The house was cool and welcoming, it rippled with the sound of bells and glass beads. They covered every window and doorway catching every fragment of wind. In her own northern lands Saura preferred to live outdoors but here in the southern heat the dwellings were designed for comfort.

Saura sipped the cold lemon wine Cora had given her and listened to Esra's recall of Seline's first scribing. She itched with something akin to fear moving in and out and around confused attitudes, emotionally torn and drained.

SELINE'S JOURNAL SCRIBED BY ESRA, CHANTED BY CORA, LOUBLES, AUGUST. SIXTH EXTRACT.

This may be my last dictation. Ragacine rarely lets me out of his sight. He is no longer my guardian, he is my gaoler. I understand nothing little sister. Neither him or myself. I am frightened to be with him and frightened to leave him and face the fears that stalk me. He is convinced that the child I am carrying is a son and therefore not his. He rambles on about how he only produces female offspring; how it is in his nature; how he has abandoned other women for lying to him about giving birth to sons of his. It is a nightmare come true. He says I must get rid of the child and has gone to seek a medical man he's met in a local bar. Shall I run or stay? Sister, how close are you? Will I see you if I turn around? Give me time, there must be a way to bring him back to health. He has become someone else. That other wicked self we all know exists. Don't close in on us now.

Esra spat into a sand tray as he finished. Saura paced around the room. Cora watched from the stove as she stirred herbs into the soup she was preparing.

'Is there more?' Saura demanded at last. Wanting to know and not wanting to hear at the same time. Outside Inso trembled as the evening air cooled.

'There is one more brief scribing,' Esra replied. 'It was two days after this one, late in the afternoon just as I was finishing business for the day.'

'Tell me,' Saura said sharply.

Esra looked towards Cora who nodded slightly.

SELINE'S JOURNAL SCRIBED BY ESRA, CHANTED BY CORA, LOUBLES, AUGUST. SEVENTH EXTRACT.

I have been bleeding for two days. The baby cannot have survived. Ragacine and the medical man came back drunk. It was impossible to talk to them. Ragacine held me while the so called doctor performed his alcoholic ritual. I refused to scream. I refused to show my fear but when he least expected it I kicked him hard on the temple and virtually knocked him unconscious. Ragacine hit me then but he could no longer hurt me, all feeling had gone. There is nothing left to live for.

Saura was sobbing by the time Esra finished. Cora wrapped her in ample arms and rocked her back and forth. From the orange grove Inso saw the shadow of a figure move across the window of an upper room in the house. Not Esra, not Cora, not Saura. As he watched for further movement and prepared to run he missed the stealthy figure creeping around the back.

'Couldn't you have done something to help her?' Saura shouted at Esra. He grunted into his chest.

'The Guild forbids us to intervene,' he said hoarsely.

'And where would we all be now if no one ever broke a rule?!' Saura yelled.

'You are taking this all too personally,' Esra said, regaining a little of his pride. 'Just the sort of mistake my daughter frequently makes,' he added loudly.

Saura had no time to respond. Ragacine burst in through the back door, his blowpipe loaded with a poison dart. Inso saw the shadow again. It moved with great speed towards where Inso guessed the staircase must be. Inso froze with indecision. It was only when he heard the teeth-shattering scream that he sprinted across the road and hurled himself through the nearest

window. Glass beads tinkled all around him as he landed with
a roll and ended up inches from Ragacine who lay dead on the
floor. The dead man's eyes stared up unseeing, but accusingly,
at Seline. In a haze Inso remembered that she'd been a cham-
pion dart blower.

The room was like a tableau, everyone staring at everyone
else. The trance was broken by Saura.

'Mother,' she sobbed as Seline held her arms open and made
no attempt to stem the river of tears on her cheeks.

'I told you so,' Cora said to Esra as he sank into a chair.

Inso said nothing. He simply marvelled at the resilience of
the women of his tribe. Saura had put her rape by her stepfather
Ragacine behind her in order to find her mother. Seline had
lost the baby, lost her love for Ragacine and lost her faith in
her own judgement. But he knew with absolute certainty that
they would both learn to love again, whereas he feared he
would never truly be able to.

'Women are such fools when it comes to loving men,' Cora
said to no one in particular.

'It's the way things are,' Esra replied.

Cora, Seline and Saura turned to look at him. Inso hoisted
Ragacine's body on to his shoulders, he would be taken to the
Annual Gathering, dead or alive.

'Things can change,' Saura said to Esra. 'Women and men
can change.'

'Maybe ... very, very slowly. When I studied to be a scribe I
had to learn all the languages in our country ... all their origins.
The earliest ideograph we found for male was also a synonym
for selfish, and I've discovered the truth of that in my long life.'
Esra grunted as he finished speaking. He took one of his
brushes, filled it with purple ink and, with a flourish, drew the
image for them. The women looked at it and thought it was
rather like a butterfly – whose wings had never fully grown.

AMANDA CROSS

The Proposition

On that particular evening when Professor Kate Fansler settled at her desk to cope with the day's mail – those letters that had arrived at home and those she had carried back from her office – she first sorted through the stack, committing to the waste-paper basket those envelopes that declared themselves to be requests for funds whether commercial or charitable, and those with less than first class postage. This left considerably fewer to be examined with suspicion and sighs. The truth was, most of Kate's mail, however first class the postage, consisted of demands for recommendations, tenure reviews, contributions (literary, not financial), and the occasional request for a book review.

Today's mail offered only one envelope not immediately identifiable: from Texas, a town called Litany – yes, Litany, Kate examined the return address and the postmark with care – and carrying the message: POSTMAN, PLEASE FORWARD IF NECESSARY AND POSSIBLE. Forwarding had turned out to be neither necessary nor possible, but, on the other hand, the letter had to have been intended for someone else. Even Kate's most distant students, teaching in odd colleges in odder places, had never achieved so unlikely an address as Litany, Texas. From whom could such a letter be, and for whom? Kate doubted that, in reaching her, it had reached its intended destination. 'Open it, for God's sake!' Reed had he been there would have demanded in his most husbandly manner. But, left to her own devices, Kate hoped to solve the puzzle without, so to speak, sneaking a glance at the answer.

In the end, she had to give up and slice open the envelope. Even so, when she had discovered the signature at the bottom of the page she was not immediately wiser. Sr Monica Robinson. Kate, she was certain, knew no Sisters in Texas, and no one named Monica. Kate was actually driven to reading the letter. 'Dear Kate,' it began:

I trust that, after a moment's cogitation, you will remember me and our long talks into the night, although I was named Leslie then; I never liked the name though you, I recall, did. I'm now Monica, and still the one who believed in God while you, I vividly remember, were the one convinced that the only true Christians you had ever met were humanists; you would have said 'secular humanists' had the word yet come into fashion. Certainly you had much reason and sound argument on your side. The harm, the cruelty, the suffering inflicted in the name of Christ is no easier to defend now than it ever was. Were we to meet today (which is what I hope for), and were we to pick up our ancient controversy (which I scarcely dare to hope for), you would no doubt take a more tolerant but no less firm stand in defence of a godless if not lawless universe. I wish we could have the discussions now as we had them when we were young and tactless and wonderfully earnest.

But I must not go on as though we had all the time in the world, as we did in our youth. I write because I need your help, as a friend and as a detective: of course, I have heard on the grapevine and from the school notes about your growing reputation as a solver of sad predicaments. I hope I may ask you for help, plainly and without excuse, on the basis of our long-ago friendship and what I remember as your generosity, called humanist by you but recognised as a kind of holiness by me. (I realise this sounds like flattery, and may offend you; believe me, I mean exactly what I say.)

But to my point. I live here in Litany with a small group of sisters who serve the rather bleak Texas communities for miles around. We perform many of the services the Church insists must rightly be performed by priests, by men properly ordained. But there are few enough of these about, and the number dwindles by the month. We live in a house built not long ago for his Church by a man who was born in these parts; it is adobe-like, with white stucco walls, and must have been quite beautiful at one time. We sisters still find it strangely peaceful and attractive too, though it is run down and worn down by the constant winds and dust. It is lonely, even desolate country hereabouts in the High Plains, where few stay if they can find a way to go. Yet some of us love it with a passion as intense as it is inexplicable. I feel sure, dear Kate, that you will not understand that passion, but I ask you to visit in the hope of your offering temporary help, not of my converting you to my strange tastes in religion and landscape. In fact, I can offer you nothing except my gratitude and my blessing, whether or not you value it.

But I have not yet reached the point; you must by now doubt that I shall ever reach it. Here it is: we had here, in our possession, I might admit as our prized possession, a painting by a seventeenth-century woman artist named Judith Leyster. Perhaps you will have heard of her. I never had, but I now know, as do we all, a certain amount about her. If you happen to own or have access to a history of women painters by Linda Nochlin and Anne Sutherland Harris and read about Judith Leyster therein, you will know all I know about that artist.

Our painting was, we were told, a rather inferior reproduction, but for all that none the less valued by us. It is called *The Proposition*, and seemed to many an odd painting for a convent. But it is the picture of an honourable woman refusing money for sexual favours, and is, according to Nochlin and Harris, the only portrayal in that genre of a firm refusal; in every other example of such pictures the proposition was accepted if the money was sufficient. That Leyster was the only woman painting in that genre is no doubt significant.

Someone, dear Kate, has stolen our painting. But why? And what, in this barren place, could they dream of doing with it? It is not hidden anywhere in Litany nor in any towns within many miles of Litany: we have ascertained that, and you must believe me. No one has left the area recently enough to be accused of having taken our picture with them.

We stare at the empty place on our wall and miss our picture terribly, I more terribly than any of the others.

Please, dear Kate, come and help us to recover our picture. That is the point of this long letter.

I add only one further personal note. The picture came here as the gift of a woman who joined our order some years ago. She was not from these parts, and I don't know how she came to be here, except that God moves in mysterious ways, to say nothing of the Church hierarchy. She was a woman I came to love, Kate. She is dead, and the picture was her legacy to me and to the other sisters, but especially to me. I want to recover it. I hope you will take some satisfaction in proving that humanistic detection can accomplish what God and prayers cannot. Or perhaps you are the answer to my prayer.

Please come, dear Kate, for my sake and for the sake of our youthful friendship.

Touching as the letter was, Kate would no doubt have responded with a regretful refusal had she not, by coincidence or the hand of God depending on your point of view, been scheduled to visit Dallas the next week. Kate remembered Monica and their youthful friendship with pleasure, but Kate had long since concluded that ancient friendships, however congenial they had been, were best left in the unresurrected past. For Kate, Heraclitus's river, into which we cannot step twice, was a rule of life as well as a description of it.

However, a call the next day to her travel agent revealed that it was quite possible to fly from Dallas, Fort Worth to Amarillo, the airport nearest to Litany; indeed, the agent surprisingly informed Kate, the Amarillo airport had the second longest runway in the United States. 'That's comforting,' Kate said. 'Is there a reason?' The reason, hardly comforting, was that the runway had been built to launch nuclear warheads assembled in Amarillo. The warheads were now being disassembled, or something like that, the travel agent cheerfully added. 'Watch out for plutonium,' she had said, signing off.

Kate's only other preparation, apart from writing to Sister

Monica with her plans, was to consult the Nochlin-Harris[1] book Sister Monica had mentioned. *The Proposition* was there, with the comment Sister Monica had referred to: 'While paintings and prints showing men making indecent proposals to women were common in the Low Countries in the sixteenth and seventeenth centuries, a work portraying a woman who has clearly not invited such an invitation and refuses to accept it is unique.' There was a colour plate of the beautiful and unusual painting. It brought to mind all the women who had had, without complaint, to fend off for so many years such unwelcome invitations.

By the time Kate arrived in Amarillo, having given her talk in Dallas, she began to wonder if, unlike the lady in Leyster's picture, she had acquiesced too easily in what was, after all, an outrageous proposition. Her worries were increased by the fact that the plane did not go immediately into reverse upon landing, as most planes on shorter runways, certainly on all New York runways, were forced to do. Having automatically braced herself for the jolt as the pilot went into reverse, she had the sensation of some failure, of the certainty that they would smash into something. But they glided to a smooth stop and taxied towards the airport building. Sister Monica, as Kate must learn to call her, was waiting, dressed as a nun, not with a wimple but with a handkerchief over her hair and a dress and skirt that were clearly part of a uniform. Suddenly, Kate felt shy and wondered again why on earth she had come.

But Sister Monica was warmth itself, taking Kate's bag and leading her to the car, all the while expressing her gratitude. 'The convent is not too far as distance is reckoned in these parts,' she said. 'I thought we might take the scenic route.'

Looking with amazement from the car window, Kate wondered what the non-scenic route could possible be like. Except for the very occasional tree, slight ups and downs on the road, a few curves, there was nothing scenic: all was fields, or plains, or prairie, or whatever they called it, with swirling dust and other evidence of wind. 'The wind is not too bad this

---

1. Harris, Ann Sutherland and Nochlin, Linda, *Women Artists 1550–1950*. Alfred A Knopf, New York, 1977.

time of year,' Sister Monica said. 'Other months, it can blow you off the road.'

Kate could not imagine that one might choose to live in such a place. But Sister Monica, questioned, said that she had chosen to come here, that she loved this country. Suddenly Kate thought of Alexandra, in Willa Cather's novel *O Pioneers!*: 'For the first time, perhaps, since that land emerged from the waters of geologic ages, a human face was set toward it with love and yearning.' Kate doubted that Sister Monica was, like Alexandra, the first to look on this land with love, but there could not, Kate thought, having been many others. Apart from ranchers and builders of nuclear warheads, why had anyone chosen to come here? Perhaps the sisters found God more accessible in this bleak place.

'There's been a new wrinkle since I last wrote,' Sister Monica said. 'For a time it looked as though the priest had taken the picture.'

'What priest?' Kate asked.

'They come on their rounds, the few priests left in these parts, to hear confessions and give absolution. There are fewer and fewer priests, and those that are here are hard-working.'

'That hardly explains one stealing a painting.'

'Well,' Sister Monica said, saluting a lone tree as she passed it, 'he has long been fascinated with the picture; his fascination took the form of his insisting on its inappropriateness for a company of religious women. We, of course, considered it a highly religious painting. The argument has been going on for years. But now the sisters are wondering if the priest may not have taken matters into his own hands.'

'You can hardly expect me to get it back from him,' Kate said with asperity. She was tired, and felt on a fool's mission. Reed, who had tried to dissuade her, was certainly right. She ought to listen to him more, and not to her strange impulses on behalf of old acquaintances.

'It wasn't him,' Sister Monica said. 'That turned out to be a mare's nest. I'll spare you the details. The mystery is as deep as ever. Ah, here we are.'

'Here' turned out to resemble not only an adobe, but Kate's idea of an adobe, which was the surprising part of it. Sister

Monica showed Kate to the guest room, cell-like as befitted a convent, but with its own bath, for which Kate thanked whatever gods there be. Later Kate met the other Sisters, including the one in charge of the order, and was soon led to the place where the picture had been. It had hung in the refectory, in the middle of the longest wall on one side of the oblong hall. The wall opposite was filled with windows looking out on a courtyard – windows admitting light, but gazing away from the world.

Kate studied the now empty wall with some puzzlement. 'How big was the picture?' she asked.

Small they told her; about a foot high and three-quarters of a foot wide. Kate was amazed. The colour plate in the book had somehow given her the impression of a large painting; inevitable, of course with one colour plate to a page, each reproduced to the same size.

'No doubt someone simply cut out the canvas and rolled it up, perhaps during the night,' Kate said. 'It would fit nicely up a sleeve or under a long skirt. Anyone could have taken it.'

'It wasn't a canvas,' Sister Monica said. 'I should have mentioned that. The picture had been painted on a wooden panel. And while it was small for so impressive a picture, it was rather too large to conceal even under the fullest skirt. No; it had to be taken away directly – it was removed from the wall. There wasn't even any likely hiding place for it; what places there are have been thoroughly searched, I promise you.'

'Are there any other facts you've omitted?' Kate asked, rather more sharply than she intended. 'Anything else I ought to know,' she added in kinder tones.

But Sister Monica was not offended, only interested in answering the question fully. 'There is only one other fact that interests me,' she said, 'but I'm sure it can't have anything to do with our problem. Judith Leyster was unique in another way: she was the only woman artist whose father had not been an artist. He was, in fact, a brewer.'

'Well, that's interesting, if not exactly helpful under the circumstances,' Kate said, smiling. 'I think I'll turn in for now. As they used to say in the fairy stories, "morning is wiser than evening".'

The next day Kate asked to be taken on a tour of the region, but nothing indicative of art theft appeared. Kate could now well understand that a stolen picture could hardly be hidden anywhere about. The Sisters were in and out of houses, they talked to everyone, Catholic or not, they knew all their neighbours. That one of these should suddenly have turned into a kleptomaniac or an art thief was beyond belief. The picture had been stolen, as all such pictures are stolen, either to be treasured in secret by some rich misanthropic collector for whom possession was its own, and the only, reward, or to be held for ransom.

'It's always been difficult to understand the theft of famous paintings,' Kate said, as she and Sister Monica rode along. 'They can't be sold; one can't even admit possession of them, as with a kidnapped person.'

'What usually happens?' Sister Monica asked. 'Do the pictures eventually turn up?'

'Mostly they do, I think,' Kate said. 'They're dumped somewhere, and returned to the museum – it's usually a museum – whence they came. But there are some mysteries remaining. The most recent theft, at least that I know of, was from the Isabella Stewart Gardner Museum in Boston. Their Vermeer, *The Concert*, an immensely valuable painting, was simply gone one morning when the curators came in, along with several other paintings, I think. The mystery has yet to be solved. The favourite guess is that it was given as ransom in some drug deal, but don't ask me how that works exactly. I suppose there is always an underground market for famous paintings. And Vermeer is particularly valuable because he painted so few.'

Kate was glad to renew her friendship with Sister Monica, and found the few days spent with her strangely rewarding. They agreed now, as in their youth, on practically nothing. Sister Monica had, however, a lasting affection for Kate, and Kate found that she felt profound respect, not easily accounted for, towards Sister Monica. No decision in Sister Monica's life seemed comprehensible to Kate; nor could she understand for a minute why anyone would want to live in this desolate, windswept place. And yet, she had not a moment's doubt that Sister

Monica's commitment was sincere and heartfelt. Kate wished she could help her to get her painting back.

But after some peaceful, refreshing days in the sister's adobe home, Kate returned to New York having failed in her mission.

Yet even as Kate took up her wholly different, far more harried life in New York City, the problem of the vanished Judith Leyster painting would not fade away. She found herself reading books on art and art collectors that she would never before have found intriguing. It was one of these books that first gave Kate the glimmer of an idea.

Being a New Yorker she did not, with Sister Monica's sweet patience, sit down and write a letter. She immediately grabbed the telephone and demanded of the startled Texas operator the number of the convent. After a certain number of false trails, Kate was given, by a mechanical voice, the number of the adobe house in Litany. Kate dialled it, and was answered by the mother superior or whatever she was, who curtly informed Kate that Sisters could not be summoned to the telephone except in emergencies. Kate, slowing down, identified herself and explained what it was she wished to speak to Sister Monica about. Sister Monica, she was finally told, would be available to speak to 'Miss' Fansler at seven that evening.

And so at eight, her time, Kate was able to question Sister Monica. 'Tell me about the man who built the building for your Order,' Kate asked, she hoped not too peremptorily.

'I don't know much about him,' came the answer. 'He was born here, went away and grew rich. He wanted to do something for his birthplace, and built this building for the Church. In time, the priest who was then in charge in these parts gave it to our Order, having nothing else to do with it. At least we have tried to keep it from collapsing entirely.'

'Where is he now?'

'Who? The priest? He retired and has not been replaced.'

'I meant the man who gave the building to the Church.' Kate said. 'Be patient,' she admonished herself; 'take it easy.'

'I don't know where he is. Do you want me to try to find out?'

'If you can,' Kate said. 'Do you know his name?'

'Yes,' said Sister Monica, giving it. 'Why, Kate?'

'I'll tell you when I've followed out this idea, if it leads to anything. If it doesn't, there's no point. Just one more question, Monica – Sister Monica.'

'Yes?'

'Would it be hard or easy for someone, a stranger, to steal the painting? I mean, are there times when no one is about, when, say a car or a person coming or going might not be observed?'

'I suppose so,' Sister Monica said. 'One or more Sisters are usually about. But we have so much to do, there are so many people who need us, that if someone were to watch and wait – yes, I suppose a car or person would not be observed. Everyone around here has a car; we have several. There's no other way to get about.'

'Thank you,' Kate said. 'I'll be in touch. I'll write, in fact, since telephoning seems an intrusion. I'll either tell you what I think happened to your painting, or I'll tell you that I have not the least idea what happened to your painting; I'll write in either case.'

'Good bye, dear Kate,' Sister Monica said. 'God bless.'

Kate, hanging up at her end, found herself pleased by the blessing. Odd, she thought.

The donor of Sister Monica's adobe convent was not hard to find. He was, indeed, famous in many circles, not least as an art collector. Kate found out a great deal about him – which took several months of intermittent questioning by her – including details of his recent travels and acquisitions. Certainly he was not known to have any painting by Judith Leyster, or indeed from that period. He specialised rather in French and Italian paintings.

In the end, Kate turned back to her books, back to where she had begun: with Nochlin and Harris. She knew by now that *The Proposition* had been acquired by the Mauritshuis Museum in 1892 as the work of an unknown artist. No recent study of the painting had been published, at least by the date of the Nochlin-Harris book. It was while reading a book by Aline B

Saarinen sometime later that Kate solved the mystery. At least, she was able to tell Sister Monica where the painting was, but it was up to Sister Monica to get it back, or to request help from the authorities to do so.

But Sister Monica retrieved the painting alone, by her own efforts. She found out where the donor of the Sister's building was living, and went to see him. What she said to him, how she managed, before that, to be shown into his presence, she told no one, then or later, not even Kate. Her gratitude to Kate was eagerly expressed; the Sisters prayed for her and blessed her as they stood in the refectory, admiring their recovered painting, as mysteriously returned to them as it had been mysteriously abducted.

Sister Monica not only prayed for Kate, and blessed her, she wrote to thank her more formally.

I wish there were some manner by which I could repay you, but I know such are not the ways of God. You honoured our youthful friendship, and I shall always be grateful and marvellously moved by that. I know that friendship to you means something of what holiness means to me, and although you will not call your commitment from God, I am, of course, free to call it what I will. Was it God or you who led me to the picture, who arranged its return to us? I shall never know. And of course, dear Kate, if you do not care to tell me, I shall never know how you managed to guide me to the recovery of the painting, for which we are all eternally grateful.

Kate did in the end write to Sister Monica to explain what she had extrapolated from her reading. Kate did so because she felt she owed it to what Sister Monica no doubt thought of as her, Kate's, secular humanism. If God exists, and operates, and affects events, Kate – never one to abandon a debate – argued, He or She has to work through human beings, and therefore His or Her existence must remain forever in question.

'As for what I guessed, dear Sister Monica,' Kate wrote,

it was inspired by an essay Aline Saarinen wrote on Isabella Stewart Gardner[2], whose Vermeer we spoke of, although that theft took place long after Saarinen's book. Saarinen pointed out that Italian families, at the time of the great American art collectors like Isabella Stewart Gardner, hated selling their pictures, hated looking at bare places on their walls, hated admitting that they were in straightened circumstances. 'When these proud aristocrats sold paintings, they usually demanded a copy to serve as a permanent "stand-in".' These ersatz pictures have 'created a certain amount of confusion in the art world,' Saarinen notes.

Well, dear Monica, I put this information, which might, I thought, apply to others besides the Italians together with the fact that when the Mauritshuis acquired your Leyster painting, they put it in the basement, since it was by an unknown painter. Sometime, who knows when, a copy – or so I suspect – was made and placed in the store room. When women's paintings became more interesting to the art world, or perhaps earlier, *The Proposition* moved up to a gallery. But was it the real painting, or an excellent copy made most carefully on an old wood panel of the same size, with paints which would have been available in the seventeenth century?

I suspected, in short, that your picture, dear Monica, had come under the eye of your rich benefactor, who believed it, not the one in the Dutch museum, to be the original, and who determined to acquire it. Whether he did, and how, only you know, and you are not telling. My guess – yet another guess – is that he meant to leave you with a reproduction, but either was unable to because of someone's unexpected return to the adobe, or decided against it in the belief that you would know the difference.

Guard your painting well, Sister Monica. You might request insurance on it from your benefactor, who would not doubt be pleased to offer so appropriate a gift. I draw no conclusions about your Leyster painting, or about the ident-

2. Saarinen, Aline B, *The Proud Possessors: The lives, times and tastes of some adventurous American art collectors*. Random House, New York, 1958.

ical one now in the Netherlands, but rest simply content to rejoice in the happy return of your property. The priest was wrong. It is entirely appropriate to the Sisterhood that owns it.

With all good wishes, Kate.

SUSAN DUNLAP

Death and Diamonds

'The thing I love most about being a private investigator is the thrill of the game. I trained in gymnastics as a kid. I love cases with lots of action. But, alas, you can't always have what you love.' Kiernan O'Shaughnessy glanced down at her thickly bandaged foot and the crutches propped beside it.

'Kicked a little too much ass, huh?' The man in the seat beside her at the Southwest Airlines gate grinned. There was an impish quality to him. Average height, sleekly muscled, with the too-dark tan of one who doesn't worry about the future. He was over forty but the lines around his bright green eyes and mouth suggested quick scowls, sudden bursts of laughter, rather than the folds of age setting in. Amidst the San Diegans in shorts and T-shirts proclaiming the 'Zoo', 'Tijuana', and the 'Chargers', he seemed almost formal in his chinos and sports jacket and the forest-green polo shirt. He crossed, then recrossed his long legs, and glanced impatiently at the purser standing guard at the end of the ramp.

The Gate 10 waiting area was jammed with tanned families ready to fly from sunny San Diego to sunnier Phoenix. The rumble of conversations was broken by children's shrill whines, and exasperated parents barking their names in warning.

'We are now boarding all passengers for Southwest Airlines flight twelve forty-four to Oakland, through gate nine.'

A mob of the Oakland-bound crowded closer to their gate, clutching their blue plastic boarding passes.

Beside Kiernan the man sighed. But there was a twinkle in his eyes. 'Lucky them. I hate waiting around like this. It's not something I'm good at. One of the reasons I like flying Southwest is their open seating. If you move fast you can get whatever seat you want.'

'Which seat is your favourite?'

'One B or C. So I can get off fast. *If* they ever let us *on*.'

The Phoenix-bound flight was half an hour late. With each announcement of a Southwest departure to some other destination, the level of grumbling in the Phoenix-bound area had grown till the air seemed thick with frustration, and at the same time old and overused, as if it had held just enough oxygen for the scheduled waiting period, and now, half an hour later, the tired air only served to dry out noses, make throats raspy, and tempers short.

The loudspeaker announced the Albuquerque flight was ready for boarding. A woman in a rhinestone-encrusted denim jacket ran by racing towards the Albuquerque gate. Rhinestones. Hardly diamonds, but close enough to bring the picture of Melissa Jessup to Kiernan's mind. When she'd last seen her Melissa Jessup had been dead six months, beaten, stabbed, her corpse left outside to decompose. Gone were her mother's diamonds, the diamonds her mother had left her as security. Melissa hadn't yet been able to bring herself to sell them, even to finance her escape from a life turned fearful, and a man who preferred them to her. It all proved, as Kiernan reminded herself each time the memory of Melissa invaded her thoughts, that diamonds are *not* a girl's best friend, that mother (or at least a mother who says 'don't sell them') does *not* know best, and that a woman should never get involved with a man she works with. Melissa Jessup had made all the wrong decisions. Her lover had followed her, killed her, taken her mother's diamonds, and left not one piece of evidence. Melissa's brother had hired Kiernan, hoping with her background in forensic pathology she would find some clue in the autopsy report, or that once she could view Melissa's body she would spot something the local medical examiner had missed. She hadn't. The key that would nail Melissa'a killer was not in her corpse, but with the diamonds. Finding those diamonds, and the killer with them had turned into the most frustrating case of Kiernan's career.

She pushed the picture of Melissa Jessup out of her mind. This was no time for anger or any of the emotions that the thought of Melissa's death brought up. The issue now was getting this suitcase into the right hands in Phoenix. Turning back to the man beside her, she said 'The job I'm on right now is babysitting this suitcase from San Diego to Phoenix. This trip is not going to be "a kick".'

'Couldn't you have waited till you were off the crutches?' he said, looking down at her bandaged right foot.

'Crime doesn't wait.' She smiled, focusing her full attention on the conversation now. 'Besides, courier work is perfect for a hobbled lady, don't you think, Mr uh?'

He glanced down at the plain black suitcase, then back at her. 'Detecting all the time, huh?' There was a definite twinkle in his eyes as he laughed. 'Well this one's easy. Getting my name is not going to prove whether you're any good as a detective. I'm Jeff Siebert. And you are?'

'Kiernan O'Shaughnessy. But I can't let that challenge pass. Anyone can get a name. A professional investigator can do better than that. For a start, I surmise you're single.'

He laughed, the delighted laugh of the little boy who's just beaten his parent in rummy. 'No wedding ring, no white line on my finger to show I've taken the ring off. Right?'

'Admittedly, that was one factor. But you're wearing a red belt. Since it's nowhere near Christmas, I assume the combination of red belt and green turtleneck is not intentional. You're colour blind.'

'Well, yeah,' he said buttoning his jacket over the offending belt. 'But they don't ask you to tell red from green before they'll give you a marriage licence. So?'

'If you were married, your wife might not check you over before you left each morning, but chances are she might organise your accessories so you could get dressed by yourself, and not have strange women like me commenting on your belt.'

'This is the final call for boarding Southwest Airline flight twelve forty-four to Oakland at gate nine.'

Kiernan glanced enviously at the last three Oakland-bound passengers as they passed through gate nine. If the Phoenix flight were not so late, she would be in the air now and that much closer to getting the suitcase in the right hands. Turning back to Siebert, she said, 'By the same token, I'd guess you have been married or involved with a woman about my size. A woman with blond hair.'

He sat back down in his seat, and for the first time was still.

'Got your attention, huh?' Kiernan laughed. 'I really shouldn't show off like that. It unnerves some people. Others, like you, it just quiets down. Actually, this was pretty easy. You've got a tiny spot of lavender eye shadow on the edge of your lapel. I had a boyfriend your height and he ended up sending a number of jackets to the cleaners. But no one but me would think to look at the edge of your lapel, and you could have that jacket for years and not notice that.'

'But why did you say a blonde?'

'Women with blond hair tend to wear violet eye shadow.'

He smiled, clearly relieved.

'Flight seventeen sixty-seven departing gate 10 with service to Phoenix will begin boarding in just a few minutes. We thank you for your patience.'

He groaned. 'We'll see how few those minutes are.' Across from them a woman with an elephantine carry-on bag pulled it closer to her. Siebert turned to Kiernan, and giving her that intimate grin she was beginning to think of as *his look*, Siebert said, 'You seem to be having a good time being a detective.'

The picture of Melissa Jessup popped up in her mind. Melissa Jessup had let herself be attracted to a thief. She'd ignored her suspicions about him until it was too late to sell her mother's jewels and she could only grab what was at hand and run. Kiernan pushed the thought away. Pulling her suitcase closer, she said, 'Investigating can be a lot of fun if you like strange hours and the thrill of having everything hang on one manoeuvre. I'll tell you the truth, it appeals to the adolescent in me, particularly if I can pretend to be something or someone else. It's fun to see if I can pull that off.'

'How do I know you're not someone else?'

'I could show you ID, but, of course, that wouldn't prove anything.' She laughed. 'You'll just have to trust me, as I am you. After all *you* did choose to sit down next to me.'

'Well that's because you were the best-looking woman here sitting by herself.'

'Or at least the one nearest the hallway where you came in. And this is the only spot around where you have room to pace. You look to be a serious pacer.' She laughed again, and slipping into the flirt persona, said, 'But I like your explanation better.'

Shrieking, a small girl in yellow raced in front of the seats. Whooping gleefully, a slightly larger male version of herself sprinted by. He lunged for his sister, caught his foot on Kiernan's crutch, and sent it toppling back as he lurched forward, and crashed into a man at the end of the check-in line. His sister skidded to a stop. 'Serves you right, Jason. Mom, look what Jason did!'

Siebert bent over and righted Kiernan's crutch. 'Travel can be dangerous, huh?'

'Damn crutches! It's like they've got urges all their own,' she said. 'Like one of them sees an attractive crutch across the room and all of a sudden it's gone. They virtually seduce under-age boys.'

He laughed, his green eyes twinkling impishly. 'They'll come home to you. There's not a crutch in the room that hold a *crutch* to you.'

She hesitated a moment before saying. 'My crutches and I thank you.' This was, she thought, the kind of chatter that had been wonderfully seductive when she was nineteen. And Jeff Siebert was the restless, impulsive type of man who had personified freedom then. But nearly twenty years of mistakes – her own and more deadly ones like Melissa Jessup's – had shown her the inevitable end of such flirtations.

Siebert stood up and rested a foot against the edge of the table. 'So what else is fun about investigating?'

She shifted the suitcase between her feet. 'Well, trying to figure out people, like I was doing with you. A lot is common sense, like assuming that you are probably not a patient driver.

Perhaps you've passed in a No Passing zone, or even have gotten a speeding ticket.'

He nodded, abruptly.

'On the other hand,' she went on, 'sometimes I know facts beforehand, and then I can fake a Sherlock Holmes and produce anything-but-elementary deductions. The danger with that is getting cocky and blurting out conclusions before you've been given "evidence" for them.'

'Has that happened to you?'

She laughed and looked meaningfully down at her foot. 'But I wouldn't want my client to come to that conclusion. We had a long discussion about whether a woman on crutches could handle his delivery.'

'Client?' he said, shouting over the announcement of the Yuma flight at the next gate. In a normal voice, he added, 'In your courier work, you mean? What's in that bag of your client's that's so very valuable?'

She moved her feet till they were touching the sides of the suitcase. He leaned in closer. He was definitely the type of man destined to be trouble, she thought, but that little-boy grin, that conspiratorial tone could be seductive, particularly in a place like this where any diversion was a boon. She wasn't surprised he had been attracted to her; clearly, he was a man who liked little women. She glanced around, pleased that no one else had been drawn to this spot. The nearest travellers were a young couple seated six feet away and too involved in each other to waste time listening to strangers' conversation. 'I didn't pack the bag. I'm just delivering it.'

He bent down, ear near the side of the suitcase. 'Well, at least it's not ticking.' Sitting up, he said, 'But seriously, isn't that a little dangerous? Women carrying bags for strangers, that's how terrorists have gotten bombs on planes.'

'No!' she snapped. 'I'm not carrying it for a lover with an M–1. I'm a bonded courier.'

The casual observer might not have noticed Siebert's shoulders tensing, slightly, briefly, in anger at her rebuff. Silently, he looked down at her suitcase. 'How much does courier work pay?'

'Not a whole lot, particularly compared to the value of what

I have to carry. But then there's not much work involved. The chances of theft are minuscule. And I do get to travel. Last fall I drove a package up north. That was a good deal since I had to go up there anyway to check motel registrations in a case I'm working on. It took me a week to do the motels and then I came up empty.' An entire week to discover that Melissa's killer had not stopped at a motel or hotel between San Diego and Eureka. 'The whole thing would have been a bust if it hadn't been for the courier work.'

He glanced down at the suitcase. She suspected he would have been appalled to know how visible was his covetous look. Finally he said, 'What was in that package, the one you delivered?'

She glanced over at the young couple. No danger from them. Still Kiernan lowered her voice. 'Diamonds. Untraceable. That's really the only reason to go to the expense of hiring a courier.'

'Untraceable, huh?' he said, grinning. 'Didn't you even consider taking off over the border with them?'

'Maybe,' she said slowly, 'if I had known they were worth enough to set me up for the rest of my actuarial allotment, I might have.'

'We will begin pre-boarding Southwest Airlines flight seventeen sixty-seven with service to Phoenix momentarily. Please keep your seats until pre-boarding has been completed.'

She pushed herself up, and positioned the crutches under her arms. It was a moment before he jerked his gaze away from the suitcase and stood, his foot tapping impatiently on the carpet. All around them families were hoisting luggage and positioning toddlers for the charge to the gate. He sighed loudly. 'I hope you're good with your elbows.'

She laughed and settled back on the arm of the seat.

His gaze went back to the suitcase. He said, 'I thought couriers were handcuffed to their packages.'

'You've been watching too much TV.' She lowered her voice. 'Handcuffs play havoc with the metal detector. The last thing you want in this business is buzzers going off and guards racing in from all directions. I go for the low key approach. Always keep the suitcase in sight. Always be within lunging range.'

He took a playful swipe at it. 'What would happen if, say, that bag were to get stolen?'

'Stolen!' She pulled the suitcase closer to her. 'Well for starters, I wouldn't get a repeat job. If the goods were insured that might be the end of it. But if it were something untraceable – she glanced at the suitcase – 'it could be a lot worse.' With a grin that matched his own, she said, 'You're not a thief are you?'

He shrugged. 'Do I look like a thief?'

'You look like the most attractive man here.' She watched his reaction to the flattery. 'Of course, looks can be deceiving.' She didn't say it, but she could picture him pocketing a necklace carelessly left in a jewellery box during a big party, or a Seiko watch from under a pool-side towel. She didn't imagine him planning a heist, but just taking what came his way.

Returning her smile, he said, 'When you transport something that can't be traced don't they even provide you a back-up?'

'No! I'm a professional. I don't need back-up.'

'But with your foot like that?'

'I'm good with the crutches. And besides, the crutches provide camouflage. Who'd think a woman on crutches carrying a battered suitcase had anything worth half a mi – Watch out! The little girl and her brother are loose again.' She pulled her crutches closer as the duo raced through the aisle in front of them.

'We are ready to begin boarding Southwest Airlines flight number seventeen sixty-seven to Phoenix. Any passengers travelling with small children, or those needing a little extra time may begin boarding now.'

The passengers applauded. It was amazing, she thought, how much sarcasm could be carried by a non-verbal sound.

She leaned down for the suitcase. 'Pre-boarding. That's me.'

'Are you going to be able to handle the crutches and the suitcase?' he asked.

'You're really fascinated with this bag, aren't you?'

'Guilty.' He grinned. 'Should I dare to offer to carry it? I'd stay within lunging range.'

She hesitated.

In the aisle a woman in cerise shorts, carrying twin bags herded twin toddlers towards the gate. Ahead of her an elderly man leaned precariously on a cane. The family with the boy and girl were still assembling luggage.

He said, 'You'd be doing me a big favour letting me pre-board with you. I like to cadge a seat in the first row on the aisle.'

'The seat for the guy who can't wait?'

'Right. But I got here so late that I'm in the last boarding group. I'm never going to snag 1B or 1C. So help me out. I promise,' he said grinning, 'I won't steal.'

'Well . . . I wouldn't want my employer to see this. I assured him I wouldn't need any help. But . . .' She shrugged. 'No time to waver now. There's already a mob of pre-boarders ahead of us.' He picked up the bag. 'Some heavy diamonds.'

'Good camouflage, don't you think? Of course, not everything's diamonds.'

'Just something untraceable?'

She gave him a half wink. 'It may not be untraceable. It may not even be valuable.'

'And you may be just a regular mail carrier,' he said, starting towards the gate.

She swung after him. The crutches were no problem and the thickly taped right ankle looked worse than it was. Still, it made things much smoother to have Siebert carrying the suitcase. If the opportunity arose, he might be tempted to steal it, but not in a crowded gate at the airport with guards and airline personnel around. He moved slowly, staying right in front of her, running interference. As they neared the gate, a blond man carrying a jumpy toddler hurried in front of them. The gate phone buzzed. The airline rep picked it up and nodded at it. To the blond man and the elderly couple who had settled in behind him, Kiernan and Siebert, he said, 'Sorry folks. The cleaning crew's a little slow. It'll just be a minute.'

Siebert's face scrunched in anger. 'What's "cleaning crew" a euphemism for? A tire fell off and they're looking for it?

They've spotted a crack in the engine block and they're trying to figure out if they can avoid telling us?'

Kiernan laughed. 'I'll bet people don't travel with you twice.'

He laughed. 'I just hate being at someone else's mercy. But since we're going to be standing here a while, why don't you do what you love more than diamonds, Investigator: tell me what you've deduced about me.'

'Like reading your palm?' The crutches poked into her armpits; she shifted them back, putting more weight on her bandaged foot. Slowly she surveyed his lanky body, his thin agile hands, con man's hands, hands that were never quite still, always past *Ready*, coming out of *Set*. 'Okay. You're travelling from San Diego to Phoenix on the Friday evening flight, so chances are you were here on business. But you don't have on cowboy boots, or a stetson. You're tan, but it's not that dry tan you get in the desert. In fact you could pass for a San Diegan. I would have guessed that you travel for a living, but you're too impatient for that, and if you'd taken this flight once or twice before you wouldn't be surprised that it's late. You'd have a report to read, or a newspaper. No, you do something where you don't take orders, and you don't put up with much.' She grinned. 'How's that?'

'That's pretty elementary, Sherlock,' he said with only a slight edge to his voice. He tapped his fingers against his leg. But all in all he looked only a little warier than any other person in the waiting area would as his secrets were unveiled.

'*Southwest Airlines flight number seventeen sixty-seven with service to Phoenix is now ready for pre-boarding.*'

'Okay, folks,' the gate attendant called, 'Sorry for the delay.'

The man with the jittery toddler thrust his boarding pass at the gate attendant and strode down the ramp. The child screamed. The elderly couple moved haltingly, hoisting and readjusting their open sacks with each step. A family squeezed in in front of them, causing the old man to stop dead and move his bag to the other shoulder. Siebert shifted foot to foot.

Stretching up to whisper in his ear, Kiernan said, 'It would look bad if you shoved the old people out of your way.'

'How bad?' he muttered grinning, then handed his boarding pass to the attendant.

As she surrendered hers, she said to Siebert, 'Go ahead, hurry. I'll meet you in 1C and D.'

'Thanks.' He patted her shoulder.

She watched him stride down the empty ramp. His tan jacket had caught on one hip as he balanced her suitcase and his own. But he neither slowed his pace nor made an attempt to free the jacket; clutching tight to her suitcase he hurried around the elderly couple, moving with the strong stride of a hiker. By the time she got down the ramp the elderly couple and a family with two toddlers and an infant that sucked loudly on a pacifier crowded behind Siebert.

Kiernan watched irritably as the stewardess eyed first Siebert then her big suitcase. The head stewardess has the final word on carry-on luggage, she knew. With all the hassle that was involved with this business anyway, she didn't want to add a confrontation with the stewardess. She dropped the crutches and banged backwards into the wall, flailing for purchase as she slipped down to the floor. The stewardess caught her before she hit bottom. 'Are you okay?'

'Embarrassed,' Kiernan said, truthfully. She hated to look clumsy, even if it was an act, even if it allowed Siebert and her suitcase to get on the plane unquestioned. 'I'm having an awful time getting used to these things.'

'You sure you're okay? Let me help you up.' The stewardess said. 'I'll have to keep your crutches in the hanging luggage compartment up front while we're in flight. But you go ahead now; I'll come and get them from you.'

'That's okay. I'll leave them there and just sit in one of the front seats,' she said, taking the crutches and swinging herself on board the plane. From the luggage compartment it took only one long step on her left foot to get to row 1. She swung around Siebert, who was hoisting his own suitcase into the overhead bin beside hers, and dropped into 1D, by the window. The elderly couple was settling into 1A and B. In another minute Southwest would call the first thirty passengers, and the herd would stampede down the ramp, stuffing approved carry-ons in overhead compartments, and grabbing the thirty most prized seats. 'That was a smooth move with the stewardess,' Siebert said, as he settled into his coveted aisle seat.

'That suitcase is just about the limit of what they'll let you carry on. I've had a few hassles. I could see this one coming. And I suspected that you' – she patted his arm – 'were not the patient person to deal with that type of problem. You moved around her pretty smartly yourself. I'd say that merits a drink from my client.'

He smiled and rested a hand on hers. 'Maybe,' he said, leaning closer, 'we could have it in Phoenix.'

For the first time she had a viscerally queasy feeling about him. Freeing her hand from his she gave a mock salute. 'Maybe so.' She looked past him at the elderly couple.

Siebert's gaze followed hers. He grinned as he said, 'Do you think they're thieves? After your loot? Little old sprinters?'

'Probably not. But it pays to be alert.' She forced a laugh. 'I'm afraid constant suspicion is a side-effect of my job.'

The first wave of passengers hurried past. Already the air in the plane had the sere feel and slightly rancid smell of having been dragged through the filters too many times. By tacit consent they watched the passengers hurry on board, pause, survey their options, and rush on. Kiernan thought fondly of that drink in Phoenix. She would be sitting at a small table, looking out a tinted window, the trip would be over, the case delivered into the proper hands, and she would feel the tension that knotted her back releasing with each swallow of Scotch. Or so she hoped. The whole frustrating case depended on this delivery. There was no fall-back position. If she screwed up, Melissa Jessup's murderer disappeared.

That tension was what normally made the game fun. But this case was no longer a game. This time she had allowed herself to go beyond her regular rules, to call her former colleagues from the days when she had been a forensic pathologist, looking for some new test that would prove culpability. She had hoped the lab in San Diego could find something. They hadn't. The fact was that the diamonds were the only 'something' that would trap the killer, Melissa's lover, who valued them much more than her, a man who might not have bothered going after her had it not been for them. Affairs might be brief, but diamonds, after all, are forever. They would lead her to the murderer's safe house, and the evidence that would tie him to Melissa. *If* she was careful.

She shoved the tongue of the seat belt into the latch and braced her feet as the plane taxied towards the runway. Siebert was tapping his finger on the armrest. The engines whirred, the plane shifted forward momentarily, then flung them back against their seats as it raced down the short runway.

The FASTEN SEAT BELT sign went off. The old man across the aisle pushed himself up and edged towards the front bathroom. Siebert's belt was already unbuckled. Muttering, 'Be right back,' he jumped up, stood hunched under the overhead bin while the old man cleared the aisle. Then Siebert headed full-out towards the back of the plane. Kiernan slid over and watched him as he strode down the aisle, steps firmer, steadier than she'd have expected of a man racing to the bathroom in a swaying airplane. She could easily imagine him hiking in the redwood forest with someone like her, a small, slight woman. The blond woman with the violet eye shadow. She in jeans and one of those soft Patagonia jackets Kiernan had spotted in the L. L. Bean catalogue, violet with blue trim. He in jeans, turtleneck, a forest green down jacket on his rangy body. Forest green would pick up the colour of his eyes, and accent his dark, curly hair. In her picture, his hair was tinted with the first flecks of autumn snow and the ground still soft like the spongy airplane carpeting beneath his feet.

When he got back he made no mention of his hurried trip. He'd barely settled down when the stewardess leaned over him and said, 'Would you care for something to drink?'

Kiernan put a hand on his arm. 'This one's on my client.'

'For that client who insisted you carry his package while you're still on crutches I'm sorry it can't be Lafite Rothschild. Gin and tonic will have to do.' He grinned at the stewardess. Kiernan could picture him in a bar, flashing that grin at other chosen women. She could imagine him with the sweat of a San Diego summer still on his brow, his skin brown from too many days at an ocean beach that is too great a temptation for those who grab their pleasures.

'Scotch and water,' Kiernan ordered. To him, she said, 'I

notice that while I'm the investigator, it's you who are asking all the questions. So what about you, what do you do for a living?'

'I quit my job in San Diego and I'm moving back to Phoenix. So I'm not taking the first Friday night flight to get back home, I'm taking it to get to my new home. I had good times in San Diego: the beach, the sailing, Balboa Park. When I came there a couple of years ago I thought I'd stay forever. But the draw of the desert is too great. I miss the red rock of Sedona, the pines of the Mogollon Rim, and the high desert outside Tucson.' He laughed. 'Too much soft California life.'

It was easy to picture him outside of Show Low on the Mogollon Rim with the pine trees all around him, some chopped for firewood, the axe lying on a stump, a shovel in his hand. Or in a cabin near Sedona lifting a hatch in the floorboards.

The stewardess brought the drinks and the little bags of peanuts, giving Jeff Siebert the kind of smile Kiernan knew would have driven her crazy had she been Siebert's girlfriend. How often had that type of thing happened? Had his charm brought that reaction so automatically that for him it had seemed merely the way women behave? Had complaints from a girlfriend seemed at first unreasonable, then melodramatic, then infuriating? He was an impatient man, quick to anger. Had liquor made it quicker, like the rhyme said? And the prospect of unsplit profit salved his conscience?

He poured the little bottle of gin over the ice and added tonic. 'Cheers.'

She touched glasses, then drank. 'Are you going to be in Phoenix long?'

'Probably not. I've come into a little money and I figure I'll just travel around, sort of like you do. Find some place I like.'

'So we'll just have time for our drink in town then?'

He rested his hand back on hers. 'Well, now I may have reason to come back in a while. Or to San Diego. I just need to cut loose for a while.'

She forced herself to remain still, not to cringe at his touch. *Cut loose* – what an apt term for him to use. She pictured his sun-browned hand wrapped around the hilt of a chef's knife, working it up and down, up and down, cutting across pink flesh till it no longer looked like flesh, till the flesh mixed with the blood and the organ tissue, till the knife cut down to the bone and the metal point stuck in the breastbone. She pictured Melissa Jessup's blond hair pink from the blood.

She didn't have to picture her body lying out in the woods outside Eureka in northern California. She had seen photos of it. She didn't have to imagine what the cracked ribs and broken clavicle and the sternum marked from the knife point looked like now. Jeff Siebert had seen that too, and had denied what Melissa's brother, and the Eureka Sheriff all knew – knew in their hearts but could not prove – that Melissa had not gone to Eureka camping by herself as he'd insisted, but had only stopped overnight at the campground she and Jeff had been to the previous summer because she had no money, and hadn't been able to bring herself to sell the diamonds her mother had left her. Instead of a rest on the way to freedom, she'd found Siebert there.

Now Siebert was flying to Phoenix to vanish. He'd pick up Melissa's diamonds wherever he'd stashed them, then he'd be gone.

'What about your client?' he asked. 'Will he be meeting you at the airport?'

'No. No one will meet me. I'll just deliver my goods to the van, collect my money and be free. What about you?'

'No. No one's waiting for me either. At least I'll be able to give you a hand with that bag. There's no ramp to the terminal in Phoenix. You have to climb down to the tarmac there. Getting down those metal steps with a suitcase and two crutches would be a real balancing act.'

All she had to do was get it in the right hands. She shook her head. 'Thanks. But I'll have to lug it through the airport just in case. My client didn't handcuff the suitcases to me, but he does expect me to keep hold of it.'

He grinned. 'Like you said, you'll be in lunging range all the time.'

'No,' she said firmly. 'I appreciate your offer, Jeff; the bag weighs a ton. But I'm afraid it's got to be in my hand.'

Those green eyes of his that had twinkled with laughter narrowed, and his lips pressed together. 'Okay,' he said slowly.

Then his face relaxed almost back to that seductively impish smile that once might have charmed her, as it had Melissa Jessup. 'I want you to know that I'll still find you attractive even if the bag yanks your shoulder out of its socket.' He gave her hand a pat, then shifted in his seat so his upper arm rested next to hers.

The stewardess collected the glasses. The plane jolted and began its descent. Kiernan braced her feet. Through his jacket, she felt the heat of his arm, the arm that had dug that chef's knife into Melissa Jessup's body. She breathed slowly and did not move.

To Kiernan, he said, 'There's a great bar right here in Sky Harbor Airport, the Sky Lounge. Shall we have our drink there?'

She nodded, her mouth suddenly too dry for speech.

The plane bumped down and in a moment the aisles were jammed with passengers ignoring the stewardess' entreaty to stay in their seats. Siebert stood up and pulled his bag out of the overhead compartment and then lifted hers on to his empty seat. 'I'll get your crutches,' he said, as the elderly man across the aisle pushed his way out in front of him. Siebert shook his head. Picking up both suitcases, he manoeuvred around the man and around the corner to the luggage compartment.

Siebert had taken her suitcase. *You don't need to take both suitcases to pick up the crutches.* Kiernan stared after him, her shoulders tensing, her hands clutching the armrests. Her throat was so constricted she could barely breath. For an instant, she shared the terror that must have paralysed Melissa Jessup just before he stabbed her.

'Jeff' she called after him, a trace of panic evident in her voice. He didn't answer her. Instead, she heard a great thump, then him muttering and the stewardess's voice placating.

The airplane door opened. The elderly man moved out into the aisle front of Kiernan, motioning his wife to go ahead of him, then they moved slowly towards the door.

Kiernan yanked the bandage off her foot, stepped into the aisle. 'Excuse me,' she said to the couple. Pushing by them as Siebert had so wanted to do, she rounded the corner to the exit.

The stewardess lifting up a garment bag. Four more bags lay on the floor. So that was the thump she'd heard. A crutch was beside them.

She half-heard the stewardess's entreaties to wait, her mutterings about the clumsy man. She looked out the door down on to the tarmac.

Jeffrey Siebert and the suitcase were gone. In those few seconds he had raced down the metal steps, and was disappearing into the terminal. By the time she could make it to the Sky Lounge he would be halfway to Show Low, or Sedona.

Now she felt a different type of panic. *This* wasn't in the plan. She couldn't lose Siebert. She jumped over the bags, grabbed one crutch, hurried outside to the top of the stairs, and thrust the crutch across the hand rails behind her to make a seat. As the crutch slid down the railings, she kept her knees bent high into her chest to keep from landing and bucking forward on to her head. Instead the momentum propelled her on her feet, as it had in gymnastics. In those routines, she'd had to fight the momentum, now she went with it and ran, full out.

She ran through the corridor towards the main building, pushing past businessmen, between parents carrying children. Siebert would be running ahead. But no one would stop him, not in an airport. People run through airports all the time. Beside the metal detectors she saw a man in a tan jacket. Not him. By the luggage pick-up another look-alike. She didn't spot him till he was racing out the door to the parking lot.

Siebert raced across the roadway. A van screeched to a halt. Before Kiernan could cross through the traffic a hotel bus eased in front of her. She skirted behind it. She could sense a man following her now. But there was no time to deal with that. Siebert was halfway down the lane of cars. Bent low, she ran down the next lane, the hot dusty desert air drying her throat. By the time she came abreast of Siebert, he was in a light blue Chevy pick-up backing out of the parking slot. He hit the gas, and, wheels squealing, drove off.

She reached towards the truck with both arms. Siebert didn't stop. She stood watching as Jeffrey Siebert drove off into the sunset.

There was no one behind her as she sauntered into the

terminal to the Sky Lounge. She ordered the two drinks Siebert had suggested, and when they came, she tapped 'her' glass on 'his', and took a drink for Melissa Jessup. Then she swallowed the rest of the drink in two gulps.

By this time Jeff Siebert would be on the freeway. He'd be fighting to stay close to the speed limit, balancing his thief's wariness of the highway patrol against his gnawing urge to force the lock on the suitcase. Jeffrey Siebert was an impatient man, a man who had nevertheless made himself wait nearly a year before leaving California. His stash of self-control would be virtually empty. But he would wait awhile before daring to stop. Then he'd jam a knife between the top and bottom of the suitcase, pry and twist it till the case fell open. He would find diamonds. More diamonds. Diamonds to take along while he picked up Melissa Jessup's from the spot where he'd hidden them.

She wished Melissa Jessup could see him when he compared the two collections, and realised the new ones he'd stolen were fakes. She wished she herself could see his face when he realised that a woman on crutches had made it out of the plane in time to follow him to point out the blue pick-up truck.

Kiernan picked up 'Jeff's' glass and drank more slowly. How sweet it would be if Melissa could see that grin of his fade as the surveillance team surrounded him, drawn by the beepers concealed in those fake diamonds. He'd be clutching the evidence that would send him to jail. Just for life, not forever. As Melissa could have told him, only death and diamonds are forever.

MALORIE BLACKMAN

Cat and Mouse

'A report just in ... The Masked Maniac has struck again.
Peter Clarkson, a twenty-five year old minicab driver, was
found stabbed to death in his cab in the multi-storey car park
above Bell Heath Shopping Precinct. Peter Clarkson is the
Masked Maniac's sixth victim. He leaves a wife and three
children. His wife Cathy Clarkson is under sedation for
severe shock. More details as they arrive ...'

Masked maniac! Who came up with that name? Some hack
into alliteration, I decided.

'I think that's terrible. The Bell Heath shopping centre is
only a few miles away. Don't you think that's terrible?' Sarah
spoke to everyone in the living room and no one in particular.

'That means all the victims so far have been men.' Paul, my
other house-mate said.

'So what?' Sarah frowned.

'So it's obviously some kind of psychotic maniac.'

'Meaning he wouldn't be a psychotic maniac if he only
attacked women?' Sarah fumed, jumping up on her high horse.

Paul sighed. 'I never said that Sarah. Don't put words into
my mouth.'

Paul and Sarah glared at each other. I carried on watching
the news, leaving both of them to it.

The three of us shared the house together. We got on fine
because we didn't try to live in each other's pockets. In fact we
very rarely saw each other. Paul was out most nights at his
girlfriend's flat where they could be alone together. Sarah was

a student, going for an MSc in Social Science, so most nights she was at the library studying. I was the one who spent most of my time in the house, rattling around like a solitary pea in a tin can. I had a nine to five job which I hated and I spent my evenings watching television, reading, thinking.

The newsreader then started wittering on about the mortgage rate going up yet again. I sighed. That meant our rent would shoot up again for the third time in as many months. Funny how it always went up, but never came down.

'Which reminds me,' Paul said. 'Does anyone have any objections to my brother Martin coming to stay with us for a while? He can sleep on the sofa . . .'

'Hang on a minute,' Sarah interrupted. 'You can't just inflict your brother on us.'

'Don't make him sound like a deliberate dose of genital crabs.' Paul said, annoyed.

'Then don't make him sound like a *fait accompli* either.' Sarah said.

Here we go again, I thought.

'He'll only be here for a month, two at the most, until he can find another place to live.'

'Well he can't sleep on the sofa. This is a living room, not another bedroom.'

'All right then. He can sleep in my room. Happy now?'

'And will he be contributing to the rent?' Sarah asked.

'Yes he will. Don't worry, he'll buy all his own food and he won't touch yours . . .'

'Why does your brother need a place?' I asked lightly before Paul and Sarah came to blows.

'He's . . . er . . . he's just been transferred up here.' Paul replied. 'So I said he could stay here until he finds his feet and gets a place of his own.'

'You had no business telling him that without talking to us first.' Sarah said what I was thinking.

'Look, I'll make sure he keeps out of the way as much as possible, he'll pay his way, he's got nowhere else to go and he doesn't have fleas. Jennifer?' Paul appealed to me.

All at once I had a strange twisting feeling in the pit of my stomach.

'I suppose if it's not for too long . . .' I said doubtfully.

'Terrific.' Paul shouted.

'Hang on a minute. I haven't said yes yet,' Sarah protested.

'The vote's two to one against you.' Paul took pleasure in telling her. 'You're out-voted.'

And so it was settled. And the strange twisting in my stomach grew worse. *By the pricking of my thumbs* . . . That one line played over and over again in my head.

Martin moved in the next day. As soon as I saw him I didn't like him. The churning, turning of my stomach told me not to go anywhere near him. He didn't look like Paul at all. Martin was fair where Paul was dark-haired. Martin was older, shorter but broader and he fancied himself like no other man I had ever met – and I've met quite a few. I was in the living room watching TV – as usual – and Sarah was at the library writing yet another essay, when Paul brought his brother into the room.

'Martin, this is Jennifer.'

'The one who's all right!' Martin smiled, holding out his hand. I pretended not to see it. He'd made that comment on purpose. Was I supposed to be charmed? Flattered? He was oilier than the fried breakfast at our local greasy spoon.

'Martin!' Paul looked scandalised at this brother's indiscretion, then he laughed.

I grinned at Paul before turning back to Martin. He looked me up and down and sideways. And it wasn't just that. His eyes . . . his eyes were so alert, missing nothing. I could almost believe that eyes like that could read my mind. I very rarely take an instant dislike to anyone but in his case . . .

After that, it seemed that I couldn't go anywhere, do anything without Martin somewhere close behind. I'd be watching TV whilst Martin pretended to read his skiing holiday brochure – but I knew he was tuned to my every movement, my very breath. I'd pop out to the corner shop only to have him walk into the shop a few moments after. I'd go for a walk in the park, only to have him turn up a few minutes after me. He'd walk by and just nod – but he was there. At first I thought I was imagining things. Why should he go out of his way to follow me when I did my best to avoid him? Why should he follow me at all? But I began to feel as if I was living in a goldfish bowl.

He was always, always there. It got so bad that even Paul and Sarah began to notice. Sarah began to tease me about it – dropping spiteful, unsubtle hints about the give-away, adoring gaze of puppy dogs whenever Martin and I were in the same room.

A month after Martin had moved in, we were all watching TV when a newsflash came up in the middle of a really crappy comedy programme.

'The Masked Maniac has struck again. Earlier today a man was found stabbed to death in Heatherfield Park. More details later in our main news bulletin.'

Sarah's gasp echoed mine. Heatherfield Park was our local park.

'I'm not going there again.' Sarah said immediately

Martin shook his head as he stared at the telly without really seeing it.

'This Masked Maniac is growing more and more confident. There's never been a killing in broad daylight before.' Paul said slowly.

'Why don't the police get off their backsides and do something?' Sarah said with disgust.

'We are doing something.' Martin snapped.

Sarah and I stared at him.

'What did you say?' I whispered.

Martin and Paul exchanged a look.

'You're a busy!' Sarah said furiously. 'I don't believe it . . .'

I stared at Martin. He was watching me, not Sarah.

Sarah rounded on Paul. 'Paul you bastard, you never said anything about your brother being a . . . a . . .'

'A pig? The filth? Babylon? You can't call me anything I haven't already heard.' Martin said.

'Why didn't you tell us?' Sarah asked.

'Because I knew what your reaction would be,' Martin replied. 'People like you make me want to puke! When you're in trouble it's 'Call the police! Call the police!' and then you can't wait to see us. Otherwise it's "Piss off you vermin and don't come back!" '

'I don't beat up and arrest innocent people to feed my ego and make my crime clear-up stats look impressive,' Sarah said furiously.

'Neither do I.'

'Son-of-a-bitch! Paul, either he goes or I go – and I ain't going anywhere.' Sarah rounded on Paul.

And all the time I just stared at Martin, unable to move. I forced myself to take a deep breath, then stood up.

'Excuse me please,' I said.

I left the room before anyone could stop me and practically ran to my bedroom. I sat down on my bed, clasping my hands together in my lap to stop them trembling. A copper! He was a copper. I should have guessed. I should have *known*.

'Can I come in?' Martin entered my bedroom, closing the door behind him.

'I'd rather you didn't,' I said without looking at him.

I lay down on my bed and stared up at the ceiling. Martin came and sat beside me on my bed.

'Are you deaf?' I asked.

'No, just stubborn,' Martin replied. 'I want to know why you don't like me.'

'I would have thought that was obvious,' I replied.

Martin put his hand on my bare arm. I flinched away as if he'd just tried to strike me.

'You're far too intelligent to dislike me just because I'm a policeman. No . . . You disliked me long before tonight. I'd like to know why.'

'Maybe I can smell a copper at fifty paces,' I replied.

'So it's the police you dislike – it has nothing to do with me as an individual?'

'I don't know what you're talking about,' I sighed. 'Now will you please go away. I have a headache.'

Martin stood up and walked to the door. I swung myself round to a sitting position.

'Tell me, Martin,' I said before he got to the door. 'How much longer are you going to be here?'

'I wondered if you'd ask me that.'

'You haven't answered my question.'

'I'm still looking for a place. Don't worry, I don't think it will be for much longer. I've got the next couple of weeks off and I intend to visit every estate agent in the town.'

I lay down again, listening to the silence that reigned until I heard Martin open my door and leave the room.

Three days later I watched through my bedroom window as Martin and Paul left the house, one to go to work, the other to visit all the estate agents he could in one morning. I told everyone I was coming down with some flu bug which was knocking me for six.

It was a lie. Which was a shame because I wouldn't have minded going to work – for once. It was a beautiful day. Cold, clear and crisp. But I had things to do.

I had to find out about Martin.

There was something about him, something about the way he watched me, something in his eyes that I liked little and trusted less. So I made up my mind to do something I had never done before. I was going to search through Martin's things in Paul's bedroom. I didn't know what I expected to find but I felt sure I would find something. There had to be some reason why he was always watching me.

Even though I knew there was no one in the house I still tiptoed into Paul's bedroom. I'd only ever been in there by invitation and I felt very strange and guilty about what I was going to do.

But I had to protect myself.

At the foot of Paul's single bed was Martin's suitcase, with his sleeping bag on top of the case. I stood absolutely still, listening for any kind of sound in the house. There was none. I took a deep breath and walked over to his suitcase. Kneeling before it, I flung his sleeping bag on to Paul's bed, before opening the suitcase. Folded, clean shirts (very unusual), folded trousers, boxer shorts – there was nothing there out of the ordinary. I delved deeper. Nothing. I searched the four corners of the suitcase. I found nothing unusual until I started searching the fourth corner.

A navy blue ski-mask . . .

Why did he have a ski-mask? I chewed on my bottom lip as I sat back on my heels, the ski-mask in my hands.

'Am I disturbing you?'

My head snapped around guiltily. There, leaning against the door, stood Martin – and he was absolutely furious. His eyes glinted like chips of ice and his lips were a straight, tight line across his face. I scrambled to my feet.

'Did you have a good search?' he asked through gritted teeth, his eyes narrowed.

I took a deep breath but didn't answer.

'I'm waiting for an explanation, Jennifer,' he said.

I watched as his fists clenched and unclenched at his sides.

'Is this your mask?' I asked, holding the ski-mask between me and him.

'That's right. What about it?'

'Doesn't the Masked Maniac wear one of these?'

Martin stared at me before he burst out laughing.

'You cannot be serious.'

I refused to speak.

'I'd be very careful about making accusations like that if I were you.' Martin said, his smile fading.

'Accusations like what?' I smiled sweetly. 'I asked you two totally unrelated questions.'

His smile had completely disappeared now.

'I'd appreciate it Jennifer if you'd put my stuff back exactly as and where you found it.' Martin said stonily.

I knelt down in front of his suitcase and tidied up the contents, keeping one eye on Martin, the other on what I was doing. He moved over to stand beside me. My hands faltered for a moment but I didn't stop. At last I finished. I fastened his suitcase and leaned forward to place his sleeping bag back in its original position. I stood up carefully as I didn't wish to touch him. My back was to the wall as he stood between me and the door.

'Don't ever search through my stuff again,' Martin said quietly.

I looked straight at him but didn't speak. We watched each other, hostility crackling in the air around us. Finally he stood aside and let me move pass him. Only he caught me by the hand just as I thought I was in the clear. I gritted my teeth, trying to pull my hand away from his as once again his touch left me feeling nauseous.

'Let me go,' I hissed.

Martin took hold of both of my wrists before running his hands up my bare upper arms. His touch was an electric shock, coursing through my body.

'Jenny, I don't want us to . . .'

'Damn it, let me go.' I was close to screaming at him now.

Desperately I pulled away from him. Martin let me go so suddenly that I stumbled backwards.

'I mean it, Jennifer. Stay out of my things,' he said softly.

I walked out of the bedroom knowing that things were drawing to a head between me and Martin. One of us would have to go.

Martin got his revenge a few days later. I dashed home from work, through the pouring bloody rain I might add, because I'd left a report I'd been amending on a floppy disk in my PC. It was meant to be a straight in-and-out job. In the house, grab the disk and back to work. It didn't work out that way. I opened the outer door to the porch, then shut that behind me but left the inner door open. After all, I was in a hurry and I wouldn't be in the house for more than thirty seconds. Taking the stairs two and three at a time, I flung open the door to my bedroom.

Martin was there – rifling through my wardrobe. He had his hands on my black leather jacket and was going through my pockets. We both froze. If I hadn't been so shocked, so stunned, I reckon I'd have burst out laughing. A crooked copper, a bent Babylon on the make! The look on his face was priceless, but it must have mirrored my own.

'Got a leather fetish?' I hissed. 'Like to sniff old clothes, do you? If you want my dirty knickers, they're in the linen basket over there.'

Martin didn't reply. I held the door wide open for him. He looked at me and left my room without saying a word. On the prying stakes we were even. Sarah was right. He was a son-of-a-bitch. And more besides. I knew exactly what and who he was. And I had to fix him. Fix him good. Because I knew now that he was after me.

I closed my eyes, enjoying the feeling of falling – almost out of control – swinging up, then down again. I love the swings! The park-keeper won't let me on them during the day, so I have to wait until dark and climb over the park railings. I closed my eyes and smiled inwardly. I knew Martin was around – somewhere – watching me . . .

He was definitely out there. I knew it because I'd led him to the park deliberately. I knew exactly what he was and I was in danger because of it. I opened my eyes to see Martin standing a few metres away from me. The full moon was a silver torch beaming down on us. Slowly, in my own time I brought the swing to a halt. I felt warm and almost happy with the thought of what was to come. Here and now, my life made sense. Such moments were rare and precious. I wore black leather gloves, a leather jacket and trousers tucked into my boots. No part of me was exposed.

'I was wondering when you'd show yourself,' I smiled at Martin.

'You knew I was following you?'

'Of course.' I jumped off the swing and walked towards him. He took one step backwards but then stood his ground.

'So what happens now?' I asked.

'You tell me,' he said.

For the first time I felt comfortable in Martin's presence. He couldn't touch me now. I tucked my hands in my pockets. There was a chill in the air.

'You're the Masked Maniac aren't you?'

'What a stupid name . . .'

'That doesn't answer the question.'

Silence.

I looked up at the moon, so bright and cold. I sighed.

'You need help.'

'Do I?'

'Don't you?'

Pause.

'Are you going to give yourself up?'

'Not in this lifetime.'

I laughed at the answer to the question. Very droll.

'You're sick . . . very sick. I'm not going to let you get away with it.'

'You can't stop me.'

Then, without warning, he charged at me, head-butting me to the ground. I hit the tarmac full force, with Martin on top of me. Winded, I let precious moments pass before I thought of what to do next. I couldn't let him get me – *I couldn't*. We both rolled around and around. He was strong, but then so was I. All I needed was to get my left hand free . . .

I plunged the blade of my switch knife downwards into Martin's back, then again and again and again . . .

He groaned deeply then was still on top of me. I pushed him off, gasping to catch my breath as I did so. His eyes were open. He lay absolutely still.

I crawled over to him. I tilted his head back and carefully placed my knife on his neck. Then I slit his throat. My calling card. The Masked Maniac's calling card.

Such a stupid name.

I thought of the minicab driver who'd tried his luck in the Bell Heath car park; the old man on the bus who'd kept putting his hand on my thigh even when I told him not to, then he'd slipped his hand up my skirt; the spotty bloke in the park who had fondled my breasts, who'd tried to kiss me – for a laugh. For a joke. All those men who wouldn't leave me alone, even when I told them nicely, then not so nicely to back off. I stood up, pulling off my ski-mask and pushing it back into my jacket pocket.

I stared down at Martin. There had been nothing in his suitcase to indicate that he or any of the police were on to me but then there wouldn't have been.

They'd catch me – one day – but not yet, not tonight. I took one last look at Martin who continued to stare up at the full moon, so bright and so cold and so far away. Martin . . . who'd never see anything, ever again.

Then I walked back home, whistling.

LINDA MARIZ

Cash Buyer

The squeaky clean policeman in my doorway had a crew cut and soft grey eyes that said he probably didn't beat on women and wouldn't tolerate anybody who did. His name tag said 'Lt Gregory' and when his gaze rested on me I suddenly put a hand on my hair to feel what it looked like. Three weeks before I had paid good money to have it coloured, and after that I put in a perm. The hairdo was now seriously wild, with spiky yellow shafts that jutted out like thunderbolts, but I really liked the effect. It made me look a little unruly and deranged, like somebody you wouldn't take on lightly.

Lieutenant Gregory stood soldier-straight and carried a clipboard under his arm. Lingering in the doorway, he checked out the corners of my back room. I keep all my inventory stacked against one wall where everybody can see it, and I think he liked what he saw.

I deal only in high-end Japanese nets and I've never known anybody yet who could resist all that lustrous green nylon, folded into rich pleats, gleaming like captured silk. For anyone who's just come from the Bellingham Co-op and looked at the brittle Thai stuff they sell, my nets make quite a contrast. Quality is all I have going for me as a small vendor; I certainly can't compete in price.

Lieutenant Gregory strode over as I straddled my hanging bench. 'Rachel Tarr?'

'Yes?'

He waited for me to stop, but I kept my eyes on the net and my ivory needle weaving through the air like sign language.

'Seen Morrie Rich lately?'

I snickered. 'What's he done now, ripped up another pool table?'

Lieutenant Gregory took out his pen. 'When'd he do that?'

'Two months ago. The Cocoanut Grove sent a bill for $540. I wrote that final check, then kicked him out.'

He smiled at me: good answer. 'And you haven't seen him since?'

'Look, Morrie works for Charlie Wallace, the cash buyer for Pacific Seafoods. The Horsefly Run opened yesterday and I'm sure you'd find the two of them out in the Straits of Georgia someplace. You can't miss *Charlie's Girl*: she's painted turquoise with dark green trim. Seriously white trash.'

'Charlie Wallace is dead,' he said. 'They found him anchored off Semiahmoo Thursday night with a bullet in his right temple.'

I stopped knotting, holding my needle mid-air like a beacon for aid. 'Morrie's okay, isn't he?'

'Morrie's missing. As is Charlie's dinghy and $25,000 cash.'

'Oh, shit.' I shook my head and the blond thunderbolts crashed around my shoulders. 'Morrie didn't kill him.'

'It'd be nice if he'd show up and tell us that himself.'

'Poor Charlie.' I pulled my hair into a rough ponytail and bound it with twine from the needle. 'Poor Morrie.'

'Know where he might have gone?'

'Morrie?' I knotted on to the next selvage and kept control of my voice. 'You might check with a woman named Eileen at the Anchorage, Alaska Airport. I believe she works in the coffee shop.' I pretended that I could say 'Eileen' as easily as I could say 'reef-net' or 'dogfish'. 'Or,' I tossed my head, 'if you're sure he's got the cash, he may be in Hawaii. He really likes it there.'

There was a sound in the drive and we looked out to see Jerry Rice backing his pick-up towards my overhead door. 'Look,' I said. 'I've got to get back to work.'

Lieutenant Gregory banged his clipboard against his thigh. 'If Morrie shows up, you give us a call, you hear?' His grey eyes were placid and deep, fathoms beyond what I was used to.

'Sure.' Standing up to open the garage door for Jerry, I looked over again and Lieutenant Gregory was gone.

'Hi, Jerry, how's it going?'

'Stinks. Like three-day-old gurry in the bottom of the boat.'

Jerry Rice is a former Bellingham High defensive end and an okay guy if you don't mind 'em a little crude. I must admit I laughed when I heard he won a Karaoke contest in Sitka by stripping down to his Jockey shorts singing 'I Gotta Be Me', but I've learned never to turn my back on him, because right away he starts telling you what kind of panties you have on – bikini or whatever – and whether they're riding up or not. Evidently being married to him was not that great a deal either, because three years ago Angela Rice packed up and moved to Medford, Oregon where she designs fancy fruit baskets for mail order.

'Why aren't you out?' I asked. Horsefly had opened yesterday, one of the best salmon runs south of Alaska.

Jerry unhooked his tailgate and gestured to the tired heap of net with its scummy brown buoys and ornamental bits of seaweed and trash. Of course he expected me to pick it clean for him, on top of whatever else he wanted. 'Net's so full of holes I can't set it, keeps getting caught on itself. I pulled it in and said "the hell with it". How soon can I have it?' His mouth stayed open, pink tongue querying his lips.

I squinted at Jerry's lusterless pile. 'I probably couldn't get it back 'til Sunday. I've got one to finish now and I need to go to bed sometime soon.'

'Sunday's fine.'

'More like Monday or Tuesday.'

'That's fine too.'

'Jerry.' I thrust my hands in my back jeans pockets. 'I'm trying to tell you I don't want to do it.'

'Well, why the hell not?'

'You still owe me from last season.'

He reached around for his black leather wallet linked to a belt loop by a chrome steel chain. 'How much?'

'Two-hundred-eighty dollars.'

'Lady knows her business.'

'Damn right.'

He flashed a clutch of bills, green Ben Franklin hundreds and heaps of twenties. He had at least a half-inch stack and he counted out 280 dollars as calmly as if he was buying a beer.

'What *you* been up to?' I asked.

He smiled like a kid with his hand in the cookie jar. 'Fished shares at False Pass with a friend from Ketchikan. We made out like bandits.'

'I'll say.'

He tucked his cash away and smiled in a hopeful way. 'Want to grab some dinner?'

My stomach was growling; clock on the wall said five pm. 'Can't. I've got to finish this for Buddy Bates. Then I'm going to start on yours.'

'I can have you in and out of the Cocoanut Grove in less than an hour: steak, salad, baked potato. What do you say?'

That was exactly what I needed to hear. 'Deal.' I tied a sweater around my waist to frustrate his underpants game and locked up the place, stuffing my new cash into my jeans pocket.

We drove down Marine Avenue in silence and at the Cocoanut Grove Jerry parked his pick-up out back. Half the world was sitting there waiting for something to happen and our coming in together lit up the place like Puget Power. Thad from the Co-op was there, drinking beer at the bar. When he saw us, he just smirked and sipped his drink.

We sat at a table by the pull-tab bar watching the optimists lay down their cash on gameboards and poke out tiny curls of paper with 'Fool' written on them. The Budweiser advertising from the Fourth of July hadn't been taken down yet and a full-size cardboard Budweiser Babe smiled from her spot between the dartboards even though it was clear her patriotic red, white and blue crotch had been the target for more than one game of darts.

'Prime rib?' asked Jerry.

'Fine.'

He ordered in a quiet, refined way, telling the waitress that 'the lady' had to be somewhere in an hour, and ordering red wine. When our salads came, he surprised the hell out of me by asking for cloth napkins. The waitress dropped them on the table, and he handed me one saying, 'Can't eat steak with a Kleenex on your lap.'

I smiled cautiously and he beamed, 'I like your hair.'

I touched the thunderbolts. 'Thank you.'

Eyeing me benignly, he asked, 'Well, gal, what do you think?'

'About what?'

'About your ex-boyfriend. Damn fool of him to knock off Charlie Wallace.'

I picked up my fork. 'I don't think Morrie did it, at least not on purpose. Although I can plenty imagine him running off with $25,000 if he thought he could get away with it.'

The waitress set a carafe of wine on the table and Jerry filled our glasses. 'Morrie ever earn that much before?'

'Probably not all at once. But I still don't think he'd kill for it. Anyway he doesn't carry a gun. Do you know what kind was used?'

'No. I just heard point blank with a handgun.' He watched a dart game that was landing more hits on Miss Budweiser's face than the target next to it. 'Know where he went?'

'Morrie? Alaska.' I crunched salad. 'He's got this thing going on with a woman at the Anchorage airport. Every time he flies in and out . . .' I waved my hand to finish the sentence.

'Yeah, we *all* know Eileen. Thing is, she isn't even that good looking.'

I put down my fork and stopped eating. 'Jerry, why do men do that?'

'Hell.' He twisted in his chair. 'That's the same as my asking you why women get so stuck on one man at a time. If I knew the answer to that, I'd know the answer to everything.' Looking at my salad, he said, 'You know, back when you were dating, the two of you would come in here and I'd see you sitting there with that black eye and I'd think: "Now what can a woman like that see in Morrie Rich?" I hope you'll pardon me for saying this, but I never could understand.'

'You never heard him play the guitar, did you?'

'No.'

'He wrote a song for me, at least at first I thought it was for me. Later on I found out he just changes the name for whoever he's with. But it is a pretty song and he really did write it: 'Rachel on a Rainy Day', or '*Sandy* on a Rainy Day', whoever.'

Jerry blinked at me several times, while over my shoulder

came this nasal California whine. 'Hi, how's business?' It was
Thad from the Co-op; he had finished his beer and was on his
way out the door.

I faked a smile. 'Busy enough, Thad. How about you?'

Thad was wearing yachtie-type chinos so expensive they were
good enough to work in. On his feet were loafers with no socks,
and over his shoulders was tied a tennis sweater to let the
Cocoanut Grove know he was slumming. Holding up his hands
to show me the calloused fingers of non-stop netting, he said,
'Too much work. Say, Rachel, I saw a sailboat ad for a Cal 35.
That yours?'

'Yeah, know anybody who wants to buy it?'

He curled his lip disapprovingly. 'Don't you live aboard?'

'Boat's in perfect condition.'

Jerry broke in. 'Hey, Thad, I got a professional problem for
you.'

'What's that?'

'I got a new dinghy and I want to paint it. What should I
use?'

Thad stuffed his hands into his 8-ounce khaki twill pockets.
'Depends on what the surface is.'

'Brushed aluminum.'

'Jesus, Jerry, why do you want to paint brushed aluminum?
You're just making work for yourself.'

Jerry ducked his head. 'Now, don't give me any grief, I want
it to match my boat.'

Thad pulled out his keys and selected one, aligning the others
into a neat fob. 'Drop by and get some Galvaleum, comes in
grey or white. If your surface is already brushed, you shouldn't
have much problem with adhesion.'

'You guys open tonight?'

''Til ten.'

'Thanks, Thad.'

We finished our meal amiably enough, talking about people's
rigs and nets, and who would fish with whom for silver season
in September. When we came to the low, ambling part at the
end of the meal where the real business is transacted, Jerry
started in about how unstable his wife had been. As a single

woman I know this part very well and I immediately bolted up. 'Excuse me for a minute.'

At the ladies' room I went into a stall and sat down. There's all kinds of graffiti on the wall and I always end up reading without even thinking about it. Right there above the toilet paper I beaded in on my name: 'Rachel, Wait for me. I'll call. MR.' I froze up like iced halibut, went out to the mirror and fluffed my hair. Calming myself with deep breaths, I walked out, almost making it to the lounge, when suddenly I wondered how Morrie knew which of the two stalls I'd go in. Sauntering back to the ladies' room, I ducked into the other stall and found the same message in the same place: 'Rachel, Wait for me. I'll call.' That made me grin.

Back at the table, Jerry paid, tipping generously and chatting up the barmaid. We drove back silently to my shop and as we pulled up he said, 'I'd invite you down to the boat for a drink but I want to have the dinghy painted same time my net comes back.'

'Thanks, but I wouldn't come anyway.' I hopped down and watched him speed off.

Next evening Morrie still hadn't called. I had finished Buddy Bates' gill-net and gotten a quarter of the way through Jerry's. Because I didn't care whether Jerry's was done on time, I went home at six Saturday night for a regular supper.

I live on a 1975 California 35: that is to say, thirty-five feet of aging fibreglass, chrome and teak that I don't have time to wax, polish or oil. Hanging on my bow rail is a sign that says, 'For Sale By Owner, $27,000 OBO.' It's been there for eight months.

Toting my bag of groceries down the dock, I was startled to see movement on a powerboat whose bridge canvas I'd never even seen off before. The boat was a twenty-six foot Tollycraft, the kind with a 'swim step' off the stern. I had always wondered who owned that Tolly because the galley curtains were home-made and seriously fruitcake, with ducks and wooden spoons and Holly Hobby girls across the bottom.

Shifting my groceries to the other hand, I peered in the open door as I passed. At that moment Charlie Wallace's widow,

Darcy, came out of the cabin carrying a red wok and some tupperware. Behind her was a woman who had to be her sister. They both wore short curly perms in their taffy-coloured hair and had on pastel sweatshirts appliquéd with flower cut-outs.

'Maybe you ought to think about this more,' said the sister. 'You might want a boat next spring.'

Darcy saw me and didn't answer; she was trying to remember who I was. I walked up to the rail of the cockpit and said, 'Darcy, I'm real sorry about Charlie.' She blinked with cola-coloured eyes. 'Thank you.' Her sister hovered near to protect her. Extending a hand to the sister I said, 'I'm Rachel Tarr. I own Nooksack Nets.'

She looked quickly at Darcy. 'Morrie Rich – '

'Not anymore,' I said, 'I kicked him out two months ago.' I turned again to Darcy. 'I'm *so* sorry about Charlie.'

'Thank you.'

I walked to my boat slip and opened up the Cal. Putting on a Garth Brooks tape, I rinsed lettuce and decided that Morrie would show up only after he had spent the cash. In the middle of that thought, a knock rattled the roof of the cabin. Peeking out, I saw Lieutenant Gregory in a baseball jacket and black-soled Nikes that would mar my deck. His gray eyes were the colour of a Pacific front.

'Come aboard,' I said.

Stretching his long legs over the lifeline, he climbed down into my cabin, his head grazing the ceiling, even in the centre.

'Have a seat.'

'Thank you.' He perched on the edge of the daybed and watched as I dipped each lettuce leaf, conservation style, in a bowl of water. Outside a rogue gust set all the sailboat stays in the harbour clinking against all the masts: wind chimes to God.

'What can I do for you?' I asked.

'Morrie Rich slept here night before Charlie was killed.'

My cheeks flushed and I nodded to where the lieutenant was sitting. 'Right there on my couch.'

Avoiding my eyes, he rippled his knuckles against the teak bulkhead but said nothing.

I stepped out from behind the counter. 'Look, until the other night, I hadn't even talked to Morrie in two months.'

'And what was so special about the other night?'

'He came to see me about a net, he wants to get back fishing for himself. He found a boat he can lease, but he needs credit on a net.'

'You going to give it to him?'

'I hadn't decided yet.'

'So you're saying the two of you just talked, then you let him sleep here?'

I slid behind the counter again. 'That's right. He had to be on *Charlie's Girl* at four a.m. and he didn't want to go all the way out to Everson where he lives.'

'Any other conversation take place Wednesday night?'

I shrugged. 'We talked about interest rates, prices at the Co-op, whether I could hang a dolphin release net if I had to.' I shook a handful of lettuce leaves. 'I can't remember.'

'What'd he say about Charlie Wallace?'

'Nothing.'

'He didn't indicate to you in any way what he might be up to in the next twenty-four hours?'

'No.'

'And when he showed up here afterwards in Charlie's dinghy, you didn't help him get away?'

'Oh, *good* try.' I ripped lettuce. 'If he does come, he's going to have to turn himself in, isn't he?'

'You better believe.' He rippled his knuckles again on the teak. 'But I still don't understand why you slept with him if you broke up two months ago.'

'I didn't sleep with him!' Lowering my voice, I said, 'The reason I let him sleep on my couch was to show him that I wasn't interested anymore; that I could take it or leave it. See what I mean?'

Lieutenant Gregory looked at the electronics above the chart table. 'You don't have a phone down here, do you?'

'I use the one at the Yacht Club.' Fussing at the sink, I muttered, 'I guess it wouldn't do to invite you for dinner now. You couldn't eat with a criminal, could you?'

Lieutenant Gregory raised himself cautiously off the daybed, standing with his head cocked to one side. 'Sorry. I'm on duty.'

As he climbed the companion way steps, I called to his back. 'Well, I'm sorry too.'

Eating in silence, I listened to Garth Brooks until I had all the lyrics memorised on both sides, then went to bed at ten o'clock. Out on the docks people were still romping up and down, barbecuing in their cockpits, enjoying the soft August night. My dinghy was tied up outside under the bow and it bumped softly against the hull, making me wonder if I should get up and line it in, or whether I should just go to sleep.

I must have dozed off when all of a sudden the dinghy bumped hard, electrifying my whole brain with the nagging question that had bothered me the first time I heard it: Thad was right: why *would* anyone paint an aluminum dinghy?

Sitting up, I peered out the porthole at the shadowy hulls. Jumping out of the sack, I slipped on jeans and my Helly fleece. Taking an unused Seattle chart from the chart table, I packed it, a pencil, and a roll of masking tape in my dock bag. Hauling out the little dinghy oars from aft storage, I climbed the companionway and poked my head out the hatch.

Things were quiet out on the docks. The boaters were all down below, behind their glowing curtains. The cooling air smelled of expensive steak fat and herby marinades. Clambering into my dinghy, I slipped the oars in the oarlocks and cast off, rowing out of the pleasure boat marina towards the commercial wharfs. Taking a short-cut under the Cold Storage dock, I came out by the fishing boats and began rowing down the empty waterway.

The leather cuffs of the oars squeaked softly in the oarlocks and the stubby blades hit the water as quietly as dropped coins. I rowed by an aluminum gill-netter with no drum housing and a nearly derelict purse seiner. I didn't really know what Jerry Rice's boat looked like or even her name, but there were only a handful of boats in port and most of those were ones that should have been scuttled after World War II. Down on the next dock I spied an overturned dinghy up on styrofoam blocks and rowed in.

The dinghy was next to a gill-netter called *Mineshaft*. Up close the fresh paint resins were so sharp they radiated in warm waves.

Tying up in the shadow of *Mineshaft*'s hull, I crept on to the dock with my canvas sack. Pulling out the old chart, I unfolded it and taped it – white side up – on to the keel strip. With the side of my pencil I began rubbing blindly across the paper, feeling the soft lead catch on unseen markings under the fresh paint. The paint fumes made me light-headed. I scribbled back and forth, then stopped, trying to read what the pencil had raised. The dock lights were too dim.

I started rubbing again in broad strokes, trying to cover the entire stern. Down the way someone suddenly slammed a locker. I froze stone-still and waited, my heart fibrillating like sonar. Rubbing the pencil as fast as I could, I ripped off the chart and stashed it in my canvas sack. Slipping quietly into my dinghy, I cast off and rowed beeline to the shadowed safety of the Cold Storage dock.

Stomach churning like a tank of bait, I tied up at home, dashing below. Locking the hatch from inside, I pulled the curtains closed and turned on the galley light. I took out the Seattle chart and opened the backside across the table. There, etched in plain script against the soft pencil rubbing were the words: 'CHARLIE'S G.' My heart beat so hard I could feel my chest move.

A knock suddenly shook my roof.

'Who is it?' Frantically I folded the chart and slipped it under the non-slip mat I use as a tablecloth.

'It's me, Darcy Wallace. I've got to talk to you.'

I got up and unlocked the hatch. 'Come aboard.'

Darcy clambered down the companionway steps with a cutesy little quilted bag on her arm. 'Rachel,' she said again. 'I've got to talk to you.'

'You just said that. What do you want?'

Behind Darcy a pair of men's legs appeared on the stairs. I waited to greet her companion.

It was Jerry Rice.

'Jeh, Jeh.' That's all I could do, stand there and make gasping noises. Jerry lunged across the cabin, beading down on me like quarry. I fell on to the daybed, opening my mouth to scream. Instantly Jerry stuffed in a crusty used handkerchief, pressing me against the cushions with his knee. I gagged and panicked as the handkerchief stuck in the back of my throat. Coughing and wrenching, unable to breathe, I tried to claw my way up. Jerry's knee crushed me down so heavily I thought my rib cage would break. He grabbed one wrist, then the other, then gathered them both in a single vice-like grip.

As I struggled against Jerry's immovable weight, Darcy fastidiously produced a roll of duct tape from her quilted bag and set it on the table.

'Hurry up,' snapped Jerry.

Darcy ripped off a six-inch strip and stood over me, trying to centre it across my mouth. I jerked my head back and forth, like saying 'no', and thrust the handkerchief out with my tongue.

'Now, stop that.' Jerry whacked the side of my head so hard I thought my jaw broke. Then he poked the handkerchief back in while Darcy neatly laid the tape over my lower face. I worked the handkerchief again to the front of my mouth with my tongue, then kicked Darcy. Cursing me, she kicked back.

Crossing my wrists as if I were a puppet, Jerry pressed them against my chest. ''Bout a foot and a half of tape, Darce. Don't let it twist up on ya.'

The widow ripped off a length of silver tape and methodically wrapped my wrists as if she were fixing her dryer vent. Jerry grunted approval and climbed off my chest. Immediately I bolted up, butting my head into Darcy. Crying out furiously, she hit me with the thick roll of tape, over and over. I dropped to the floor to avoid the blows, using my heels like hammers on her feet. She tap-danced backwards out of the way, swinging her tape role and cursing under her breath.

Jerry cackled loudly, enjoying the fight. Calmly reaching down, he grabbed my ankles and held them perfectly still. 'Rip some more tape, will you, honey?'

They bound my legs, then Jerry picked me up and threw me over his shoulder like a sack of potatoes. My back brushed the overhead and I ripped my shirt on a hanging locker.

'Find that chart she was rubbing,' Jerry said.

Darcy checked the chart table, then her housewife's eye caught the bulge under the table mat. She slipped it into her quilted bag.

'Is anybody outside?' asked Jerry.

Darcy poked her head out. 'All clear.'

I wiggled and squirmed, and in retaliation Jerry banged me purposely against every locker, light, and bulkhead in the place. Toting me up the steps with great difficulty, he swung my wriggling body around to clang my head against the boom. White light filled my eyes for a full second and I decided to hold still.

At the end of my boat slip Darcy's Tollycraft was tied broadside. Striding over to the swim step, Jerry climbed up the ladder into the cockpit. Darcy followed, unlocking the cabin door and turning on the lights. As Jerry threw me on the settee, Darcy cast off and started the engine, running the boat gently out to the breakwater, then throttling into high gear across the open bay.

I had chewed the handkerchief to a sodden mass, sweet-tasting and nasty. In Darcy's galley drawers, I knew, were sharp surfaces that I could use to cut the duct tape. All I needed was a chance.

We raced across the inky void of Bellingham Bay and Jerry raised a settee cushion, lifting out a handful of thick white-wrapped line. This was followed by more handfuls, and more. Fear shot through my body like a hormone: he had at least twelve fathoms of lead-filled line, the weighted stuff we use at the bottom of nets.

'Must have bought this at your shop,' he said. He dragged the lead-line over and sat beside me like a patient father. Methodically he began wrapping me in the thick nylon-covered stuff. I saw that he had left the tail end free and I watched alertly as he wrapped my body, weaving in and out my bound arms, then up and around my legs in a figure–8. 'Want to know how much Darcy and I are going to gross this season?'

'Aaugh.'

'Tell her, Darce.'

From the helm, Darcy called, '$600,000.' She grinned. 'I believe that's from the Mutual of Omaha run.'

They looked at each other and burst out in nervous laughter, the tension shattering like the back windows of a warehouse. Through his guffaws, Jerry huffed. 'That's right. Big fish run in Nebraska.' After a moment he wiped a tear from his eye and asked, 'Think buying Charlie a cell phone and VCR were worth it now?'

They mugged like old school chums and Jerry saw the confusion on my face. 'That's what so great about cell phones these days. She calls up and asks him what movie he wants, she'll run it out to him at anchor. We put on out to Semiahmoo, me here in the cabin. She climbs up: 'Hello, Dear, sorry I couldn't find *Rocky*.' Bang! He doesn't even know what hit him. Not only do we clear his $25,000, we get the lucrative Mutual of Omaha fishery too. Only thing is, Rachel, why didn't you go to the cops with your graffiti from Morrie? That sure would have helped us out.'

'She's too loyal,' offered Darcy.

I watched intently as he wound the dense line around my legs, knowing that I had the skill to undo anything he could tie. But as he worked, the weighted line fell heavier and heavier on my body: even breathing was an effort. Darcy cut the engine and Jerry finished winding the last fathom of line around my torso. I knew I could still free myself if I had the time because not many people know how to work lead-line. But when Jerry got to the end, I watched in horror as he picked up the first tail and looped it with the end into a lover's knot. A lover's knot is the only thing that'll hold two ends of leadline. And that's when I knew I was going to die.

'Stand up,' he said.

I planted my feet, trying to rise, then slumped back on the settee. I was simply too heavy. Not as heavy as I pretended, but still too heavy to get up.

'Walk!' He pulled me by the armpits, but even he couldn't budge me.

'Darcy, I can't move her.'

'Take off some of the rope.'

'We can't. She's a hundred-thirty pounds, she's going to need at least this much to keep her down.'

'Dammit, Jerry, if we can't move her. . . .'

His temper flared. 'Well, I'll be damned if I'm going to unwrap her.'

Patiently Darcy examined the cabin floor. 'Can we drag her?'

Jerry grunted, and like a practised team, they lugged me down to the floor and hauled me across the carpet, Jerry clutching under my arms and Darcy lifting my seat by the lead-line. It took them at least a minute to get me to the entry, and they were both sweating and breathing hard by the time Darcy slid back the door.

The chill night air rushed into the cabin and the two of them collapsed on the settee to rest. They left me laying with my head out on the cockpit deck, my legs still in the cabin. I looked up at the blue-white stars, brain filled with images of .caught fish flopping futilely on the deck.

'Ready?' asked Jerry.

They got up and resumed their positions, bracing themselves for a few seconds against a passing wave. Then, with immense effort, they pulled me several more feet out into the centre of the cockpit. The cockpit on a Tollycraft is like a big playpen fenced on all sides by three-foot fibreglass bulkheads. On top of the bulkheads runs a chrome railing that hits most people about waist level. The only break in the railing is where the stern ladder leads down to the swim shelf. Darcy analysed the situation. 'How are we going to get her over?'

'Just like we're doing. I'll pull, you push.'

They dragged me to the stern and Jerry climbed into the ladder opening, straddling the bulkhead. Gripping with his knees, he grabbed me under the arms, pulling me almost upright. I slumped inert, making myself as heavy as possible.

Needing more room for leverage, Jerry climbed entirely over the stern and stood halfway down the ladder to the swim shelf. Reaching back over the bulkhead to grab me under the arms, he waited as the boat rolled with the waves. I felt Darcy pause too, steadying herself against the rocking boat. A split second later they both relaxed their grip, ready to go back to work. And at that moment I suddenly slumped to the deck, pivoted on my back like a turtle, and smashed Jerry in the face with my feet.

'AARGH!' He fell in the water with a cry like an air raid siren.

Darcy screamed too, then yelled, 'Swim, Jerry!' She dashed inside and came back with a yellow horseshoe buoy. Pausing to tie the buoy line to a stanchion, she suddenly stopped and stared over the stern. On her face, clear as day, was the thought that she really didn't need Jerry anymore.

'Throw it!' Jerry's voice sounded like a third-day drunk.

I shimmied back towards the cabin as fast I could.

Darcy dithered with the horseshoe and buoy line, still deciding Jerry's fate. Biting her lip, she looked once more at Jerry in the water, then resolutely turned away to start the boat. Stumbling over me on the deck, she panicked, suddenly realising she couldn't get rid of me on her own.

'No, wait!' She turned and snatched the horseshoe again, throwing it across the waves.

'TOOOOT!' A thunderous boat horn sounded all the way down to my hip bones. Raising my head, I saw a Pac-Can seiner off our port, running back to Cold Storage with a full load of fish simply because Charlie Wallace wasn't out there buying.

'What's the problem?' called a voice through a megaphone. A sudden floodlamp switched on, beaming daylight over the Tollycraft.

'Man overboard!' cried Darcy, squinting into the beam of light.

'You got a raft?'

'No,' she called.

'We'll get ours.' Then he paused. 'What's the matter with the man on your deck?'

I wriggled away from the bulkhead that partially hid me from view. Darcy looked down calmly, punching me with a toe. 'He's seasick.'

Frantically I hoisted myself up on one elbow and tossed the blond thunderbolts for the purse seiner to see. There was an unnatural silence up on her bridge and then an inflatable raft went over the side for Jerry. Following the raft was a man in a red flotation suit. Unable to hold myself erect any longer, I collapsed back on the icy deck and waited. Up on the dark fishing boat things were still very quiet.

Darcy looked off the stern at the rescue going on, trying to pretend that I didn't exist. Then the megaphone blared, 'Ma'am, I'm sorry, but we have a 30.06 and a flare gun aimed at you and we're on the phone to the Coast Guard. Is there anyone else inside?'

'Oh, shit.' Darcy shook her head and called, 'No.' Then she kicked me, hard. I could barely feel it through the lead-line.

Things fell into place pretty quickly after that. The Bellingham Police found the rest of Charlie Wallace's payroll in the Tupperware of Jerry's galley. As it turned out, Mutual of Omaha had already started an investigation on Darcy: two months before she had upped the coverage on her beloved Charlie from $150,000 to $600,000 and – as it was explained to me – anytime someone dies that helpfully within two years of a policy being written, all the little bells and whistles go off in insurance-land.

Still, no one heard from Morrie. Darcy and Jerry were staying mum, so on an outside chance, I called Eileen at the Anchorage Airport. She turned out to be real nice but said, no, she hadn't seen him either.

Finally, in mid-September after the first heavy storm of the season, some kids found Morrie's body washed up on the beach at Semiahmoo. His mother came up from Ballard and collapsed all over me for the next few days. And as for me, I must admit I even cried a little myself when they told me they'd found him wrapped in lead-line tied with a lover's knot.

ROBYN VINTEN

The Man in the Hat

The man in the hat is coming back, climbing down the steps
from the pier. He's older than I thought, the lights in the pub
are misleading. He's older and he's not so flash either, when
you look close his suit is frayed around the end of the sleeves.
I don't know how Val could have thought of going with him.
He's only touched me once and I thought I was going to be
sick, all that fat, that sweaty, slimy fat. I don't see how she
could have liked that stuff, the kissing and things. I use to watch
her at the youth club, some boy all over her and her just loving
it. I don't see how she could.

It's bloody cold tonight, it was warm that night, not cold and
windy like tonight. And it was darker too, there's a moon out
tonight when the clouds blow away, and it's earlier, so the lights
on the pier are still on.

I wish I'd brought my mac, but it's supposed to be bloody
summer. This dress is silly, so thin and the wind is blowing right
up around my knickers. It's one of hers, and even though I
haven't hardly eaten anything all week it's too tight around my
waist and it doesn't do all the way up at the back. Mum nearly
had a fit when she saw me in it, I thought she was going to rip
it right off me, but she just started crying again, and I ran out
of the house. I thought it would be right, to do it in one of her
dresses, and besides I've got nothing but jeans, and he mightn't
have gone for me in jeans.

He's close now. I know it was him. Rubes pointed him out
to me. She'd seen them together, she'd pointed him out to the
police too, but they'd just patted her on the head and sent her

along. Just because she's short and really fat and has beer bottle-bottom glasses no one takes her seriously. The police didn't believe her, but I do, she said he was the one and I believe her.

I sent him back to get my cardy, I left it in the pub. I knew he'd want to come down here to the beach. This is where I found her, I was the one that found her first. I'd had a real bad feeling all day, we were down here on our Youth Club outing. She'd gone off with her friends so I didn't see her all day, but that was all right because I didn't see any of her friends either. I thought they'd be off somewhere chatting up the boys. I'd gone off with my friends, we'd mucked about on the pier, ate fish and chips and candyfloss. I'd saved up my pocket money and had £3.00 to spend.

I tried not to worry about Val, she hated it when I made a fuss, but she was so pretty and so trusting of strangers, especially of strange men. I'd tell her to be careful, but she'd just laugh, she was always laughing at me. Said I was too careful, said I'd end up like our Mum. 'You can't be too careful.' That's what our Mum always says. I suppose there are worse thing I could end up like, like I could end up dead.

When it was time to go, we were all getting on the bus. Her friends were there but she wasn't. They said she'd gone off with some flash bloke, gone off to the pub. She was only fourteen, she shouldn't have gone off like that.

The bad feeling I had got worse then, like all the chips and things I'd eaten were going to come back up again. But I didn't do anything, I just sat on the bus with the others, feeling worse and worse. I have that sick feeling now thinking about me sitting there, doing nothing. She hadn't been dead long when I found her, Mum says if I hadn't have been so stupid she'd still be with us.

We waited half an hour, then Brian, the youth leader said we'd have to go without her. Well I was off that bus like a shot, stupid wanker, what would Mum say if I went home and said we'd left her there. Hit me around the head she would.

So I ran off the bus, Brian shouting after me. I ran off and down the beach, the bad feeling getting worse and worse, and that's when I found her. Back up the beach a bit from here.

And he's coming back with my cardy now. I left it under the seat where he wouldn't notice. It's Val's cardy too, I don't have any good ones like that. I sent him back, said Mum would kill me if I lost it. Said I wasn't going to do anything till he went and got it. I didn't know if it would work, but it did, like a treat.

He's walking across the pebbles towards me. The sea is in front of me, I can see the white tops of the waves and hear them crashing, and I can hear his footsteps, crunching like broken glass. That's one good thing about this beach, no one could sneak up on you. Not that that helped Val, it didn't help her because she was already with the bastard.

And here he is, he's got my cardy, her cardy. He's holding it up in front of him and he's smiling, like he's giving me a present. I take it off him, he tries to grab my hand but I pull it away. I hug the cardy to me, it's warm and smells of smoke from the pub, smoke and booze. He moves in closer, he smells of smoke and booze too. He's still smiling, he looks stupid when he smiles. I try and smile back but my lips kind of wobble. I hug the cardy and I think of Val.

'A shining light', that's what the minister called her, and Mum must have agreed, because she cried really hard when he said it. She cries all the time now, except when she's yelling at me and the way she looks at me sometimes now, when I've done something stupid, I can tell what she's thinking, she's thinking that she wished it was me that got killed.

Val was wearing this cardy in the picture they had in all the papers. I was in the picture too, only they cut me out. She was laughing, laughing at me probably, because I was worried about something and she said I shouldn't. I'm too young and I'd be old before my time, like Mum.

I start to cry and that's not what I had planned so I get cross with myself. I brush the tears away, he looks at me kind of strange, like he's embarrassed. My hands are shaking, I think I might miss if they shake too much. I remember the knife suddenly and feel inside my bag for it. I can't find it and panic for a moment and then I find it inside my book. It is cold, bloody cold, even colder than I am. I feel the blade against my hand, it's like ice. My palm is sweating, it's funny my palm is sweating when the rest of me is so cold.

He's moved in real close now, his hand is on my chin, lifting my face to look up at his. His skin is hot and clammy, slimy. I want to pull away, but I make myself stand still, like Val would have done. He brings his face right up to mine, licking his lips. His breath smells like the cardy, of the smokes and beer he's been chucking down his throat all night. He puts his smelly mouth over mine, his tongue slides out and slips along my lips and teeth.

'Come on baby, open up.'

I clench the knife in my bag, clench it hard in my sweating hand, until the handle hurts. I close my eyes and open my mouth a little. His tongue barges in there, pokes around inside my mouth. I take my hand out of my bag, I put my other hand around his waist, I can feel the rolls of his fat against my stomach. The hand I've taken out of my bag, it has the knife in it. I shove it up through those rolls, it goes in real easy, like a hot knife through butter, Mum would say.

He gives a kind of grunt and I feel my hand go wet. He leans heavily into me, I push him away. He falls backwards and lands with a crunch on the pebbles. He looks at me surprised, Val had that same look on her face when I found her. Her eyes wide open and surprised looking.

I kneel down beside him, he watches me. I still have the knife in my hand. I run the blade across the front of his throat, it sticks in something, a bone or something. He puts his hand up to stop me, I push it away. I try the side of his neck, the knife goes in easier, then it hits a vein or something, because all this blood spurts out, hits me right in the chest. There's so much of it, it just keeps coming and coming. It soaks through my dress, Val's dress. It will leave a stain, a real bad stain, blood does that, and Mum will kill me, say it's typical, I can't even look after anything, not Val's dress, not Val, not anything.

I start to cry again, 'cause I know Mum will be mad and Val won't be there to make things okay like she did, and because no matter how hard I try I can't be like Val. And the blood is still coming out, still soaking the dress, and I think, 'Salt water',

I need some salt water to wash it out. That's what I use to get the blood out of my knickers. I'm kneeling beside him, beside the sea wishing I had some salt water, and I realise I've got a whole bloody sea of it, the whole bloody English Channel full of it.

I stand up, he's still watching me, so I put the knife across his eyes, I drop it on so I don't have to touch him again and he can't watch me any more. Then I walk into the sea, it's gone calm now, dead flat and the wind's dropped and it's not as cold as I thought it would be, not once you get used to it.

The water lifts the dress up, it billows around me like a balloon for a moment, then the water pulls it down. For some reason I remember Rubes, her standing there pointing the man out to me, that night after the police had put ropes around Val's body and a crowd had gathered to watch.

'The one in the hat.' She said.

The water is up to my tits now, the dress moves backwards and forwards under the water. I look back at the man on the beach, the moon's come out from behind a cloud and I can see him quite clearly for a moment. He looks like he's just sleeping, lying back, his stomach sticking up in front of him.

I remember Val, so small and thin, and I remember how she hated fat men. Hated them because they were like Dad, hated Dad for what he'd done to Mum, to us. Absolutely hated them, how she said she'd rather died than let one touch her.

Then I see him, the other man in the hat, standing by the pier, in just about the place I reckon I found her, and I remember Rubes again, her pointing and there being two men in hats, but I decided she couldn't had meant the tall one, he looked too smart, too rich, too thin.

Suddenly it goes dark and I think it might be my eyes for a second, then I realise it's the pier lights, they've turned them off. I know I should get out of the water, I'll catch me a death of a cold, as Mum would say, but I'm so tired, and this dress is so heavy.

Red Office

One week, over several consecutive days, our office was painted red. No, it was mainly painted a peculiar colour called Serenade, like vomit, someone said, except that vomit can be different colours, so this was not a precise description. Like oyster or magnolia, the colour of a cheaply converted flat, all smooth and shining, before ominous patches of damp appear where the rain is overflowing from the blocked up gutters and penetrating the walls. Yes, exactly that colour, but enlivened in our office's case by dashes of bright and lurid red – red pillars, red filing cabinets and red radiators.

Word got around. People made special visits from the first, third and fourth floors to view the dramatic spectacle. They blinked and smiled uncertainly, or laughed loudly. Carol said that our filing cabinets were the talk of the lately established smoking room, next to the managing director's office in the basement, its walls sticky with nicotine, air heavy with gossip and cigarette fumes, where Grace might be found, if through hurt pride I were not studiously avoiding her, because she cancelled our lunch date and talks to other people in union meetings. My mind closely enfurled in jealousy like the leaves of an artichoke.

The new colour scheme was Luke's idea, because the colour red motivates people, or so he told Muriel, his secretary. Luke does not enjoy a calm office atmosphere, no, he stirs the murky depths of the settled pond, he pokes the ants nest, or it might be said he revels in the use and misuse of power.

After suffering a severe headache two days running, I traced its source to the red pillar situated directly behind my Apple Mac. 'A number of factors may contribute to cause eye strain, including seemingly insignificant matters such as the office colour scheme' I read in a Health and Safety Executive booklet on new technology. It seemed reasonable to suppose that if red motivates people, it might also give them headaches. I went to get some paracetamol from the first-aid cupboard, but it was locked and Philip Sidney of the Computer Department informed me that anyway it was empty of useful drugs, in accordance with EC regulations, to guard against the possibility of staff, whether by accident or by design, taking fatal overdoses and their grieving relatives bringing legal actions against the company.

The first-aid cupboard now contained only a couple of bandages, judged harmless, and a tiny blue-glass bottle of smelling salts, as used by bridesmaids at royal weddings. The first-aid book dangled on a piece of dirty string above the photocopier, permanently open to announce that 'On 1 July 1987, at 10.30 am in the PRD administration offices, 1st floor, a ceiling tile fell off and hit Iris Hancock on the head whilst she was sending a fax. Although shocked, she was not badly injured and will not require hospital treatment.' No further entries appeared, although surely some minor injuries had occurred in the five years since Iris was assaulted by a piece of polystyrene. The glue on those tiles is no more reliable now than it was in the late 1980s, although to the sharp-eyed observer they give clear warning signs of their impending detachment. Threatened by redundancy in these post-Depression years, dragging ourselves into work with period pains, cured of Monday and Friday-itis, staying grimly till 6 or 7 pm, maybe we also find it harder to admit to physical injury. '20 May 1986. Jane Marsden was fetching an elastoplast for a colleague with a cut finger; the lid of the first-aid cabinet failed to open properly at first, then fell down sharply, cutting her head. There was a small amount of blood.'

I stuck pieces of A4 white paper to my red pillar with sellotape, so effectively screening the section of it that was giving me a headache. Feeling pleased with this solution, I then wrote on it 'Headache pillar' in green felt-tip pen. It was now beginning to resemble a surrealist work of art. My colleagues looked at it, then at me, in fearful apprehension – they already knew I was odd, but now it occurred to them, I might have a serious mental illness. 'Has Luke seen that?' Carol asked. She is my immediate boss, one down from Luke in the office hierarchy, so it was her responsibility, we both knew, to tell me to remove the paper, but she was pissed off with Luke because he keeps cancelling important meetings at short notice; this counted in my favour.

'He hasn't been in today,' I replied, disingenuously. Luke operates an efficient spy network: his personal eyes might not have rested on my pillar, but its transformation would certainly have been described to him, in hurried phone calls.

'Well it all seems very petty,' Carol said. 'Couldn't you just ignore the pillar?'

'No, I'm sorry, but you see it stands right behind my computer, in my direct line of sight, so I'm sorry, but I can't possibly ignore it.'

Carol's lips twitched. 'You know, the decorators painted a pillar red in Luke's room by mistake and he was so furious, he ordered them to repaint it straight away. I head him shouting at them at six o'clock yesterday morning – telling them it was contrary to his clear instructions and an insult.'

Insult. The word reminded me of hospitals, my father and the medical phrase 'an insult to the brain'. Wiping out the body's memory, like the Etch-a-Sketch, that expensive toy he once allowed me to have, the plastic screen with two knobs you could turn to make angular scribbles, then shake the screen to see its miraculous powers of erasure.

'Well it is an insult,' I said 'to think you can motivate your employees with red paint, instead of pay rises.' Our managing director had circulated a memo to all staff, expressing his smooth regret that there would be no pay reviews this year, due to recent 'extraordinary expenditure' – in particular, the cost of redecorating the building. Adding injury to insult. 'Um – why were you in here at six o'clock in the morning?' I asked.

'Oh, you know, Luke gets in early and it makes a good impression. As I mentioned to you in your quarterly assessment, Annie, we not only have to do our jobs, we have to be *seen* to be doing them. Make that a conscious and deliberate part of your career strategy. And by the way – '

Muriel came in, waving a knife. Its blade flashed dangerously in the bright overhead lights. 'I can't stand it anymore,' she said, her breath coming fast and shallow, her forehead shiny with sweat below her parted and strained-back hair. 'They're all picking on me and talking about me behind my back, the atmosphere's terrible, it's like a witch hunt.'

Carol slipped into her office and closed the door. With her career in mind, she would not wish to be seen associating with Muriel, a stroppy, independent-minded woman and therefore an obvious target for victimisation by Luke's sycophants. The writing was on the wall, or on the red pillar – Luke would sack her soon. In fact, as I happened to have noticed while scanning the job columns of the local free newspaper, he had already placed an advertisement for a new secretary. Muriel was going on holiday next week, so the preliminary interviews were probably scheduled for then.

'So I've brought the post in here to open.' Muriel sat down at an adjacent desk and began slitting a pile of envelopes. 'My faith gives me strength, otherwise I'd probably top myself. But I'm a Christian.'

Muriel often tells me she is a Christian: in a low, prideful voice, as if revealing a special secret close to her heart. Once I almost reciprocated by confiding that I was a lesbian, but as I think she belongs to some evangelical sect, I am glad I kept my mouth shut.

'Maybe I'll start applying for other jobs.'

'That's a good idea.'

'Because I might be paranoid, but I think he's looking for an excuse to sack me. For instance, the night before last, I worked till past eight o'clock doing the media packs like he'd told me to, and at half-past seven, the phone rang. Well, I knew it must be him, checking up on me – who else would ring the office at half-past seven? I was going to answer it, but then I decided, no, I'm too busy to play stupid games. I don't need to justify myself. So I just let it ring. And the next day, before I'd even had a chance to say good morning, he called me all sorts of vile names, accusing me of having left early. But I told him, "I was here, I must have been down at the photocopier when you rang." And he can't prove I wasn't, can he?'

'Why should you stay till half-past seven, anyway? You don't get paid overtime. The bastard.'

'I think he's planning something.'

By now it was lunchtime, so I went for a walk in the park. I was suffering from a painful fit of unrequited love, the kind I commonly get in melancholy late autumn, but this particular attack had lasted three years already, its intensity not noticeably diminishing with the changing of the seasons. Grace must know how I felt about her, otherwise why had she cancelled our arrangement to go out for a drink at lunchtime? Besides, I blush easily and my face is as WYSIWYG as my Apple Mac screen. No, the only thing to do was avoid her scrupulously from this day forward, to preserve my last remnants of dignity by never again using the PRD photocopier even if ours was genuinely out of order and going straight down the back stairs to the sandwich queue, rather than taking the slightly longer route along the first corridor, in the hope of catching a glimpse of her.

I crossed a stream and began sloshing uphill towards the wood. The park is of the country kind as opposed to the urban. It incorporates a golf course and a miniature farm, as well as most of Middlesex University. Students were out combing the grass for magic mushrooms; they held small plastic bags and looked seriously intent. In the wind, rain and fresh air, my head began to clear, my heart to lift. The park is a reliably work-free zone, since my colleagues toil through their lunch hours or go to the pub. Once Muriel asked me dubiously if I wasn't frightened of being 'attacked'. No, I feel safer out here.

Muriel, Luke, Carol, Philip Sidney and even Grace were all, it occurred to me, if not exactly figments of my imagination, yet aspects of my karma, of the imprisoning morass of earthly concerns and preoccupations within which my soul struggles, like a seagull caught in an oil slick.

I had the foreboding sense of something being about to happen. Some minor or perhaps major disaster. Already that week I had witnessed a masked raid on a security van and seen a chimney fall off a block of flats. Misfortunes tend to come in threes, don't they?

Musing thus, I almost tripped over two Middlesex University students, male and female, lying entwined in the long wet grass. They were both wearing duffle coats and jeans, untoggled and unzipped. Careless passion. I'm 36, I thought, and I've never made love in a duffle coat. Life is passing/has passed me by. I wish I had a lover. Or even a friend, yes, a friend would be nice. I did have some, but they seemed far away. In another Travelcard zone or lifetime. What I needed was a friend within the company. Then I would feel less of a misfit, less lonely.

Arriving back in the office, I found a note on my desk from Carol. 'Annie, I have gone home to catch up on a huge backlog of work. Please tidy up the office, *put your disks in the disk holder*, clear all the work surfaces and leave nothing on your desk when you go home tonight.'

So. Carol was taking the afternoon off and I would have peace, for what remained of Friday. Even the Busy Bees playgroup had packed up for the day, leaving the neighbouring church hall sombre behind its French windows. Likewise the builders, who over the past several years have been mending the church's flat roof, had removed their asphalt sheeting, their tar buckets and themselves. The weathercock had seemingly flown away too, an illusion that occurs whenever it turns on its steeple point to the north-west. I thought I might practise my yoga exercises in this lovely solitude.

A piece of paper fluttered to the floor, from the desk next to mine. A leaf from a notepad, with a pretty blue flower printed in the corner. 'Let the wicked be ashamed, and be brought down to hell. Let deceitful lips be made dumb. (Psalm 30, A prayer of a just man under affliction.)' I recognised the neat, precise handwriting as Muriel's. While reading it, and wondering how close to the edge she was, I felt the first ominous twinges of a tension headache. Something just beyond my range of vision was making strenuous efforts to be noticed. Like a silent shout, or a loud silence. I looked up. My red pillar had been striped naked, its paper veil torn down by violent, hasty hands and crumpled in the bin. Only a scrap of sellotape remained.

I began to tremble. This is war, I told myself. Luke is trying to break my spirit, to crush me. Well, he's got a choice, it's this pillar or me. Me or the bloody colour scheme.

Muriel stood in the doorway. 'I know who was responsible for that,' she said. 'It was – ', naming one of Luke's henchmen. 'I just had a phone call from His Majesty. He dictated a memo to me, saying I was sacked. I've got to type it up. He's coming in to sign it later this afternoon.'

'Oh, Muriel!' I went over and tentatively put my arms around her. It was like trying to hug a rock. Her eyes blazed with a strange, distant light.

'You must take it to a tribunal.'

'The Lord is my tribunal.'

She went out again. Muriel was stronger than me, she could endure being alone at such a time. Tears were streaming down my face. He is a madman, I thought, a serial killer, he is like Robert Maxwell, he enjoys hurting people, destroying our lives, it gives him a kick. I paced back and forth. Then I found myself downstairs in Grace's office, without exactly understanding how I'd got there. I had been aiming for the coffee machine.

Grace looked exhausted. She was writing out sticky labels for the filing cabinets, in a desultory way. PRD had recently moved two doors up the corridor. Their office, too, had that Friday afternoon deserted feeling. I sat on an upturned plastic crate. She gave me a cigarette, with instructions to waft the smoke out of the window. She has pale skin and light red hair, a beautiful, soothing shade of red, quite different from my pillar, and clear, perceiving eyes, so unlike Carol's or Luke's.

'The man's a right prick, isn't he?' she said, when I paused for breath. 'Tell Muriel to get herself straight along to the Citizen's Advice Bureau.'

'She's placing her faith in the Lord.'

'Fuck that.' Grace has an extreme antipathy to things religious; even the word 'spiritual' makes her jerk backwards in disgust. 'What a place this is, eh, everyone's a bloody nutter. On your corridor.' She laughed, pulled a cigarette from the packet and lit it, tipping her chair back. 'So how are you, anyway? Haven't seen you for *ages*.'

By your choice, not mine, I thought, but managed to restrain myself from saying. Safer to dodge the main issue, as usual.

Immediately you develop a crush on someone, it completely ruins your prospects of having an intelligent conversation with her, of getting to know her better. It reaches the point, as a friend of mine observed, where you're not even sure if you like her anymore – and you're *still* behaving like a plonker.

I do like her. It's myself I have severe doubts about.

I opened my mouth, hoping a coherent sentence would emerge, although the blood was now fizzing through my veins like lemonade and my heart was the squeezed lemon, but fortunately I was interrupted by noises above. Voices rising in a crescendo, followed by a huge crash.

'Bloody hell!' Grace leapt to her feet. We both stared at the ceiling. In the square gap left by a long-ago-fallen polystyrene ceiling tile, a red stain was spreading. Slowly it spread wider. It filled the square. Like a Rothko painting. Like a bleed ad. Darker in the centre. A drop splashed down on Grace's desk.

'Is that red paint?' she said.

'No. Grace,' I said, 'I think I'm in love with you.'

Grace walked round the desk and took a gentle grip on my arm. 'Annie' she said, 'You're not. What you are is, bored. Frustrated in your job, isolated in your office. And I'm the only other dyke within a quarter mile radius.'

Something big fell past the window. A black dustbin bag. Gretchen, the cleaner, throws them out of the office windows into the skip in the car park. Starting on the fourth floor.

'What d'you think's happened?' Grace changed the subject, but kept a reassuring hold on me.

'Muriel's got a knife. She uses it for opening the post.'

'Hmm. Of course, he might just be badly wounded. I guess we should go and investigate.'

As we reached the second-floor landing, Grace said thoughtfully, 'The laws on provocation are shockingly biased against women. Although it's getting better – a woman who beat her husband to death with a rolling pin and buried him in the garden got off with two years' probation last year. Mental state impaired by years of sustained abuse. Muriel could offer the same defence.'

'But Luke's not violent, at least not physically. He's just a bully.'

'Yeah, but men get off scot-free after killing their "nagging wives".'

'That's domestic violence.'

'We live here, most of the time.'

All the lights were off along our corridor and the street lamps cast an eerie orange glow through the outer offices. As Grace pushed open the swing door, Muriel emerged from Luke's private office, buttoning up her coat.

'Oh, hello.' She looked at us, blankly. 'I was just going home.'

'Muriel, um, are you all right?' I faltered.

'Fine, thanks.'

'We heard a noise – like someone falling on the floor – '

'Oh, did you?' She locked Luke's office door and slipped the key into her coat pocket.

'Has Luke been in?'

'Oh yes. We parted on good terms. Agreeing to disagree. It's the Lord's will,' she added, ambiguously. 'He has pointed out a new path for me. I'm going to Africa, to be a missionary.'

I suppose I should have challenged her more strongly. But already I felt compromised, complicit. I might so easily have killed him myself.

'When are you leaving the country?' Grace asked.

'Tomorrow morning. So it's goodbye and God Bless. I've always thought well of you,' Muriel said, addressing me directly. 'You're a quiet little thing and a good listener' – not exactly an effusive tribute, but I felt touched by it.

Elspeth Buchan, Her Book

My cousin William seemed to believe that writers perform a kind of voodoo and scoop up characters like toe-nail clippings. 'You'll be putting us in a book, Elspeth, so you will.' He made the same tired old joke whenever we met, his tone implying that I didn't really work, not like someone who ran a garage chain in Greater Glasgow.

This time he said it at Nettie's graveside and added a knowing smirk. I knew then that he was up to no good. When we were children he showed sharp practice towards my pocket-money. William was fifty-nine, a year older than myself.

The St Pitten cemetery is set among fields that stretch to the edge of sandstone and basalt cliffs in south Fife. Nettie was buried on a crisp September morning; the barley stubble and the sky and the Firth of Forth were drenched in that amazing blue-golden light. The service was held in a chapel at the east end of the harbour; it had once been a fish-curing shed. We'd walked uphill behind the minister; William and five more men carried Nettie's coffin on their shoulders. I brought up the rear with the other women. Now only Ellie was left, Nettie's twin. My parents were dead and so were William's. Our four uncles had emigrated before we were born.

There was a great throng of St Pitten people at the cemetery and I recognised many of them from childhood and student holidays with my aunts. Yet there had been only two dozen at the service. Even the most tolerant find Third Advent Buchanites deeply embarrassing. I didn't belong to the sect but family funerals had hardened me to their chanting and archaic ritual.

Since the sixties, as a minor concession, they have allowed women to follow the coffin. I was glad that the cemetery was so close to the harbour. The Tabbies, as St Pitten people call them, disapprove of mechanised burial, and my funeral shoes were killing me.

William, Bella and their four sons had booked into a luxury hotel on the outskirts of the town. I'd driven over from Edinburgh the day before and was staying with Ellie. As soon as I arrived my aunt astounded me by saying that she didn't intend to go to the funeral.

'I'd only let you down,' she whimpered. 'I'd be greeting all the way.' And she burst into tears.

Third Advent Buchanites are the kindest bigots I know; my relations always abash me by the warmth of their welcome. I'm also outraged by their cruel self-denial. They think it disgraceful to grieve over death because every Buchanite goes straight to Heaven. Ellie had lived with her twin for eighty years. All evening I tried to convince her that sorrow was natural, but she stubbornly maintained that it was a sin.

On the morning of the funeral William and his family arrived to collect us at half-past eight. Ellie was still refusing to leave the house.

'Outside,' he commanded, pushing Bella and the young Buchans back into the street. They ranged from seven to twelve. Like his mother he married late. He was flushed with annoyance, but wisely kept his voice down. Aunt Ellie, barely five-foot tall, was as responsive to being leant on as the Bell Rock lighthouse. In a very short time – and I may say his approach was much cruder than mine – she accepted his dictum that it would cause a scandal if she missed her sister's funeral.

'I'll do what you say, William, but bide a wee.' She went upstairs and returned five minutes later looking even paler, though composed. She had put on her gloves and the sealskin coat was wrapped tightly across her thin little body. She threw off my arm quite crossly when I offered to help her to the chapel. She had given in because William was Isa's son.

Isa was our eldest aunt. She was a bossy woman who sang contralto in the Tabbies' choir. Over much of their lives she and William looked so alike that each could have been the other in drag. They were tall and bulky with massive heads and springy white hair. 'One helluva strong lady', an American cousin wrote when we buried Isa fifteen years before Nettie. She had two children, but William never saw his sister.

I ought to have taken Ellie's compliance as an omen rather than fuming at another example of brainwashed Tabby women. All the same, I was glad that William had succeeded. My aunt's conscience would have martyred her if she had missed the funeral.

Tabbies go back to the Buchanites who traipsed round Scotland after the eighteenth-century prophet Elspeth Buchan. Most of her followers were young women, including a lovely lass on whom Robert Burns had evil designs. (I like to think of our Rabbie being foiled for once.) My family is supposed to be descended from Elspeth Buchan; our great-great grandfather was born in the prophet's village and Elspeth is a family name. If we did bring the cult to Fife the transplantation must have induced some startling changes. Elspeth Buchan was another strong lady: she'd have scourged the sexist practices of her modern followers with fire and brimstone.

On their wedding day Third Advent Buchanite wives have to hand over all money and property to their husbands; a female child can inherit a house only if all her brothers are dead. Of course she loses it again on marriage.

We left Aunt Nettie under her white lilies and returned home for the dredgie, or reception. The men still marched soberly in front, while the women straggled more informally behind. We passed the chapel once more and walked along the street that lies between the harbour and the terrace of fishers' houses. That and the rows of council flats that climb up to the main road are all there is to St Pitten. Hardly any real fishermen live there now. A few boats still use the tidal harbour to go out for lobsters but most of them cater for day-trippers who want to visit the gannets nesting on the Bass Rock.

Ellie's house stands out because it isn't colour-washed like the rest; it is rendered in plain rough-cast studded all over with shells. In the tourist leaflet there's a photo of the Shellie House; my aunts were annoyed when they saw it.

I knew that Bella would be in on William's plans, but as we

walked home she was more concerned that the weight of the coffin might have affected her husband's blood pressure.

'It's an awfy worry, Elspeth. Dr Campbell warned him again last week.'

I tried to reassure her by mentioning William's zeal for fresh air and exercise. Well, his elbow was exercised pretty frequently in the golf club bar.

'Aye, but you'll mind his mother went the same way.'

What killed Isa wasn't high blood pressure but cheated hopes. She married a St Pitten grocer and galvanised him into opening another branch in St Andrews. After living above the shop for two years they bought a large stone villa overlooking the Old Course. The day before the removal Bob Leslie went on a fishing trip and drowned. William's sister was a posthumous child.

William let her down too. Isa wanted to see her son Provost of St Pitten, population one thousand but still a Royal Burgh. William disappeared west as soon as he was into long trousers and Isa had to sell the two shops to her managers. She went back to living with her sisters.

I could see that Bella's fingers were twitching to take out her packet of king-size, but smoking in the street would have shocked the Buchanites. She distracted herself with another subject. 'Did you see yon lassie at the service? She wasn't family, no even the Newcastle lot. Right cheeky to sit at the front like that.'

Indeed I had. Attractive, dark and thirtyish; her blue jeans and anorak had displeased the older Buchanites. There was a scruffy rucksack beside her on the pew. She soon gave up the baffling order of service and tried to catch my eye. When we formed up for the procession she had vanished.

The Shellie House was cluttered with Edwardian furniture and bric-a-brac, all cheap and ordinary when bought and now worth a tidy sum. What belonged to whom was unclear, but the Buchanites used to go through a token destruction of worldly goods when one of their members died. The items were usually put out in the bin. William's thoughts had no doubt been winging towards Old Tyme Curios fifty yards along the street. I hoped he wouldn't go so far as to cheat my aunt.

By five o'clock the guests had all gone. William glanced round the sitting-room as if seeing it for the first time, although he'd lived at the Shellie House for fourteen years. His eyes lighted on a Bell's punchbowl and became pensive. Battle was going to commence. Bella unearthed a bottle of twelve-year-old Talisker. She'd hidden it in a cupboard that morning before William thrust her out. She sat down at the crumb-strewn table and pushed away the empties.

'Too good for those keelies,' she said, twisting out the stopper. I winced at the noise and her remark. She poured the whisky with her head askew, squinting along a cigarette tethered to her scarlet lips. Bella wore tight blonded curls and flashy rings. Her self-confidence was brass-plated, and I'd once supposed that her gruffness protected a generous heart.

Ellie had already disappeared to stack dishes in the kitchen. I went to help her clutching the whisky in my hand. My aunt was tipping a kettleful of hot water into the sink.

'Elspeth, when you go to your room, mind to look in the bottom drawer of the chest. Friday past, I was turning out Nettie's clothes and papers. I canna think how all your stuff got among them.'

'Come away in, Aunt Ellie,' cried Bella. 'Elspeth will see to the dishes later.'

We returned to the sitting-room. Ellie refused the whisky, but this was only personal taste. The Buchanites pre-date the Temperance movement and find spirits and sanctity entirely compatible. She said, 'You've been awfy good to me, William, you and the bairns baith. I'd like to treat the six of you to your supper, but I'll no come mysel. I'm that wabbit I'll away to my bed with some porridge.'

That's spiked his guns, I thought, but both Bella and William looked surprisingly relieved.

Three of the boys were crawling under the table making jungle noises. Their heads swayed up like cobras when they saw Ellie take her purse from the sideboard. Iain, the eldest, was homing in on the whisky bottle. Bella slapped his hand away and lit another cigarette.

'I'll bring your porridge to you, Aunt Ellie.' She gave her husband a significant look.

'Oh, aye. We've our supper booked at the hotel. Just you get away to your bed, auntie. We'll be back tomorrow forenoon as soon as we're able.'

Ellie slipped the purse into her apron pocket, gave William a grateful smile, and left the room.

I wouldn't like you to suppose that Ellie was unappreciative of anything Bella and I did for her; but that's a woman's job, isn't it? It's a black shame to trauchle bairns before their time, and you must be grateful when the menfolk put themselves out for you. William was giving up three days of his working time.

'What about this lot?' William poured himself another glass of Talisker and jerked his thumb at the four backs crowded against the window.

'Wee pitchers, eh? When I've put the porridge on I'll take the bairns back to the hotel.'

There was a simultaneous 'Oh, Ma, no!' from David, Roderick and Jimmy. Iain was still trying to creep up on the Talisker. They were spoilt, selfish and disorderly, but I too had been a cooped-up child with muscles twanging like rubber bands.

'Why don't you let them go to the beach? You can keep an eye on them from the window.' There isn't a real beach at St Pitten, but when the sea retreats there are spits of gritty orange sand between the reefs outside the harbour wall. The tide was well out. Seagulls were strutting up and down the smelly green banks of the Pitten burn. At high tide it floods with salt water but at present it was trickling round the foundations of the Gauger's Inn where I'd hoped to take Ellie for dinner.

I remembered Aunt Nettie sitting at that window with her head turned seawards. Her eyes looked like opaque agates because she'd been blind since her twenties. Except in the coldest weather the window was kept open. Using only smell and hearing she could tell the exact moment when the tide turned.

William agreed it was a good idea and the four junior Buchans exited with whoops and yells and routine warnings from Bella.

'Thank God,' she groaned, stretching her legs and reaching for the packet of cigarettes.

'Her porridge,' William reminded menacingly.

'Aye, aye.' Bella kicked off her shoes and went to clatter about in the kitchen. I longed for them to go. William refilled my glass; he made time-filling remarks about the funeral and distant cousins who had resurfaced. Eventually I couldn't put up with any more.

'What do you want to discuss, William?'

His reply startled me. 'What should we do about Aunt Ellie? She can't go on living in the Shellie House on her own.'

'Why ever not? She's fit and active, and she has dozens of friends in St Pitten.' This wasn't what I had expected at all.

Bella's head appeared at the door. 'D'you want me in with you, pet?'

'Take her up the porridge, Bella!'

It was the repeated 'her', rather than the tone in which he said it that alerted me. It wasn't to be only the bric-a-brac. I thought, You have a timeshare in Majorca, a cottage in Ullapool and a yacht on the Ayrshire coast. What more do you want? I heard Bella's feet thud up the stairs and down again.

'Ellie's eighty, nearly eighty-one,' said William. 'We want to keep an eye on her but it's a long drive over.'

'You could arrange for her to pay you long visits, if she's willing. That way you'd soon find out if there were any problems. Frankly, I think she'll see us all out.'

'The kids would drive her demented. You know that, Elspeth.'

'Then we'll all keep an eye on her, won't we? I'll try to come over more often.' I wondered what he could be working up to.

Bella joined us and plumped herself beside William on the sofa. She bent her head to light a cigarette, but she kept her gaze on me. William began to show annoyance.

'Have you forgotten what went on with Bella's mum? We don't want to leave it too late this time.'

Bella's jowl became weighty. 'Yon was an awfy business, Elspeth. Never again, I promised myself. Never again.' William patted her hand.

No, I thought, it can't be that. Not even William would go as far as that. But he would.

'There's a good residential home on the Ayr road. It's only five miles away from us, near enough to go over every day.

Bella's seen over the accommodation. The manager buys her car from Buchan's . . . What's the matter? We'll not ask you to help with the fees.'

Every day. For how long? I must confront him. 'What about the Shellie House?'

'It needs modernising. Central heating, a new kitchen and bathroom, that sort of thing. Re-decorating, naturally.'

'New carpets,' added Bella. She stared at the rag-rug in front of the fender. I'd knelt so often on that rug toasting a slice of bread at the red-hot bars of the range. Teatimes were even better after William left home. Sentimentality laced with hatred is a powerful drug. I was speechless.

'Come on, Elspeth. We wouldn't let it go out of the family. We'd let you stay here whenever you wanted. You could sit upstairs scribbling like you used to when you were a kid.' He was mocking me. Bella had crinkled her eyes above her fifth cigarette since Ellie went upstairs.

I found my voice. '*You* would let me – ! If you paid for Ellie to stay at Gleneagles you'd still be stealing the house from her. You can't remove her like a piece of old furniture. If she left St Pitten she would – she – ' It seemed indecent to conclude that sentence so soon after the funeral.

'*Steal*, is it?' growled Bella. 'You'd better watch your tongue, my lady.'

William then dropped his bomb-shell.

'We spoke to Ellie before you arrived. She agrees it's not the same now there's only herself. She thinks the house should belong to me because I am Isa's son.'

I said incredulously, 'You don't believe that Tabby nonsense any more than I do! Anyway, the house would revert to me. It belonged to my father. I haven't any brothers.'

It was only a debating point, not a claim, but I saw alarm jump into Bella's eyes. 'Don't you go upsetting Aunt Ellie, Elspeth!'

'She won't,' snapped her husband. 'Come on, we'll be missing our dinner.' He turned back at the door. 'We'll talk again in the morning, Elspeth. When you've got back your temper.'

They left me to clear up the litter of empty bottles and cigarette butts. I saw Bella shouting at the children from the harbour wall. When the four kilted figures had scampered back to base the whole family disappeared round a corner to the car park.

The light was waning, and the street was quiet except for a noisy queue at the fish and chip shop. I decided to buy myself a carry-out; no seafood dinner at the Gauger's Arms tonight.

I slumped into the buttoned armchair. It wasn't cold enough to light a fire, but it was too chilly to sit there all evening. I thought of my first encounter with William at my grandfather's funeral. Grandpa Buchan died a few months before the war broke out and we came up from Birmingham on my father's rail pass. After the service I was whisked home to watch my mother and aunts laying out sandwiches and whisky for the dredgie. The whisky was for the men. There was sweet sherry for the women.

Cousin William counted as a man, even at the age of six, and he was allowed to follow the coffin. I was bitterly jealous. 'I mustn't tell you,' he replied, when curiosity overcame my hurt pride. It was no consolation that we were both restricted to drinking Barr's Irn Bru.

When I was a child we changed home frequently because my father was moved around by LMS railways and we always moved with him. He'd long since escaped from the Tabbies, while my English mother, staunch C of E, kept me away from them as long as possible. James, my father, was the only surviving son. Despite having lived outside Scotland for ten years he was told by the Third Advent Buchanites that it was his duty to take on ownership of the Shellie House. The minister did it at the reception after the burial, saying he spoke on behalf of the family. My father had a childish zest for stirring things. He replied that he was shocked to the marrow: did they expect him to turn his sisters out on the street? There wouldn't be any dramatic eviction; both my father and the Tabbies knew that. They merely wanted him to play along with their charade. They couldn't admit this, so they chewed things over for a week and then sent a pompous letter which provoked him into engaging a solicitor. A declarator inserted in the local paper named my aunts as legal owners of the Shellie House. They were so morti-fied that they wouldn't have anything to do with us while my father was still alive. They would have found it less shaming to be seen naked in the street.

I went upstairs to my attic bedroom. It had a coom, that is sloping, ceiling and was stiflingly hot because the sun had been beating on the slates all day and I'd forgotten to open the skylight. I did that now and stood on my toes to peer across the milkily amethyst Forth to the hills of Lothian. The Bass Rock and Berwick Law stood out darkly against glimmering pastels. I could smell brine and seaweed.

I remembered what Ellie had said and knelt to open the pine chest. There was a pile of papers inside, mostly letters I'd written weekly to my aunts in the late forties, after my father was killed in the last month of Hitler's war. They had been overwhelmingly kind to my mother and her three children. I was glad it was getting too dark to read. I'd had quite enough churning-up for one day.

There was something thicker below the letters. My fingers explored around until I realised what it was. At the age of twelve I had informed my aunts that I wanted to be a writer. Isa snorted, 'You'll as likely turn into a porpoise. Just you set your mind on the teaching. There's good holidays and your pay aye going on.' Nettie said nothing. Ellie, who worked in the local newsagent, brought home a chunky pad of paper and stitched it into covers which she cut out from a shoe-box. On the outside she inscribed in red block capitals: ELSPETH BUCHAN, HER BOOK, and gave it to me at breakfast. The pages were too small for the rhyming couplets of my never-finished Celtic epic, but the gift confirmed her as my favourite aunt. I had been named after Ellie, although she never used the full form of Elspeth.

I clutched the pad against me, wondering how far I'd go to stop William stealing the Shellie House. Would I be prepared to murder him? Yes, if I could do it without upsetting Ellie. But that was where William had me stymied. He wasn't just William; he was Isa's son, Ellie's surrogate child. I was aware that my hatred was fuelled by a lot more than altruism. I wasn't proud of myself.

'Is that you, Elspeth?'

I put the book down. I went through to Aunt Ellie's bedroom and sat on the side of her bed.

'Why aren't you asleep?'

'I canna seem to drop off, hen.' She squeezed my hand. 'Dinna be angry at me, Elspeth. I have to do the right.' So she had overheard our conversation.

'May I light the candle?' There was electricity downstairs but when the gas lamps were replaced my aunts decided it would be extravagant to light the bedrooms as well.

She nodded, and I groped for the Scottish Bluebell matches. When the soft flame steadied I could see Ellie lying back on the pillows with her hair in its usual night-time plait; she looked much calmer than I'd expected. I restrained my urge to argue, and waited.

'Isa was good to me once when I was in awfy trouble. Long syne, you wouldna mind on it.' Her fingers twisted the end of the grey plait. 'William's the nearest kin I have, forbye yoursel.'

And William is a man. I said, 'I just want to be sure. Are you really willing to leave St Pitten?'

She turned her head on the pillow and I saw tears. Careful, I told myself.

'William is Isa's bairn.'

'Suppose something happened – never mind what – but if William couldn't look after the Shellie House, would you like to go on staying in St Pitten?'

She was silent for at least a minute. Then she said, 'If that was the way of it, I'd have to stay. I canna give the house to just anybody.'

I stood up and lifted her tray. 'Shall I blow your candle out, Aunt Ellie?'

'Aye, Elspeth. You needna bide in for me.' I think she hoped that I'd go and make my peace with William.

'Maybe I'll take a short walk before I go to bed. It's still a bit early for me. Don't worry, I'll lock the door when I go out.'

I kissed her good night and blew out the candle.

There was still enough light to tell rocks from sand so I ate the fish supper as I headed towards the stepping stones that spanned the Pitten burn. I trod across them gingerly. On the other side some steps led up to a breakwater and the back street that came to a sudden halt beside it. I went the long way round to the Gauger's Arms, throwing the greasy paper into a bin outside the hotel. I wanted a drink, but not with William and Bella. There was a lounge bar upstairs fitted out with ships' wheels, lobster pots and other maritime miscellanea, all of them faked. Its one plus point was the lack of Muzak. It was a good place to think. There was only one other person in the room apart from the barman.

'Hullo again. What are you doing here?'

I said this to the dark-haired women with the rucksack. She smiled at my remark and tapped her table. I took over my Belhaven and sat beside her.

She said, 'I'm looking around before I start my course at St Andrews. D'you think I could find some digs in St Pitten? I'm staying at the Youth Hostel tonight.'

She had a Londonish voice, and must be a mature student.

'What are you studying?'

'One of the anthropology options.'

'Good Heavens! How many are there?'

She laughed, but didn't reply.

'Was going to the service some kind of field study? There can't be many Third Advent Buchanites outside Fife. . . . I'm Elspeth Buchan.'

'Friends call me Spetty.' She didn't offer a surname. 'So Janet Buchan was a relation of yours? I saw that notice on the door. Do you belong to the – the Third Advent Buchanites?'

'No, I came over from Edinburgh for the funeral. Nettie was my aunt.'

'Are you a large family?'

I began telling her how I remembered Grandpa Buchan in his stiff serge trousers and the checked cap he wore inside the house. I was fascinated by the way he removed his pipe from his mouth and leant forward to spit into the fire. His moustache was stained a browny yellow.

'My grandmother died before I was born. She was Mary Buchan. I can remember my *great*-grandmother, another Elspeth. She died much later. She wore black taffeta and had tickly white hairs on her chin. She was working in a Dundee jute mill when the Tay Bridge blew down. When I was four my father put me on her lap and told me to listen carefully. She went with her friends to gawp the day after the storm.'

'Cor,' said Spetty, 'you're living history, you are.'

I felt silly. A funeral opens doors you didn't know existed.

'I wasn't ribbing you. I really am interested. Go on.' We bought ourselves another drink, although I was having qualms about leaving Ellie alone for so long. At eleven o'clock I asked, 'Is there a curfew at this youth hostel?'

'You could always put me up at the Shellie House and tell me some more family history.'

Like heck I could. That was pretty cheeky too.

Spetty suddenly turned serious. 'It's all right. I have a special late pass. But I genuinely do want to find out more. I saw the death notice in the *Fife Herald*. I've been ordering it in Hackney for the past year. I came up on purpose.'

'Why?'

She gave a self-conscious smile. 'I think we're related. Spetty is short for Elspeth, and I've taken my grandmother's surname. So I'm Elspeth Buchan too. I felt such an idiot when you told me your name. I suppose I should have mentioned it sooner.'

'Coincidence. The same name often runs in families.' I decided she was sending me up and didn't believe a word of it. But she was fun, and very, very attractive. 'If you'd introduced yourself we would have invited you to the reception.'

'It's not just names that run in families,' she said meaningly, with a straight look to my eye. Oh, I see, I thought. She must have some reason for wanting to con me.

The generation gap restored itself.

She told me that her mother had been adopted as a baby by a couple living in Humberside and later married a postal worker who moved to north London. That was where Elspeth and her two brothers were born. Her mother first mentioned the adoption five years ago.

'I didn't think much about it at first. I had my own life – married, split up. No kids, fortunately.' Her face let through unpleasant memories. 'Anyway, I was picking up enough bits of paper to start a degree course. I wasted my time at school.'

'Don't we all, one way or another?'

'The two ideas grew together. Wanting a degree and becoming obsessed with my mother's family.' Her personal story was beginning to sound plausible, but I still didn't believe we were related.

She had tracked down the agency that took in her mother. All that time ago only minimum information was given to adopting couples, but the regulations had now changed; they had shown Elspeth their records. Her mother was born in St Pitten, Fife.

'I had to get Mum's permission to start looking, but she wasn't really interested. She said she'd had a good childhood; her birth parents were probably dead and she didn't want hassle with their other children.'

'What about your father?'

'Poor old Dad had an accident at work and had to retire early. I think he died of depression. That was ten years ago.'

Elspeth had gone to Somerset House to hunt down the family surname. The agency had deliberately expunged this from its records when the baby was given out for adoption.

'I knew Mum's date of birth, of course. I took a copy of the full birth certificate. Could you explain how she fits into the family?'

If I'd guessed her own age correctly her mother had to be between late forties and early seventies. I knew the family background of all the Buchans who fitted into that age range and had been born in St Pitten. None of them could possibly be related to this young woman. Every other detail of her story could be true: that would be why it sounded so convincing.

Unless I am terribly angry I can't challenge people who tell me lies. I'm ashamed of this weakness, but there's nothing I can do about it. I didn't ask to see the certificate. Things would have turned out so differently if I had. I stalled.

'Did you decide to take the name Elspeth too?'

'Oh, no. That's what I was christened. I forgot to say that a message was left with the baby, that if she had a daughter of her own she was to call her Elspeth.'

I bit my lip in case I burst out laughing. Come off it!

'What's your mother's name?'

'Mary, and she was born on the tenth of June, 1934.'

The room did a somersault. Not because that was my own date of birth, but because I was born on the same day as Isa's second baby. This was becoming sinister. She must have prepared her hoax long before tonight and done hours of delving at Somerset House. I concentrated desperately on a scratch at the side of the table.

Elspeth touched my arm. 'You don't believe me, do you?'

I forced myself to look at her. Her eyes were full of concern, not for herself.

I said, 'There was a Mary Buchan who was born on that date in 1934. She was my cousin. She died when she was ten months old.' I hoped she would concede defeat and leave quickly.

'She didn't, not according to the agency. The adoptive parents sent them a photo of my mother's fifth birthday party.'

'Children change a lot in four years. They could have sent someone else's photo. I expect they were frightened to admit that the baby died, in case they were had up for negligence.'

She turned round and unzipped a pocket of her rucksack. 'Are you calling me a liar? Look at this.' She held out a small black and white photograph cracked across one corner. 'This is an earlier one which they let me take away. Mum's birth mother sent it with the message about my name.'

The snapshot was fuzzy; it could have been of any baby, if I hadn't already seen it in Ellie's photo album.

I said, 'Let's have another drink. You don't know what you've done, Elspeth.'

I explained that most of the family thought the baby had died. It would be a terrible shock to everyone when they heard that her grandmother had lied. As the implications of this sank in we both became subdued; we didn't even speculate on why Isa should do such a monstrous thing. Both of us needed time to think. Before we parted we arranged to meet in the same bar at ten o'clock next morning.

I lay awake most of the night listening to the incoming tide and waiting for it to go out again. William had a right to know that his sister was still alive. And Ellie – I didn't know how I was going to tell Ellie.

He turned up at nine o'clock saying that Bella and the boys were still at breakfast. His voice was simmering with anger. I took him for a walk along the beach. The tide was now coming in and the weather had turned unsettled. I repeated Elspeth's story.

'Preposterous!' he bellowed into the wind, before I reached the end. 'Trust you to fall for another bampot. She'll clean you out like the last one.'

He fell into worried silence when I described the photo. Like me he had seen it in Ellie's album. Then he said, 'It can't be the same one! You're doing this because we had that rammie yesterday.'

'Don't be stupid, William. It is the same one. It must have been taken just before Isa gave Mary away. I don't understand why she sent a copy to the orphanage, but there is no way Elspeth could have got hold of it unless her story is true. Shall I ask her to show it to you?'

That defeated him, but he seemed curiously undented by his overnight acquisition of a sister and three nieces and nephews. He was far more anxious to stop the Buchan family from imploding in a mega-sized scandal.

Bella and her sons appeared on the harbour front, and William waved to them frantically. I saw Bella hand some money to the children, who then streaked towards an ice-cream shop. She stood on the wall refusing to sink her heels into the sand. When we reached her William was panting noisily, but he suggested a stroll to the end of the pier. Bella agreed with reluctance, wrinkling her nose as we passed a pile of lobster pots. She listened hard, flicking her ash into the harbour mud. 'You'll have to shut up that wee bitch. How much d'you think it would take?'

'I don't know,' replied William savagely. 'This could change everything.' I didn't see why.

I said, 'The way to keep Elspeth quiet is let her rent the Shellie House when Aunt Ellie goes into the home. She understands the situation. Maybe you could persuade her to go back to using her father's name.'

That would keep the Shellie House in family circulation if I couldn't stop William and Bella in their tracks; but I hoped that the presence of her great-niece would override Ellie's compulsion to give the house to William.

'You sneaky besom!' cried Bella, her face turning bright red. 'D'you think I came up the Clyde in a barrel? I see what you're at, and I'm going to tell Ellie before we leave!' She stormed on and on, her language becoming as highly coloured as her cheeks. Most of the time Bella convinced herself that I was a sexless spinster, but she could become frenziedly homophobic. I'd heard it all before, so I didn't rise. Finally she burst out, 'If you think we're keeping Ellie's manky old hovel for you and your wee chancer, you're dancing on ice, the pair of you. No danger! There's gonny be a new Buchan garage on the bypass by the end of this year.'

William's expression will be imprinted on my mind for ever.

'He's a bastard,' I told Elspeth the next morning. 'To him the Shellie House is just a piece of real estate.'

She curled her legs around the bar stool. 'But if he's so scared of scandal, would he have the nerve to sell the house?' She'd waded through a whole module of anthropology in the last half hour.

'Ellie's the last Buchan left in St Pitten. Once she's away he doesn't need to show his face here. He won't dispose of the house until he has her safely tucked up at Journey's End.'

'I wish I could do something to help.'

'You can. Go and confront him while the boat's still rocking. Wave that birth certificate at him. You don't have to make any threats. Call him Uncle William and say you're going to visit your great-aunt Ellie.'

'How would that help?'

'William and Bella appear to think it will change everything if Ellie meets you, so let's try it. If that doesn't work we'll think of something else. Go to their hotel. By the time you reach the Shellie House I'll have broken the news.' I crushed forebodings about Ellie's reaction when she knew that Isa had deceived her.

I returned home to find her mixing a cake for our tea. She usually rose at seven, but she was much later that morning and had missed my cousin's visit.

'Have you no brought William and the bairns with you?'

I said they were looking around the shops and would call in

later. I asked her to sit down. Then I told her that when I'd gone out the previous night I'd met someone who'd been at Aunt Nettie's funeral service. I had heard something astonishing.

Ellie chafed at my slowness in getting to the point. In the end I managed to speak out.

'Aunt Ellie, this woman said Isa's baby was given away for adoption. Is that true?'

Her eyes became hard and shallow. 'Was it Jean Moultrie's lassie telt you? Jean promised she'd never let on!'

'I don't know either of them. Who are they?'

'Jean was the St Pitten midwife before they went in for all yon fancy stuff at the Victoria. She's no with us now. . . . Aye, Elspeth, wee Mary did go for adoption, but it all came to the same in the end. I canna think what business it is of yours.'

Something warned me to stop right there, but of course I didn't. I wanted to be quite sure of the facts. 'Was it the agency that told you when the baby died?'

'The agency? How would the agency speak to me? Mary was Isa's baby.' I thought that a strange answer. Her mouth had begun to quiver.

'Then it was Isa who told you.'

'Who else?' Her hands were shaking. I took hold of them.

'I don't want to know why Isa told you that the baby was dead, but it wasn't true. Mary grew up and married and she's now a widow living in London. Yesterday I met her daughter.'

I've never heard anything as dreadful as the sounds that came out of Ellie's mouth. They were far worse than screams. She rocked to and fro on the sofa, cowering and hugging herself as if to avoid the blows of a stick. I put my arms round her, and the moans began to subside. After five minutes she sat up and pushed my hands away. Her eyes were completely dry.

'It was my baby, not Isa's. I wanted to keep her but I had to let her go. You couldna live with a thing like that when I was a lassie. No like nowadays.'

I didn't dare ask how she'd concealed the pregnancy or why they didn't bring up the baby themselves when they'd already passed her off as Isa's. I was too appalled to wonder who the father was. What would happen when William and Bella turned up at the house? How I wished I'd never spoken to Elspeth Buchan!

Ellie went on flatly, 'He was a lad I met in the war. One of the airmen frae Leuchars. They shot him down over the North Sea. He never heard about the bairn.'

'Oh, Aunt Ellie! Did you tell his family?'

She was stony-eyed again. 'Of course not. I should have kent better at my age. I was thirty past. I let him go too far ... All the same, he forced me.' She stood up. 'Elspeth, we'll never speak of this again.' She returned to the kitchen.

I continued sitting on the sofa. Then my brain began to function. How could the father be a Polish or Norwegian airman? Mary was the same age as myself; she was born five years before the war began.

If there is good reason, Buchanites are allowed to lie; but they must tell the truth before death. I visited Isa in hospital the day before she died. She had succumbed to a stroke. It was probably the effort to speak to me that finally killed her. She grabbed at my hand; her weight almost pulled me over. We both tried, again and again, but I couldn't understand her mumblings. Now I realised she had wanted to say, 'Baby – baby – not dead.'

I watched Ellie spoon the cake mixture into a tin. The gas roared softly when she opened the oven door; the noise blurred into a shrieking wail outside that rose and fell, fell and rose. Ellie straightened herself as she took off her thick gloves. Our conversation never had taken place.

'There's the ambulance on the St Andrews road. Let's pray they get to the poor soul in time.'

But they didn't. William died on the way to hospital. While I was talking to Ellie the hotel clerk rang from reception up to suite 302; he told William that a Miss Elspeth Buchan wanted to speak to him. William took the lift down, and expected to see me waiting in the foyer. That was enough to send his blood pressure soaring, never mind a face-to-face encounter with the other Elspeth. She told me that he was very truculent; he demanded to see the birth certificate and collapsed after reading it.

I am not a Third Advent Buchanite or even a Christian. I

don't believe in survival after death. Nevertheless I'm convinced that when we were drinking in the Gauger's Arms, what stopped me asking to see Mary's certificate was the collective spirit of all those women who share the name of Elspeth Buchan. We all helped to murder William. I don't regret our crime one bit.

I read the details on the certificate later, after I brought Elspeth to meet her grandmother.

MOTHER: Elspeth Buchan. FATHER: Robert Strachan Leslie.

William's father.

You'll have noticed that Buchan women are great survivors. Buchan men don't seem to do so well. We managed to straighten everything out in the end. I think the first Elspeth Buchan would have approved. Ellie and her grand-daughter get along fine in the Shellie House, and I go over there most weekends. We're taking Ellie to London before Christmas so that she can meet her daughter. We let Bella and the boys crowd us out for an occasional visit, but no one except ourselves knows the exact nature of our three-way relationship. We don't want to cause a family scandal.

Biographical Notes on the Contributors

Malorie Blackman has written over twenty books for children as well as numerous short stories for both adults and children. Her first collection of short stories, *Not So Stupid!* (Livewire Books for Teenagers, The Women's Press, 1990) was a Selected Twenty Title for Feminist Book Fortnight, 1991. Her first novel, *Hacker*, won the W H Smith's Mind Boggling Books Award 1994. Her latest novel, *Trust Me*, has recently been published by Livewire Books for Teenagers (The Women's Press, 1992). She is currently working on her first adult novel.

Loveday Blakey is a pseudonym.

Amanda Cross is the pseudonym of Carolyn Heilbrun, Avalon Foundation Professor in the Humanities Emerita, Columbia University. She has published eleven mysteries including *No Word from Winifred*, *A Trap for Fools*, *Players Come Again*, and *An Imperfect Spy*. As Heilbrun, she has written several works of non-fiction, including *Writing a Woman's Life* and *Hamlet's Mother* (The Women's Press, 1989 and 1991), and a biography of Gloria Steinem, published in 1995.

Susan Dunlap has written fourteen mystery novels featuring forensic pathologist turned private investigator Kiernan O'Shaughnessy (*High Fall*), Berkeley, California Homicide Detective Jill Smith (*Death and Taxes*), and public utility meter reader Vejay Haskell (*An Equal Opportunity Death*). A former president and founding member of Sisters in Crime, she has also been a social worker and taught Hatha Yoga. She lives near San Francisco.

Kitty Fitzgerald was born in Ireland in 1946 but came to live in England as a child. After leaving school at fifteen she did a variety of jobs, including waitressing, shop and factory work, until going to college as a mature student in 1976. She began writing seriously in 1982 and her novel *Marge* was published by Sheba in 1985. She has written extensively for film, theatre and radio, as well as continuing prose writing, and in 1994 producing a first collection of poetry, *For Crying Out Loud* with Valerie Laws. She was a member of Amber Films Workshop between 1988 and 1993 when she wrote the script for the internationally acclaimed feature film, *Dream On*.

Val McDermid worked as a journalist for fourteen years and currently works as a full-time writer. Her Lindsay Gordon mysteries are published by The Women's Press, *Report for Murder* (1987), *Common Murder* (1989), *Final Edition* (1991) and *Union Jack* (1993). She is also the author of the Kate Brannigan series *Dead Beat* (1992), *Kick Back* (1993) and *Crack Down* (1994).

Iona McGregor began to write historical novels for young adults while teaching in London. After moving to Edinburgh she became involved in gay politics, which has influenced all her later writing. She has published two historical crime novels for adults, one, *Death Wore a Diadem*, with The Women's Press (1989), and is currently toiling at a sequel!

Linda Mariz lives on the Pacific coast thirty miles from the Canadian border. A former junior college history instructor, she is the author of the Laura Ireland mystery series published in the US through Bantam Crimeline. An avid competitive swimmer and triathlete, Mariz's current obsession is long distance open water swims.

Pam Mason was born in Liverpool in 1961. She wrote her first story (about a lost dog) at the age of six, and has never looked back since. She has had articles in *Modern Review, The Pink Paper, Spare Rib* and *Cat World*; short stories broadcast on BBC Radio Merseyside; and a piece published in The Women's Press anthology *Mustn't Grumble: Writing by Disabled Women*, edited by Lois Keith (1994). She is currently working on a novel entitled *Helen Kelly.* She lives in the countryside with the inevitable cat.

Meg O'Brien lives in California. She has written four full-length mysteries featuring Jessica 'Jesse' James, all published by The Women's Press: *The Daphne Decisions* (1993); *Salmon in the Soup* (1993); *Hare Today, Gone Tomorrow* (1993); and *Eagles Die Too* (1994).

Sara Paretsky is the author of a number of mystery novels featuring Chicago-based private investigator V I Warshawski, including: *Indemnity Only, Deadlock, Killing Orders, Bitter Medicine* and *Toxic Shock.* She is president and co-founder of Sisters in Crime. She lives in Chicago.

Rosie Scott has written four critically acclaimed novels, *Glory Days* (The Women's Press, 1989), *Nights with Grace, Feral City* and *Lives on Fire* published in Australia, New Zealand, the UK, USA and Germany. Her play was the basis of the film *Redheads,* winner of five international awards. Her latest novel, *Movie Dreams* is currently in production. She lives in Sydney, Australia.

Penny Sumner was born in Australia and moved to Britain as a postgraduate student and part-time tutor at Oxford. She now lives in Newcastle upon Tyne where she lectures in contemporary English literature at the University of Northumbria. *The End of April*, the first of her crime novels featuring private detective Tor Cross, was published by The Women's Press in 1992.

Robyn Vinten was born in New Zealand in 1961, and ran away to London in 1986 in search of the bright lights. She plays football for Hackney Women's Football Club, and belongs to

Slip of the Tongue Theatre Group. This is only her second published story and she would like to thank her writing group, especially Val and Helen.

Mary Wings began her writing career with *She Came Too Late* (The Women's Press, 1986), which launched the bestselling career of intrepid detective Emma Victor, and was followed by *She Came in a Flash* (The Women's Press, 1988) and *She Came by the Book* (The Women's Press, 1995). She has also written the bestselling gothic detective novel, *Divine Victim* (The Women's Press, 1992), which won the Lambda Literary Award in 1993. Mary Wings lives in San Francisco, and her work has been translated into Dutch, German, Japanese and Spanish.

The Women's Press is Britain's leading women's publishing house. Established in 1978, we publish high-quality fiction and non-fiction from outstanding women writers worldwide. Our exciting and diverse list includes literary fiction, detective novels, biography and autobiography, health, women's studies, handbooks, literary criticism, psychology and self help, the arts, our popular Livewire Books for Teenagers young adult series and the bestselling annual *Women Artists Diary* featuring beautiful colour and black-and-white illustrations from the best in contemporary women's art.

If you would like more information about our books, please send an A5 sae for our latest catalogue and complete list to:

The Sales Department
The Women's Press Ltd
34 Great Sutton Street
London EC1V 0DX
Tel: 071 251 3007
Fax: 071 608 1938

Also of interest:

Jen Green, editor
Reader, I Murdered Him

With original stories from Sara Paretsky, Barbara Wilson,
Amanda Cross and many more, *Reader, I Murdered Him* (the
prequel to *Reader, I Murdered Him, Too*) showcases sixteen
suspenseful murder mysteries by some of the best women crime
writers in the world today.

A classic of the genre and runaway bestseller, this exciting
collection offers razor-sharp solutions to the problems of the
outgrown husband, the office bozo and the holiday bore...

'Entertaining and witty.' *Living*

'Splendid yarns.' *Ms London*

Fiction £5.99
ISBN 0 7043 4159 X

Helen Windrath, editor
The Women's Press Book of New Myth and Magic

'But some folks say no, it's not that mountain sitting back watching over us, and it's not that black lake reaching, and it's not that old white-trunked, yellow-tipped tree next to Blue's that Reverend Daniles swears covers a hole leading from this world to the next. The thing that makes Pearl a funny kind of place is all that whispering we hear coming up from the ground.'

In this entrancing, powerful and acclaimed collection, women explore alternatives to society's highly prized values of finance, commercialism and practicality, illustrating their relationship to mythology and magic, both in terms of women's great inner strengths, and in their interaction with the outside world.

'A delicious, delirious brew . . . a lot of fun.' *Everywoman*

'You will be hooked . . .' *The Voice*

Fiction £7.99
ISBN 0 7043 4347 9